Submission

By

Kimberly Zant

Erotica Romance

New Concepts   Georgia

Be sure to check out our website for the very best in fiction at fantastic prices!

When you visit our webpage, you can:
* Read excerpts of currently available books
* View cover art of upcoming books and current releases
* Find out more about the talented artists who capture the magic of the writer's imagination on the covers
* Order books from our backlist
* Find out the latest NCP and author news--including any upcoming book signings by your favorite NCP author
* Read author bios and reviews of our books
* Get NCP submission guidelines
* And so much more!

We offer a 20% discount on all new Trade Paperback releases ordered from our website!

Be sure to visit our webpage to find the best deals in e-books and paperbacks! To find out about our new releases as soon as they are available, please be sure to sign up for our newsletter (http://www.newconceptspublishing.com/newsletter.htm) or join our reader group (http://groups.yahoo.com/group/new_concepts_pub/join)!

The newsletter is available by double opt in only and our customer information is *never* shared!

Visit our webpage at:
www.newconceptspublishing.com

Submission is an original publication of NCP. This work has never before appeared in book form. This work is a novel. Any similarity to actual persons or events is purely coincidental.

New Concepts Publishing, Inc.
5202 Humphreys Rd.
Lake Park, GA 31636

ISBN 978-1-60394-272-0
© copyright June 2008 Kimberly Zant
Cover art (c) copyright 2008 Alex DeShanks

NCP books are available at special quantity discounts for bulk purchases for sales promotions, premiums, fund raising, or educational use. For details, write, email, or phone New Concepts Publishing, Inc., 5202 Humphreys Rd., Lake Park, GA 31636; Ph. 229-257-0367, Fax 229-219-1097; orders@newconceptspublishing.com.

First NCP Trade Paperback Printing: November 2008

Chapter One

Luke glared at his computer and finally lifted his head to study the narrow, two story house across the street. It was her address alright and the damned tracker led straight to it.

He muttered a curse under his breath.

Her image rose in his mind. He didn't know why it had taken him so long to notice her unless it was because she didn't look like much more than breath and britches at a glance. She wasn't much over five feet tall despite the ridiculously high heels she wore every day—trying to make herself look taller, no doubt—along with the thick, dark hair she piled on top of her head. He'd caught a flash of red in it in the sunlight, but usually it just looked deep and dark and as deceptive as her face.

She wasn't flashy, that was for certain.

She wasn't even beautiful, certainly not in the classic sense, although there was a touch of the exotic about her because her eyes tilted upward faintly at the outer corners. Her narrow little nose ended with just the hint of an upward turn that, along with her heart shaped face and her diminutive size, gave her the look of a pixy. Her mouth was narrow, her lips modest rather than either full or thin, but the shortness of her upper lip gave them a bow shape that was damned appealing. Even the little knob of a chin she had tilted upward, forming a chin that somehow looked stubborn and vulnerable at the same time.

And yet the first time he'd locked gazes with her ….

She had the eyes of a fawn. He wasn't poetic by any stretch of the imagination but that was the first thing that had popped into his head. They were huge for her small face, and he didn't doubt that was part of what had spawned the notion, but mostly it was the look in her eyes.

Vulnerability—gentleness—defenselessness. It was the kind of look that made a man fall all over himself to rush to her rescue.

As if she *needed* rescuing, he thought derisively! The vixen!

He should've known no woman with a body like that could possibly be as innocent, or as helpless, as she looked.

Oddly enough, it had taken him a while even to notice her figure—really odd because generally when a woman had that effect on him he immediately checked out the rest of the package—or he checked out the package before he checked the face. Then again, he usually saw her behind the counter, virtually hidden except for her head and shoulders since she was short even *with* heels.

Beyond that, it seemed to him that she went out of her way to downplay her figure in the way she dressed. She always had the look of someone struggling against their nature to appear neat. Whenever he saw her, her blouse was tucked unevenly, there were ink stains on her hands or clothes, and there was usually a stray hair falling from her bun—not artistically and deliberately, but random chaos.

Despite tucking her blouse to appear neat, she always wore blouses that looked a little too big for her and ditto the slacks—too loose to tell much about what lay beneath which was what made him suspect it was a deliberate attempt to hide her assets.

He'd studied her hard enough, though, he had a damned good idea what she was hiding—a damned fine pair of breasts that were larger than average and still firm, an unbelievably tiny waist, and a heart shaped ass that made his cock twitch with interest every time he got a look at it.

He just didn't know why she seemed to go out of the way to look ordinary, to fade into the background, when she was anything but ordinary.

Or he hadn't before today.

Now, he was afraid he knew.

Reluctance tightened in his belly, but he knew what he had to do. All roads led here.

* * * *

The thunderous, imperious knock on my front door so early on a Saturday morning startled me so badly I jumped all over and sloshed hot coffee over my hand and spattered my favorite, disreputable sleeping t-shirt. My heart knocking against my ribcage like a bad valve on a car engine, I stared down at the mess with dismay and dawning anger.

I'd be the first to admit that I just wasn't a 'morning person'—far from it. Even on my 'good' days, I was grouchy when I first got up and not particularly sunny even after I'd downed a cup of coffee to rev my engines—just slightly more alert.

The weekends, though—those were sacred, the one time of the week when I could actually sleep until I woke up naturally and then ease into my day.

Weekdays, I tolerated what I had to, but anyone who bothered me on the weekend was just asking for it.

The thunderous knock came again. It didn't startle me the second time, but it certainly pissed me off. Setting my coffee cup down, I made a stab at licking the coffee/heavy cream/and sugar off my hand,

and then swiped the rest off on my already stained sleeping t-shirt since there wasn't anything else handy. Trying to ignore the stickiness, I stalked to my front door ready to blast whoever the asshole was on the other side with my temper.

A shockwave hit me like a physical blow as I snatched the door open and glared at the man standing on the other side of the panel, though.

The expression on his face was every bit as thunderous as the knocking had been. I registered that, vaguely, feeling the glare fall from my own face as it went slack with shocked recognition.

He looked me over from the top of my wild, bed head to the tips of my unpolished toenails, missing nothing in between.

I didn't see a speck of recognition in his expression when he met my gaze again, and not a lot of appreciation for my dishabille for that matter.

Somewhere in the back of my mind, that disturbed me. I decided I must look a lot worse than I'd realized if the man couldn't even appreciate the fact that I was standing at the door in nothing but panties and a ratty t-shirt that barely grazed the tops of my thighs. That thought probably wouldn't have occurred to me at all except for the fact that I'd lusted over this particular young, virile male almost from the time I'd started working at Thorne Bank and Trust.

Naturally enough, that fact made my heart skitter to a brief, painful halt, and then jumpstart into overdrive, sending first a blast of heat then a blast of cold through me and a million thoughts I had no business thinking.

Like the possibility that he'd noticed me, as well, and had finally decided he wanted to get to know me a little better.

His expression wasn't exactly conducive to that thought, but one could hope, and one did.

And one was seriously disappointed the moment he opened his mouth because it instantly became clear that romance wasn't what was on his mind.

"Ms. Bridges?"

"Uh ... Yes?"

"Can I come in?"

Since he followed that question by pushing past me into the foyer, I realized immediately that it was a mere formality. I turned to gape at him blankly as he halted in the center, feet apart in a stance that radiated hostility, his hands balled into fists and planted on his hips as he surveyed my house. Dragging my gaze from him after a moment, I glanced outside. There were two dark vehicles parked outside—one in my driveway behind my beat-up economy car and one in the middle of my slightly overgrown lawn. Three of the bank's security guards stood just outside the cars, surveying my house from the outside.

Frowning, feeling my belly begin to flutter with nerves, I closed the door and turned to look at Luke Thorne questioningly.

"You have a computer?"

It was said with a questioning lilt, but it was clearly a statement. Another shockwave washed over me. The question instantly connected in my mind with my son. "My s...." I broke off abruptly, feeling another frigid bite of fear and glanced up the stairs toward my son's room guiltily. "What's this about?"

Eagle-eyed, he'd caught the direction of my gaze.

I dashed around him and stood on the stairs, blocking his path even as he took a step in that direction. He didn't even pause. His hands shot out. He grasped me beneath the breasts as one might a young child, lifted me straight up, and then set me to one side. I was so flabbergasted, both at the move and the gall of the man, that he was nearly at the top before I recovered enough to charge after him. "Don't you *dare* go in my son's room!" I bellowed at him, galloping up the stairs behind him and flinging myself at him like a linebacker.

He staggered a step as I tackled him but regained his balance. I heard a frantic spurt of movement within my son's room, heard the window shoved up the sash. Apparently Luke heard it, too. He peeled me loose from his waist, set me aside, and strode toward Jimmy's room. I raced around him, slammed my back against the door, and braced a palm on either side of the door frame, barring his path.

He plunked his hands on his hips, glared at me a moment, and then grabbed me as he had before and set me aside.

The door was locked.

I'd just breathed a sigh of relief when he slammed his shoulder against it. The door flew open. I tried to beat him inside but it was like an economy car battling a tank. He stepped on my foot as he plowed past me. I let out a yelp and hobbled into the room behind him, wondering if the elephant had broken one of my toes but too intent on guarding my son from his wrath to stop to examine it for damage.

The window was open. Shoving past him, I raced to it and nearly fell out in my rush to see if I could see any sign of my son. Luke grabbed me and hauled me back inside, but not before I'd caught a look at the security men who'd accompanied him. They had my son.

I plunked my hands on my hips, glaring at him as he drew his head back inside the window. "What the hell's going on here?" I demanded.

He shoved his face into mine until we were practically nose to nose.

"As if you didn't know!" he growled, drawing away almost immediately and scanning the room.

Jimmy's computer caught his eye and he crossed the room in two strides and began pecking at the keys.

"This is against the law, you know!" I pointed out to him with what little bravado I could muster considering I had a fair idea by this time of what was going on.

He slid a dark, narrow eyed glance at me. "You think bank robbery isn't?"

Oh my *fucking* god! I felt the color leave my face, felt a wave of dizziness wash over me. Denials sprang to my lips but I couldn't find my voice to utter any of them.

He straightened, fixing me with a look filled with intent. I felt my eyes bug, took a step back as he advanced on me and fell over a pile of Jimmy's clothes that were lying in the floor at the foot of his bed. Luke made a grab for me as I toppled backwards and ended up sprawling out on top of me on the bed.

* * * *

Jesus! It needed only that, Luke thought with a mixture of disgust and raging lust. It wasn't bad enough that he'd been battling between lust and rage from the moment she opened the damned door in nothing but a flimsy t-shirt that emphasized her breasts more than it hid them?

If she'd had any sense of self-preservation, or any idea how badly he wanted to push her down on any handy surface and fuck her unconscious, she wouldn't have been throwing herself in harm's way.

He knew it was a mistake the moment he made a grab for her and realized he was too off balance to stop her fall.

And he still hadn't realized he was off-balance enough to sprawl on top of her.

Falling into her was nearly his undoing, though. Bent backwards from the knees because she'd fallen over the footboard, her jutting pelvis made almost painful contact the moment he landed with the raging hard on he'd been trying to ignore. Her soft breasts flattened against his chest.

For a handful of moments, he was more interested in thoroughly enjoying the opportunity she'd handed him than getting off of her.

Until it dawned on him that it might not be as accidental as he'd thought.

And he realized he was seriously contemplating dismissing his suspicions and focusing on what he wanted.

It cooled his ardor with sickening speed—not completely. It left a dull, throbbing pain in his groin that was like a toothache—impossible to totally ignore.

* * * *

I let out an inelegant grunt as Luke squashed the breath from my lungs. He weighed a fucking ton! We wrestled for several moments because that was how long it took me to figure out that he was trying to find a place to put his hands to push himself upright. He finally managed to get leverage and pushed himself off of me, dragging me with him by way of a handful of my t-shirt.

Did I mention that it was old?

The neck stretched as he levered me up and one boob came within inches of popping clean out of the damned shirt.

He paused, his face flushed, his breathing ragged, but I had a feeling it was his attempts to contain his rage that was responsible for it, not lust.

Maybe a little lust. He thoroughly examined what he'd exposed before he lifted his gaze to meet mine again. "We tracked the IP to your place," he said, an odd mixture of anger and complacency in his voice.

I blinked at him. I didn't have a fucking clue of what an IP was, but I had a bad feeling that Jimmy and I were in serious trouble. "IP?" I echoed cautiously.

"The hacker that breached our system and transferred eight mil to a bank in the Caymans."

I blinked a little more rapidly. "Eight mil?" I asked weakly.

"Million dollars."

I stared at him in disbelief. What the *hell* were they thinking to keep that much money in one place? Wasn't that just *asking* for trouble? Sure it was a bank, but people *knew* banks had money.

"Let's go," he growled.

I tried balking, for all the good it did. "Where?"

"Downtown."

My belly cramped. Everything had happened way too fast for me to fully assimilate what was going on, particularly when I'd hardly had two sips of my damned coffee! But I was beginning to put things together and I didn't like the picture that was emerging. "Like this?" I asked weakly.

As if he hadn't noticed before that I was half naked, he paused and looked me over thoroughly. Instead of commenting, he escorted me across the hall to my room and shoved the door open. "Put some pants on."

Scared as I was by that time, I sent him a resentful glance before looking around for the jeans I'd been wearing the night before. I spied them in a pile by the bed where I'd dropped them before climbing in and shrugged his hand off. "Do you mind?" I asked tightly when I'd picked the jeans up, waiting for him to leave or at least turn around.

"I do," he retorted grimly, "but I think it would attract a lot more attention than I want at the moment if you waltz into the bank in your panties."

I gaped at him. My belly clenched again, but a tiny flicker of hope came to life. Was it better, though, that he meant to take me to the bank? Or was that just the first stop? Or were the cops waiting there?

Deciding that it might be best not to antagonize him any more, I shook my jeans out and stepped into them, slipping my feet into a pair of flip flops that had been lying beneath the jeans on the floor. He was studying me intently when I looked up from fastening the jeans, wondering if I could talk him in to stepping outside while I searched for a bra and clean shirt.

He met my gaze. "That's good enough. Let's go," he said as if he'd read my mind.

It wasn't good enough for me. I still felt exposed and disadvantaged, but it occurred to me just then that Jimmy was downstairs with his gorillas and probably scared shitless.

As if *I* wasn't!

Of course *he* should be, the little shit! I knew in my heart he'd done something he shouldn't have or we wouldn't be in this mess. I didn't want to believe it. I was still hoping it would all turn out to be a huge mistake and I could threaten the Thornes with a lawsuit, but I wasn't betting on it.

I would've liked to at least comb my hair, but I had a feeling that part of Luke Thorne's determination to drag me out of my house half dressed was to keep me off balance and I wasn't about to ask him. Shoving my hair out of my face, resisting the urge to glance at the mirror to see just how hellish I looked, I stalked past him and down the stairs. He caught my arm as we reached the foyer again, manacling one hand around it.

I glanced at his hand, flicked a look at his hard face, and then decided to ignore it. He walked me out to one of the black cars and opened the back door. Jimmy, owl eyed, his freckled face flashing first white then red, was already seated in the car.

Resisting the urge to reassure him, I gave him a look that promised retribution if I managed to talk our way out of this, settled beside him, and fastened my seatbelt.

"Mom?" Jimmy whispered in a croaking voice as the car pulled in behind the bank and Luke and the driver got out.

At least he'd held his silence during the trip from our place to the bank and waited until Luke got out before he even attempted an explanation. I shook my head at him. "Don't talk now!" I hissed at him. "We'll discuss this later."

I wasn't entirely certain of when that might be. Clearly, they intended to question us at the bank before they called the police in.

Maybe I could figure out a way to talk them out of pressing charges, I thought hopefully?

Then I saw that the men who'd followed us in the other car had gotten out with Jimmy's computer and my heart sank. I had a bad feeling that whatever it was that Jimmy had been up to was in there, just waiting to hang us.

The bank was dead quiet and gloomy when we were escorted inside—tomb-like, I thought. It sent a shiver through me, almost as if it was an evil omen. We were escorted down a corridor that I'd never taken before and then up a narrow flight of stairs and along another dim corridor. It didn't make me feel any better that it wasn't in the basement. It still felt dungeon-like.

Or maybe that was only because I had every expectation that the next stop was going to be the modern equivalent of a dungeon—jail?

Jimmy and I were pushed into a small cubicle of a room and the door shut behind us.

We turned to look at each other questioningly once the door closed.

"The bank has security cameras all over the place," I said as casually I as I could in warning.

Jimmy's eyes rounded again. He tipped his head up, surveying the ceiling, and finally nodded, turning his attention to examining the room. There was a small table, or desk, and a couple of chairs. Ignoring the chairs, he moved to one corner, planted his back against the wall and slid to the floor, huddling in a knot.

I studied his posture for several moments, struggling with the urge to go to him and comfort him as I always had. He wasn't a little boy anymore, though.

He wasn't a man either.

After a moment, I crossed to where he was sitting and claimed a place on the floor beside him, patting his knee reassuringly. I wanted to ruffle the unruly tangle of blond hair standing up all over the place on his head, or finger comb it into some sort or order, but he'd established his independence before he was even five and made it clear that he didn't appreciate being treated like a 'baby'. At sixteen he was six feet tall, even if he didn't look, or act, like a grown man and it had been years and years since I'd either cuddled him or spanked him.

I felt like doing both at the moment, but I was pretty sure I wasn't up to the task.

I felt a knot of emotion well into my throat. "You've been hanging around with *those people* again, haven't you?"

He lifted his head from his knees long enough to give me a look that was a mixture of guilt, resentment, and remorse. "I didn't do anything wrong, Mama. I swear it."

I released a shaky breath. It was just as I'd feared. My heart sank.

He didn't have to say anything else. I knew *exactly* what he'd been up to.

I should have *known* he couldn't be trusted with a computer, I thought with rising anger aimed mostly at myself. He hadn't *denied* hanging with the hacker crowd that had nearly landed him in juvenile detention several years earlier, which meant that that was exactly what he'd been doing. It took all I could do to keep from bursting into an angry tirade. The only thing that kept my tongue firmly between my teeth was the certainty that we were under observation and the fear that anything I might say in my anger could and would be used against us, or at least Jimmy.

We were left waiting for over an hour. I wasn't certain if that was a deliberate attempt to break us down with anxiety or if it was because they spent that time going through Jimmy's computer and collecting evidence, but it certainly put me on edge. I was a nervous wreck by the time the door opened again.

Luke summoned me. "You wait here," he said to my son when Jimmy surged to his feet.

I was about to point out that they couldn't question my son without me present, but Jimmy bowed up at Luke, dropping a possessive—or maybe protective?—arm across my shoulders. It was a side of my son I hadn't seen, but he obviously didn't like the way Luke was looking at me.

Although in all honesty, and with a good deal of disappointment, I have to admit I certainly couldn't see anything in Luke's demeanor myself that might have brought out Jimmy's male need to protect and stake his prior claim.

Regardless, it forced me into the position of switching gears.

"We should stay together," Jimmy muttered mulishly.

I gave him a quick hug. "It's alright. You wait here. I'll find out what this is all about and then call a lawyer if I think it's necessary."

I could feel Luke's speculative gaze as he walked me down the corridor. "How old is your son?"

I felt my face redden. I've no idea why but something about his tone brought out a sense of defensiveness. "Sixteen."

He escorted me into the offices of the president of the bank, Gavin Thorne. I forgot all about my defensiveness as we crossed the reception area. I'd lusted over Luke, but it paled beside the fantasies I'd entertained about his elder brother, Gavin.

I instantly began to suffer agonies about my appearance when it should've been the furthest thing from my mind. There was something completely demoralizing about having to face Gavin Thorne looking like a bag lady, though.

I slunk into Gavin's office when Luke ushered me in and settled in the interrogation chair that awaited me, wishing I could dig a deep hole and crawl into it.

* * * *

For the third time, Jared glanced impatiently at the two way mirror that looked into the room where his cousin was waiting for the culprit Luke had dragged in. He wasn't used to standing around with his thumb up his ass. He always had places to go and things to do and he wasn't keen on standing in one spot. He'd paced the small room he stood in with his brothers until he was starting to get fucking dizzy.

"What's keeping him?"

Jessie shrugged. "Damned if I know any more than you do. You might as well cool it. There's no telling how long the interrogation will take. Luke seemed to think she was a cool one."

Jared shook his head. "But the money's back, right?"

"Pending. It's sitting there. Waiting for transfer when the bank opens."

"Well, it doesn't make any fucking sense to me. Why take it and then put it back? Luke's sure it wasn't just some kind of weird glitch?"

"That's what we hope to find out," Bret, his younger brother said dryly. "That's usually the point of an interrogation, to figure out the motive, the means, and the accomplices."

"It wasn't a glitch," Jessie said tightly. "Maybe it was supposed to look like one? Maybe the idea was to randomly transfer different sums several times, until we were convinced it was just a glitch and then drain the bank's resources and take off?"

Jared stared at him. "I don't see any point in that," he said tightly. "That doesn't make any damned sense either!"

"It's a woman. Need I say more?" Bret said.

Jared sent him an irritated look. "So speaks the man!" he said dryly. "Those twits you usually hang with might pull something like that—if they had enough brains to actually figure out how to do it at all, but this one is supposed to be smart and wily."

Bret shot him a bird. "Bite me!"

"In your next life—maybe. Depends on whether or not you come back with tits and ass."

Bret shrugged. "So I like veggies. I'm a shallow bastard. I'll take looks over brains, thank you very much."

Jared snorted. "Try a real woman sometime—looks *and* brains is better. You'd know that if you'd ever lived with any of those bimbos you go for. Nothing can piss a man off quicker than to discover he's saddled himself with a completely useless female! Maybe you can find one that's smart enough to act dumb and make you feel all manly."

"Keep it up, asshole!" Bret growled. "When I'm ready to settle down, maybe I'll take your advice. I'm not looking for anything permanent. It doesn't matter to me if they aren't useful outside the bedroom."

"And you've had so much luck with that!" Jessie retorted dryly. "When was the last time you got laid—I mean got past dragging that club of yours out?"

Bret reddened. "I get plenty," he muttered.

"Right!"

"Fuck you, Jared. You're just pissed off you aren't hung like me and Jessie!"

Jared laughed. "Like hell! You keep on thinking that—Is that why you're always chasing after the light brains? You think they'll be easier to convince to take that on? How's that working out for you?"

"I get plenty," Bret repeated through his teeth.

"Jared's right," Jessie said, not without sympathy. "You'd have better luck with an experienced woman—older. One with a couple of chicks would be even better. Once they've had babies, they *know* they can handle something like that without being ruined. A virgin can't, and they're too scared their pussy would be permanently disfigured to want to try. The young non-virginals you're always chasing—same thing. Too young, too inexperienced, too focused on themselves. An older woman is also more likely to take pity on you and give it a try even if she isn't particularly anxious to take it on. Take my word for it. I've been there."

Bret, thoroughly pissed off by now, was on the point of informing them he wasn't a fucking virgin—because it seemed to him that was what they were implying—when the door in the other room opened.

He forgot what he'd been about to say when he saw the woman Luke escorted through the door. Time seemed to stand still—at least for him. He couldn't speak for the others, mostly because he forgot they were there.

Jared sucked in a pained breath, feeling like he'd just been kicked in the gut.

The first thing he noticed was the yard of thick, dark hair swirling around her shoulders and all the way down to her hips as she walked into the room, but it sure as hell wasn't the last. The unfettered breasts that bounced and swayed with each step caught his attention in the next instant, and when she turned to look at the chair that had been set out for her, the snug fit of her jeans gave him a view of a heart shaped ass that just begged to be fucked.

"God damn that's a beautiful woman," he breathed, unaware that he'd spoken aloud.

Bret, his gaze glued to her bouncing breasts, was prompted by that to check the face that went with the beautiful pair of tits outlined by her thin t-shirt. He didn't have to guess whether she was wearing a bra or not. He could see, clearly, that she wasn't. Her nipples were standing erect and tenting the material.

He felt his cock tent his jeans. He thought for a moment he'd black out when his jeans hit maximum capacity and began to feel like a torture device.

He discovered with a good bit of disappointment that he couldn't actually see her face.

"Is she?" he asked a little hoarsely. "I can't really see her face. Move and let me have a look."

"Fuck you," Jared snarled. "I like the view from here just fine."

"Don't be a fucking asshole," Jessie growled. "Change places with me. I can't see her worth a fuck."

Bret glared at him indignantly. "I was the one that asked!"

Jessie lifted his bird finger absently.

"Shove it up your ass!"

"I'd rather shove it up that tight little ass of hers."

"Not if I get to her first," Jared said. "That is one MILF."

Jessie glanced at him. "MILF?" he asked blankly.

"One mother I'd like to fuck—make that love to fuck. Jesus! She's been working in the bank for months and neither Gavin nor Luke have fucked her?"

Jessie frowned. "It does seem unlikely, doesn't it?"

"You think the bastards have been holding out on us?" Bret demanded. "Shit! You're right. No way did both of them keep their hands off of her. You can bet your ass one of them has."

"Look at the look on Luke's face. That sly son-of-a-bitch! Man is he ever pissed off. I'll bet he feels like a fucking idiot. Been chasing that sweet thing and she's done stumped him!"

* * * *

Neither Luke nor Gavin said anything for several moments after I'd plopped weakly into the chair assigned to me. When I finally nerved myself to lift my head high enough to see if I could tell what was going through their minds from their expressions, I discovered that Luke had parked himself at the door. Leaning his broad shoulders against the panel, he'd folded his arms over his equally broad chest.

I couldn't tell anything about his expression beyond the fact that he was still totally pissed off and his face looked like it had been carved from stone.

Gavin was seated at his desk. His expression closely mirrored Luke's.

As usual, he looked immaculate—not a hair out of place. I returned my attention to my lap, idly scratching at a scaly patch of dried food on the leg of my jeans that I hadn't noticed before.

Last night's supper, if I wasn't mistaken.

I was a born slob. There was no task that I could perform without wearing half of whatever it was I was working with. If I picked up a pen, it sprang a leak. If I cooked, I was wearing a sampling of everything on the menu before I was finished. If I ate, I always managed to drip at least one glob down the front of my shirt or in my lap. I worked hard at being neat, but it never seemed to last more than five minutes.

I supposed that was one of the things that attracted me to the Thornes—they were always neat—sheer perfection.

Aside from the fact that they were sinfully handsome, built more like football players than bankers, as suave and debonair as Bond, and filthy rich.

I was so sunk in my own reflections that when Gavin abruptly broke the silence, I jumped all over. Something flickered in his eyes when I met his gaze, but I was damned if I could tell what it was.

It didn't look like empathy, though, so I decided it probably wasn't something I wanted to know.

In a perfectly calm, cool, completely controlled voice, he laid out my 'crimes' before me while I struggled to look blank since that was as close as I could come to looking innocent. Unfortunately, I couldn't do a damned thing about my complexion. I could feel the color leave my face and then return, flash with heat and then drain from my head again until I felt vaguely ill just from the fluctuation of blood flow. I'd been trying to convince myself that it couldn't possibly be as bad as it had seemed like it was when Luke and his bullies had stormed my abode and dragged me and Jimmy off like terrorists, but I discovered it was.

The question was, what did they plan to do about it?

When Gavin finally stopped speaking, I merely stared at him, waiting.

His lips tightened. "You've got nothing to say?"

I was pretty sure he'd covered everything. I searched my rattled brain, trying to think what sort of reaction I should have if I was innocent, but nothing came to me. I realized a moment later that that was probably just as well. If I claimed complete ignorance then everything fell on Jimmy and I wasn't about to allow that to happen when I had no idea of what it would mean in the long run.

Of course, I *was* ignorant. I hadn't had a clue of what Jimmy was up to, but I had to protect him, didn't I?

Maybe I should just say I was sorry, I thought a little weakly?

Wouldn't that sound like an admission of guilt, though?

"Does this mean I'm fired?" I mumbled after a prolonged moment of thought when nothing else came to mind.

* * * *

The feeling I'd had since I'd entered the office, of finding myself caught up in some sort bizarre dream, magnified as my boss' verdict pounded through my skull, defying comprehension. This was the third meeting in little over a week regarding the 'situation' but instead of growing accustomed to the interrogations and less anxious, I'd grown steadily more unnerved, knowing that, eventually, things were going to come to a head, that I was careening toward Armageddon. I couldn't help but wonder if all of the built up anxiety had finally resulted in a breakdown. "Uh," I finally managed after mulling things over the best I could for about ten minutes or so. "Could you run that by me again?"

Luke didn't look particularly happy at the question. At least, I thought that might account for the thunderous scowl and the muscle ticking in his jaw, as if he was grinding his teeth.

Gavin looked a tad peeved, too. I saw a muscle work in his lean jaw at the question—must have been a family habit. He flicked a look at his brother and his cousins before settling his cool blue gaze on me again. "You wanted to keep this out of the courts. As it happens, we do, too. We'd actually like to keep this as quiet as possible and, as long as you cooperate—fully—we can.

"Since you claim you masterminded the robbery, we'll expect you to serve time, too—as our submissive—six months to two years … depending."

I blinked as he tossed that out. *That* was the word that kept throwing me.

It *sounded* like he was saying I was going to be their sex slave.

Chapter Two

That couldn't be right, I decided. Gavin must mean it in another context.

I couldn't think of another context he might mean, though.

After studying his handsome—very hard—face again, I glanced at the other men. They were all young, all extremely attractive—and rich. Why in the world would they have any interest in *me* playing submissive? Assuming, of course, that I could manage such a feat, which totally went against my personality.

I was *old* compared to them! Well, not really compared to Gavin and Jessie. Gavin had turned thirty two recently—the bank had celebrated. Jessie, I was pretty sure, was around thirty one. Luke was only two years younger than his brother, Gavin, but I knew Jared and Bret, Jessie's two younger brothers, were closer to their mid-twenties than thirty.

They didn't even *know* me! Why would they want to screw me? Any of them? Particularly when they were the most eligible bachelors in the tri-county area—at least—maybe in the state.

It hit me then. They *didn't* know me. They didn't *want* to know me. They just wanted safe, easy, accessible pussy that didn't come with any strings, and I—or my son—had put me right into their hands.

I still couldn't figure out what had put that particular form of 'punishment' into their heads and it made me uneasy. The sex—well, they were men, young men at that. I'd heard of a study once that concluded that men thought about sex, in some context, almost constantly. I suppose it hadn't taken a great leap to arrive at using me for a sex toy—woman equals pussy equals sex equals 'owes us big time'.

There were times, I reflected in a vague, detached corner of my mind, when shock was a good thing, when it prevented a person from acting on impulses that might be contrary to self-preservation. I wasn't certain what my instincts might have prompted me to do, but I was sure it was a good thing that all I could really manage was a blank stare.

I was screwed. I was about to be *seriously* screwed, and it wasn't even my fault … this time, I thought when I finally managed to break the lock my boss had on my gaze and scan the faces of the other men in the room for any sign that they might be joking.

Their eyes were gleaming, alright, but not from amusement.

I considered my previous internal denial of culpability and realized I had to revise it. Technically, it *was* my fault that I was totally screwed—about to be—unless I could think of a way out of this. That seemed unlikely, even to me in my current near vegetative state given the fact that my brain was scrambling like a hamster on an exercise wheel and not actually making a lot of progress toward producing an excuse—or even an objection.

It *was* my son that had robbed the bank, after all—for a cool eight mil, as he'd put it when I'd finally had the chance to confront him and demand answers. Or … maybe he'd put it another way? I couldn't really recall anything before or after he'd admitted taking the eight mil.

He was a teenager, which meant that, under the law, I was responsible for everything he did. I had to consider that I might have blighted him at conception and that that was what had led me to my current predicament. At the very least, I had to take responsibility for the person I'd molded him to be after birth, didn't I?

In a way, I was resentful of that. I'd done my best. It hardly seemed fair that the parents were always blamed for everything their children did when they'd pounded the rules in day in and day out and it just hadn't taken. It was one thing to be considered a failure when you were too fucked up to try to instill a sense of right and wrong, something else entirely when you *had*, but you hadn't managed to make it stick.

Was it *my* fault that my son thought he'd discovered a 'gray' area where it came to stealing? Well, I was going to pay for it. I was willing to. I'd volunteered to in order to protect my darling idiot and keep him from completely ruining his life, but was it my fault? That was the part that bothered me most.

It was the 'I only borrowed it' clause. *I hacked into the bank where you worked, just to see if I could*—because it was there. *And I moved eight mil over to a bank account I'd set up off shore so I could prove to my buddies that I'd succeeded, and then I put it back. No harm done!*

I'd nearly collapsed into a coma of shock when he baldly admitted what he'd done—as if he was talking … sand! … not millions of dollars. There hadn't been much in the way of brain activity and what there was was the product of instinct not real thought. My motherly instincts had kicked in and my only focus had been to protect my son from his folly at all costs, whatever it took.

I could kill him later, I reasoned.

Once I had him safe.

When I'd regained the ability to string words together and make thoughts, that 'I borrowed it' clause began to boil and fester. I realized I should've kept a score board, because I couldn't recall how many times I'd told Jimmy that taking without asking, without permission, wasn't 'borrowing'. It was stealing. Returning it after use was certainly at least half right, but it didn't change the fact that it was stolen to start with. I wasn't certain if kids in general, and mine specifically, just couldn't grasp the fine points between borrowing and stealing, or if they just thought as long as they took it back afterwards that they could play dumb and *pretend* it wasn't really stealing.

It wasn't as if I didn't grasp the difference myself or that I hadn't tried to get it through to him and yet, here I sat, after years of punishing my son with everything from tongue lashing, to ass whupping, to 'jail time' in his room for 'borrowing' my personal belongings whenever the mood struck him.

I knew it was certainly at least partly my fault that this had happened. Jimmy was brilliant with a computer, had been since he was so little he'd had to stand in a chair to reach the keyboard, and, like any parent, I was proud of any and every accomplishment. Somehow, in trying to balance my pride in his abilities with trying to instill a firm grasp of right and wrong, I'd fallen down on the job.

At sixteen going on 'I know everything' this was now so apparent I wondered how I could've missed it and it began to look like my failing was going to ruin the life he had before him.

Unless my big brother, who was currently putting the culprit through a rigorous 'boot camp', could succeed where I'd failed.

I prayed he could. As much as it bothered me to think of my baby being put through hell I knew it would be worth it if he came out on the other side as a man—a responsible individual who stopped to think before he acted.

Not that that was going to help me, now, but it was something to hold on to—the possibility that my sacrifice might save my son.

It flickered through my mind that if Jimmy had just been a little better, as good as he thought he was at hacking, we still wouldn't be in our current predicament. I'd tried not to think to think about it that way, but maybe that was my defect?

We were lucky, I thought, that the bank had decided to handle it internally instead of alerting the police. I realized that that wasn't as a favor to me, even though I was an employee. It was because they couldn't afford for it to get out that a sixteen year old had by-passed their high dollar security. I didn't suppose any bank would want that bandied about, but it was especially true of Thorne Bank and Trust, a small, independently owned banking firm.

That knowledge might have been useful to me except for the little fact that I wasn't in any position to use it. Jimmy was their ace in the hole. As long as I behaved he was going to be alright. He wasn't going to end up serving time, and with a record, before the age of twenty for bank robbery.

That went both ways. They'd drummed it into Jimmy that his good behavior was also my protection. He would pay penance by enduring the six months of boot camp my brother was going to put him through and then he would work off two years 'probation' for the bank as an unofficial consultant to help them ferret out any more weaknesses in their security. As long as he did as he was told, I wouldn't be charged. I'd claimed responsibility, however, and if Jimmy got out of line again, I would be charged along with him and sent to jail.

They hadn't actually gotten around to telling me what my punishment was going to be for spawning the demon child that had breached their security—until today. I'd strongly suspected that that was because they were trying to figure out what they could do—maybe what they could get away with.

"Ms. Bridges?" Gavin prompted me impatiently.

It trembled on the tip of my tongue to disclaim any knowledge of the alleged crime—maybe even disclaim my son. I bit down on the impulse, mentally berating myself for my cowardice. Maybe I wanted to beat the pure shit out of the little snot myself, but I sure as hell wasn't going to let anybody else touch him—not while I had breath in my body.

He'd given it all back, without even being threatened—everything except the transfer fees, of course, I thought a little resentfully—proof positive that he hadn't actually, really and truly, meant to rob them.

My boss—bosses, the board members of Thorne Bank and Trust—hadn't been amused by the 'exercise'. I thought that might be partially because, as luck would have it, the accounts my son had decided to hack to drain for his proof of success were their personal accounts.

Groveling might've worked on some people, but I had a bad feeling it wouldn't work on the Thornes—plural. Thorne Bank and Trust was a family enterprise. It had been started by the fathers of the men currently in power when they hadn't been any older than their sons were now—fresh out of college. They—the founders—had come from money, of course, being the sons of well-to-do farmers who, if not actually rich, weren't far from it. Apparently their hearts had still been in farming, but when they'd finished college in their mid-twenties, they'd decided to parlay the family fortunes and diversify. By the time their sons had graduated from college, they'd had three branches and were already looking forward to retiring from banking and focusing on running their farms. They'd groomed the eldest—Gavin and Jessie—to take over the banking and dropped it in their laps. As the younger Thornes completed college, they, too, were inducted into the banking business, and now made up the board, including Luke, who evidently preferred the security end of the business.

Gavin was president of the bank, I supposed because he was the eldest son of the eldest founder.

I had assumed, when the secretary had said 'Mr. Thorne' that that was who she was referring to, and it had made my stomach knot a little tighter. I might be older than him by several years, but I was a lamb. He was a wolf, scarier even than his brother, Luke, who was pretty damned scary himself.

I wasn't sure if it was their size I found most intimidating—they were farm born and bred 'boys' and looked it—which was to say not one of them was less than five ten and all of the Thorne's looked like they could plow the fields without a tractor—or if it was because they were powerful in the sense of 'loaded with money'. If it was because they were my bosses, or it if was because I'd found myself in a very bad place. I didn't suppose it mattered either.

When I'd entered Gavin's office today to hear my 'sentence', I'd discovered much to my dismay, that the entire clan was there—not the elders—but the banking Thornes—Gavin, Jessie, Luke, Bret, and Jared.

One would've been hard enough to face! Did they have to gang up on me, I thought a little resentfully?

Gavin had surveyed me from the top of my carefully demure, if somewhat old fashioned, hairstyle to the toes of my cheap, only slightly scuffed, high heels. I had the feeling that he'd assessed the value of everything in between in that brief survey and nailed the price tag within pennies. It made me feel at a disadvantage, which had made me defensive. I'd managed to gather enough backbone to lift my chin at him challengingly.

Something flickered in his eyes. He lifted a hand, gesturing toward a chair that had obviously been set out just for me. As appropriate, I supposed, for the condemned, it was set apart from them, so that I would effectively be 'on stage' as it were once I took my seat, in clear view of all of them.

Quaking inwardly, I'd marched across the office and dropped into the chair with what dignity I could muster.

My poise, staged to begin with, began to deteriorate rapidly beneath the cold, assessing stares of the five Thornes. Even the youngest, Bret, who I knew couldn't be much more than twenty six, had the cold, Thorne haughtiness down to a science, the ability to make anyone squirm just by fixing them with the icy blue eyes that were a family trait that they all seemed to share. Their Irish heritage was evident in their swarthy complexions—although I supposed that might be from time spent in the fields since it was known that they had actually *worked* their farms throughout their youth since their parents apparently considered it 'character building'—and the inky black to the next-thing-to-black hair three of the five had. Bret and Jared were blonds—Bret's ash and Jared's a dark, more golden color—and I wondered if they'd inherited their coloring from their mother.

For that matter, I supposed they'd all inherited a good bit from their mothers. I'd seen the portraits of the founders. Neither of the two were particularly exceptional in the looks department—not bad looking men, but not nearly as handsome as their sons, whose good looks sprang from their fine, almost classical features.

Obviously money had brought beauty into the family to add to the brains.

Gavin stood up from his chair abruptly and moved around his desk, making me jump even as it brought me sharply out of my reverie. When he was facing me, he propped a hip on the desktop, folding his muscular arms over his broad chest.

He looked like a man who would've been more at home on a football field than in a banker's swivel chair, but there was no getting around the fact that he set his expensive tailored suit off to advantage.

Some people had everything, I thought morosely.

"We have an unorthodox situation here," he'd begun coolly.

I met his gaze with an effort. I wasn't sure it was all that unusual. People robbed banks all the time. Of course they weren't usually sixteen years old and they didn't generally do it with a computer without ever coming anywhere near the bank, but even so ….

"Your son's settled with your brother?"

I was surprised at the seeming change of subject. Finally, I nodded. "Buddy called last night to tell me he'd arrived."

His lips tightened. "You think your brother can handle him? Drill some discipline into him?"

I resented the implication that my son needed it, but there was no getting around the fact that he did. "He was a drill sergeant in the Marines," I said dryly. "I'm pretty sure he can handle Jimmy."

Gavin's eyes narrowed at the sarcasm that had crept into my voice. It made my heart go pitter-patter. I struggled to look contrite.

He stared me down until I was sweating bullets before he finally relented enough to glance around at the other Thornes. "To be honest, we discussed this situation a good bit, trying to come up with something we'd consider … adequate restitution."

My stomach knotted.

"Keeping you on the job, but under constant surveillance, hardly seemed like fair compensation … to us. Firing you was so far from adequate punishment that it was downright laughable. A fine? You don't make enough to pay even a reasonable fine within a reasonable time frame."

I tried not to look resentful about the pay. After all, I worked for them, damn it! If I didn't make enough to pay a healthy fine, who's fault was that? I bit my tongue to keep from suggesting they give me a raise so that I could pay a bigger fine.

"There was one thing we did all agree on," he continued grimly, his expression growing noticeably harder, "and that was that we took this very personally … particularly since the money that was 'borrowed' came out of our personal accounts."

Inwardly, I winced at the reminder. It was almost as if Jimmy had gone out of his way to get caught!

It occurred to me, though, that he might have had some strange idea that he was playing Robin Hood.

I was glad he was with my brother. I couldn't strangle him, something I was sure I'd regret once the deed was done.

"We finally agreed that the compensation we're seeking would have to be *as* personal."

I blinked at him, feeling my belly tighten. "How personal?" I asked warily.

His eyes narrowed. I could see he thought I was being deliberately obtuse. "Intimately personal."

I felt perfectly blank. "Intimate?" I asked in a strangled voice. "How intimate?"

He unfolded his arms and leaned toward me until we were almost nose to nose. "Completely and totally intimate."

That sounded *really* personal. I was having a hard time gathering my wits, though, when he was so close to me that I was beginning to feel dizzy, as if he was sucking up all the air. Then again, maybe it was just his cologne?

"Define intimate," I said a little hoarsely.

For the first time amusement seemed to flicker in his eyes. "On your back, with your legs spread," he said crudely.

I felt my jaw slide downward with shock. I *really* hadn't expected him to put it quite that bluntly.

"And any other way we want it," Jessie contributed.

I thought it was Jessie. I couldn't see who'd spoken—Gavin was totally blocking my view—and I wasn't really familiar with their voices, but I knew Jessie was second in command. It seemed logical.

It was pretty insane, to my thinking, but that part seemed logical.

"You can't be serious!" I managed finally.

Gavin straightened, thankfully, before I passed out. "Consider it time served."

I stared at him in disbelief. When I finally managed to drag my gaze from his, I carefully studied the other men in the room. I couldn't see anything in a single face that indicated they'd gone off the deep end. I was pretty sure I didn't detect lust there either.

Discovering my mouth and lips felt like the Mohave because I'd been gaping at them and panting like a winded horse, I snapped my jaws together, trying to gather a little spit to moisten my mouth and finally licked my lips when I'd mustered a little moisture.

The sense of unreality I'd felt since I'd entered the lion's den increased. "Uh," I finally managed after mulling things over the best I could for about ten minutes or so. "Could you run that by me again? I think I might not have understood."

Gavin's dark brows rose. "What part do you think you misunderstood?"

I felt my face redden. "Did you …? Was that … uh … a proposition?"

Amusement flickered in his eyes again, but anger glittered there, as well. "No, it wasn't. It was a demand."

I blinked at him. "Yes, but … for what?"

"Whatever any of the five of us want."

The heat that had surged into my face began to pulse so that I was starting to feel like a neon sign. I licked my lips again. "As in … sex?" I asked weakly.

Gavin glanced around at the others.

"You're a woman of experience—A lot I'd say, considering you have a son going on seventeen and you're only thirty three," Luke said dryly.

I gaped at him, but I felt a slow rise of anger. "I got knocked up when I was sixteen," I snapped. "That doesn't mean I've had a lot of experience!"

Truthfully, I supposed I had, but the vast majority of it had been while I was going through my wild teens—and with other teens who didn't know a hell of a lot more about what they were doing than I did. Regardless of what it apparently seemed like to them, I doubted very much I'd be a challenge to them. They were young, drop dead gorgeous, and wealthy. I didn't doubt they'd had far more experience than I'd had and, if they'd tried anything wilder than sixty nine, they'd explored more kink than I had.

That seemed to give them pause. I saw that they were exchanging questioning glances. Before I could feel even a little relief, however, they seemed to dismiss it as unimportant.

"All the better," Gavin said pointedly, adding with a touch of grim humor. "Consider it *your* boot camp."

I gaped at him. I couldn't believe we were having this discussion—at all—let alone that I'd found myself ... haggling with them. "You seriously expect me to ... serve six months of a ... servitude as ... uh ... doing ...."

Jessie narrowed his eyes. "You like the alternative better?"

As in jail? No, actually, I didn't. Particularly since I was liable to *also* find myself as a sex toy inside the slammer. It wasn't that I objected to *them*—It actually made me feel a little dizzy considering the possibility. I wasn't heady enough over it, however, that it hadn't occurred to me this wasn't going to be like a relationship where I was an equal and could object any time I wanted to. In fact, it had finally occurred to me that that was at least one of the things that appealed to them—power. They controlled every other aspect of their lives, but they had far less control when it came to their personal lives—girlfriends.

People talked. I knew they'd had a string of girlfriends since they were old enough to date. Gavin and Jessie were the only two who'd tried marriage and it hadn't worked out that well for either of them, according to rumors. Gavin and his wife had separated in less than a year, although the divorce had taken a good bit longer. Jessie had had a little better luck—sort of. He'd been married for three whole years before he'd discovered his wife in bed with another man.

All I could think was that there were some damned crazy women out there if they couldn't behave themselves enough to lasso some of the most eligible bachelors around—polished gentlemen, good looking, personable, wealthy .... They had to have some unsuspected flaws was all I could figure.

Although—maybe it was the power thing? I was pretty independent myself, used to doing things my way. I doubted I'd handle a double harness all that well.

Feeling more than a little overwhelmed, I finally gathered enough spine to request clarification, even though it made me wince inwardly to do it. I wasn't walking into this blindly.

Not that I really had a choice.

"I think … I need an outline here."

Gavin and Jessie exchanged a look. "Six months," Gavin said coolly. "For six months, assuming good behavior, you belong to us—as our submissive. You are completely at our disposal—whatever any of us ask for. Safe sex. We have you checked out thoroughly. If nothing pops up, this is how you'll make restitution."

"What's good behavior?" I asked uneasily.

"Doing what you're told—without question, without demands, without expectations, without throwing screaming fits—you keep your temper under control."

The punishment aspect worried me.

I'd begun to consider, as it slowly sank into my brain that I hadn't misunderstood them, that serving time under the five of them wasn't going to be any huge hardship. They still had the look of farm boys despite their high dollar suits—strapping young lads, healthy, strong, muscular. They could've looked like Quasimoto and still been attractive given they were all wealthy, powerful young men, but they didn't. They actually looked more like models for some upscale men's clothing magazine—except for the brawn even their expensive suits didn't hide.

"Exactly what does being a submissive entail?" I asked cautiously.

I could see surprise flash in Gavin's gray-blue eyes. He flicked a glance at 'the rat pack'. I wasn't certain if he was looking for suggestions in explaining or wondering how I could possibly have reached such an advanced age and not know what 'submissive' was.

I thought my seeming ignorance might've thrown him. I had the feeling they'd expected me to know a lot more than I actually did because I was pretty sure that, by this time, they'd gone over my life with a microscope and that there wasn't much they'd missed. They knew how old I was just from my application for the job since I worked for them—the bank. It couldn't have taken them long to add up my age and my son's and come up with 'born slut'. People inevitably did when they realized I'd 'gotten myself knocked up' when I was barely sixteen—which no doubt accounted for Luke's previous, nasty, comment.

And I'd never been married.

My boyfriend, Jimmy's father, had vanished when he'd discovered that (a) I wasn't quite as old as I'd claimed, (b) I'd gotten myself knocked up in spite of the condoms, and (c) he was either going to land in jail because I was underage or find himself saddled with a child bride and a squalling infant.

I'd tried to remedy the 'never been married' part for a while, not because I was deeply concerned about my reputation—the one I had was already bad and couldn't be fixed—but because I'd decided my darling needed a father figure and a few siblings. When I'd finally realized the string of boyfriends I'd dragged up weren't interested in anything but the proof that I 'put out' and either ignored Jimmy or were downright mean to him because they didn't want him around, I'd lost interest in the hunt. I'd hardly dated in the years since and occasionally wondered if 'it' had grown up from lack of use but, although I hadn't had much experience in years and years, I was still a world away from innocence—which still didn't equate to any knowledge or experience regarding the world of 'kink'. I didn't get 'it' often enough to be jaded.

I knew just enough to be deeply worried.

Beyond that, rich kids with a desire to 'own' a living, breathing sex toy had a seriously high scare factor in my book.

"You do what you're told when you're told to do it … without questions, whining, or complaints," Luke said sardonically.

I focused my attention on him when he spoke, blinking rapidly while my mind tabulated that. "Yes, but … could I have a sort of list of what I might be told?"

There! I'd established my iron will!

"Jail sounds better?"

I turned to look at Gavin when he spoke, considering that.

Maybe. That depended on what they might expect. At the moment, being cellmates with somebody called Big Bertha was way down on my list of 'want to experience', but I was seriously allergic to pain and if they were 'in' to BDSM I wasn't certain but what I might be just as well off with Big Bertha.

"This isn't a negotiation," Gavin said tightly, obviously tired of waiting for a response. "Yes or no?"

Chapter Three

"What did you make of that?" Jessie asked, breaking the lengthy silence that had held them from the time Luke had escorted Stephanie Bridges from the office.

Gavin had been glaring at the surface of his desk, idly drumming his pen on it as if it was drumstick. At Jessie's question, he looked up and met his gaze absently for a few moments before his eyes focused. A derisive smile twisted his lips. "She didn't exactly leap at the suggestion, did she?"

"You thought she would?" Jared asked with a mixture of surprise and, oddly enough, a touch of admiration for Stephanie.

Gavin shrugged irritably. "It isn't as if there's anything wrong with any of us. I could see it if we were old, paunchy, and balding," he retorted tightly.

"Maybe that's because you misjudged her," Bret put in, his own voice tight with irritation. "I know you find that hard to believe, but you are wrong occasionally."

Gavin narrowed his eyes at his young cousin. "Misjudged? She has a history for wildness."

"Christ!" Jared snapped. "Because she got in trouble when she was a teenager? If everybody was judged by the things they did in their teens, there wouldn't be many upstanding citizens! Besides, you know damned well she didn't have anything to do with the break-in—whatever she said. She only said that to protect her son—who's *also* a teen."

Gavin gave him a look. "As wild as she was when she was that age, obviously. What are you suggesting? That we should've just given them both a slap on the wrist? If I remember correctly, *you* were the one who suggested it."

Jared reddened faintly. "I *said* she was a MILF. I was just thinking out loud."

Jessie looked amused. "Which is what put it in our heads."

Bret's lips twisted derisively. "Yeah, right! Don't sit there and tell me it didn't run through your minds, too, the minute Luke dragged her in here that day. If I'd seen her like that before, I would've already made a play to get in her pants."

"It's against policy to fuck employees," Gavin reminded him shortly.

Bret and Jared exchanged a speaking look before Bret met Gavin's gaze.

Irritation flickered across his features since he knew damned well what that look was for. He and Jessie, both, had met their wives when they'd come to work in the bank. "Which is exactly why we adopted that policy," he retorted in response to Bret's knowing look.

"I hate to point it out, but Steph *is* an employee," Jared said.

"And this is an entirely different situation," Gavin responded irritably. "It's restitution, which we're entitled to. Whether the money was returned or not, it was taken, and for all we know that was just a trial run. Besides—whether she actually took part in the damned robbery or not, she took responsibility. A court of law would've held her accountable and prosecuted her. A few months of putting up with our demands isn't that great of a hardship. At least, maybe, it'll make her keep a tighter reign on that kid of hers! We all agreed on that. What's bothering you now?"

They *had* agreed on that. Jared finally realized, though, what was really bothering him about it and, he suspected, them, as well. "Yeah, well the reality of it isn't quite what the fantasy seemed like at the time," he said finally. "I don't especially like the fact that she didn't jump at it, if you want to know the truth. I thought it didn't matter how she felt about it as long as she agreed to it. Now—well, shit! I've never fucked a woman that didn't want to fuck me, damn it—or at least *pretended* she wanted to because she wanted to get into my wallet as badly as I wanted to get into her pants!"

"Maybe she didn't bother to pretend because she knows she won't be getting into the wallets?" Gavin retorted dryly. "If you don't mind a pretense, why worry about it? She'll *act* enthusiastic to protect her son."

* * * *

I was still in a state of shock when Luke dropped me at my place again, informing me that he'd be back to collect me when the test results were in.

The examination had been a nightmare. I never had really liked doctors and steered clear of them unless I just had to have one. Money was only part of the reason—I couldn't really afford to have a doctor on retainer—but the other was that I just hated being poked and prodded.

Apparently, that was something I was about to get used to.

They assumed I'd check out alright. I supposed that should have comforted me. It didn't particularly because it seemed to me that they'd done a lot of checking into my background to be so certain.

It seemed to indicate that they'd known all along that my sex life was virtually non-existent, which made me wonder where they'd gotten the idea that I was such a 'worldly' woman.

So maybe they hadn't thought so any of the time?

It made me uneasy in an indescribable way to think that might've actually had something to do with their decision—that I was practically a born again virgin, a woman mature enough to have had enough experience to at least know my way around men. And yet I hadn't progressed much beyond first experimentation so I couldn't possibly challenge their own experience—and the fact that I couldn't refuse them whatever they wanted was just icing on the cake, I supposed.

Was it a power play? I was sure that had to be part of it. Maybe not having to worry about their partner was part of it, too? In this day and age sex had become like Russian Roulette. I had the feeling that, once they had an all clear, they meant to see to it that there was no chance of 'contamination' of their pussy.

It was a little comforting to think that, because the only way they could insure it was to make sure they were also safe and keep it that way.

Beyond that, the fact that it was me was immaterial, I was sure. They weren't particularly attracted to or drawn to me. I'd just very obligingly put myself into their clutches.

Maybe the temper thing was telling, too? They wanted access to uncomplicated, unemotional sex. They couldn't get that with wives or girlfriends, and using prostitutes, for men obviously conscious of the health risks, wasn't appealing enough to consider that route.

It didn't make me feel particularly good about myself to realize that I'd just agreed to prostitute myself to save my son's future, but then I wasn't going to regret that. It wasn't as if it would become widely known. They were just as anxious to preserve their reputation and the reputation of the bank as I was to preserve at least a façade of respectability for my son's sake.

Jimmy didn't ever have to know what I'd done to keep his record clean and keep him out of jail.

That was all that really mattered, I told myself. Jimmy would be saved from his folly and, hopefully, my brother would knock some sense into him, the close call and the realization that I'd also paid for his mistake would keep him from making another, possibly, more costly one in the future.

All I had to do was get through my six months of 'boot camp'.

It was the fear of the unknown that made my belly cramp. I wouldn't have worried about straight sex. I had a feeling, though, that I was going to be expected to do things I might not particularly like.

They'd assured me they weren't 'in' to sado-masochism, thank god!

I was allergic to pain.

Deep down, though, I realized I was scared to death that their idea of pain and mine might not be the same.

* * * *

I was to continue working at the bank as before in order to prevent any gossip from arising because it had been agreed that I would continue to draw a paycheck and appear to go about my business as usual. Since I had financial obligations I couldn't ignore, I was almost tearfully grateful for this concession even though I found it very difficult to 'act normal' when my entire life had been turned upside down and I suspected the paycheck was to insure they had proof my services had been paid for if I was stupid enough to report it.

Of course, that would still put them in the uncomfortable position of paying for sex, but they couldn't be charged with anything as nasty as blackmail or slavery.

Fortunately, the test results didn't come back until after my first week back from 'sick leave'. I supposed it was fortunate, anyway, because although I was tortured with dread I could at least put off the beginning of my 'sentence' a little longer.

I'd always been 'in' to procrastination, figuring anything I could put off long enough might actually go away.

It didn't in this case. The first Friday after the results were in, Luke offered to give me a 'lift' home. It raised eyebrows. I could see speculation in the other clerks' eyes, but since gossiping about fellow employees or customers was grounds for termination, I supposed Luke wasn't particularly worried about it.

He didn't take me home, needless to say, but I was in such turmoil that it wasn't until we passed the city limits sign that it penetrated my self absorption enough for that to register. "Where are we going?"

Luke slid a narrow eyed look at me.

I felt my belly tighten.

Folding my lips, I looked out the window on my side. Apparently, I wasn't allowed to even ask.

When I didn't say anything else, he deigned to enlighten me. "We have a house that's reasonably accessible to all of us … not as convenient as we'd like, but a short drive for any of us."

And, of course, that was all that really mattered!

My tension increased. To my surprise and dismay, however, it wasn't all nerves. Some of it, as much as I hated to admit it, was anticipation.

I wouldn't have admitted it, even to myself, except my pussy had started clapping and that was pretty hard to dispute.

It occurred to me fairly quickly that convenient to them probably meant a long drive for me if I was to continue working at the bank. I decided to keep my thoughts to myself, though. It seemed pretty obvious the five of them had carefully worked out every detail and they'd already been very clear that I was just to do as I was told.

The drive took an hour—at Luke speed—which was to say that he didn't pay a lot of attention to the speed limit signs and didn't pass other cars poking along at the limit so much as he slalomed the highway. I was pretty sure I'd left nail prints in the door. I'd stomped the 'brake' on my side enough times that Luke was beginning to look like a thundercloud by the time we pulled up in front of the neat little ranch that looked like it was in the middle of nowhere.

As *if* the experience I had ahead of me wasn't enough to sap the starch out of my knees!

Some of the anger glittering in Luke's eyes seemed to dissipate, however, when he helped me out of the car.

No doubt it was the whiteness of my face. His gaze flickered over my face and amusement joined the anger. "Did you enjoy the drive?" he asked coolly as he walked me to the door.

I managed a weak smile, suppressing the urge to tell him, sarcastically, that I was *so* looking forward to the drive back. There was the little 'no complaints' clause to consider, but at that point I was more worried that he might take it as a challenge and *really* put the car through it's paces.

Gavin, Jessie, Bret, and Jared were already inside, I discovered, trying not to feel too dismayed. I hadn't realized until that moment that I'd hoped—actually expected—that it was going to be a one-on-one sort of thing even though I'd known I was to be passed around. It was unnerving to think I might have to get used to the idea of 'serving' all of them at once.

Maybe, I thought, trying to look for a silver lining, it was only sort of an initiation? I was just starting out and they all wanted to be present for the 'launch' or something like that?

I would've come to a halt the minute I spied them if Luke hadn't had a firm grip on one arm. Either he didn't notice my attempt to balk, or he chose to ignore it, escorting me into the center of main living area, which was a lot larger than I'd expected.

The group, with the exception of Luke, had discarded their formal business suits. Attired now in comfortably casual clothes, it was hard to imagine them as the hard faced business men I'd known up to that point.

Particularly since they each had a long necked bottle of beer.

That made me uneasy. My experiences with drinking men hadn't led me to trust them. I couldn't see that any of them looked drunk or even high, but that, I was afraid, was subject to change as the evening wore on.

Luke abandoned me in the middle of the floor, striding toward the only empty chair and sprawling in it.

Gavin looked me over assessingly—they all did. "Strip."

I blinked at him as if the word was completely alien to me. "What?"

His lips tightened. I could see he was debating whether he felt like going back over the 'rules'. "We want to see what we have. Take your clothes off."

I glanced around at the men surrounding me. They were all eyeing me with varying degrees of annoyance and anticipation.

I hadn't expected anything like this, but then I hadn't known *what* to expect. Uncertain if they expected me to perform like a strip tease or just to undress, I reached for the top button of my blouse, telling myself I might as well get used to it. They were all going to see me naked eventually. There was no avoiding that.

I would still have far preferred a darkened room.

I could well imagine the brightly lit room I was standing in wasn't going to leave my flaws undisclosed. When I'd reached the last button above the waist of my trousers, I pulled the shirt free and unbuttoned the last, shrugging out of the blouse.

I looked around a little uncertainly for a place to put it and finally just dropped it on the coffee table in front of me when I saw that the couch and every chair was already occupied. Pushing my heels off with my toes, I kicked them under the coffee table so I wouldn't stumble over them.

My underwear wasn't anything to excite them—just plain, ordinary—cheap—stuff like everything else I owned, but I was thankful it was at least relatively new. Unbuttoning my trousers and sliding the zipper to the bottom, I pushed them over my hips and stepped out of them, pausing to look around a little hopefully.

Gavin gave me a look.

Uttering a shaky breath, I unfastened the bra and dropped it on the growing mound and then slid my panties off, staring at a distant point and trying not to think about the fact that they were studying me.

The silence was so prolonged, though, that it unnerved me.

I discovered when I finally flicked a curious glance at them that I had their full attention—as I'd thought. In point of fact, they seemed a little stunned. I didn't know whether to take that in a good way or a bad way. I'd figured, especially considering my age and the fact that I'd had a child, I was in good shape. I'd been fortunate enough to have a good figure and I'd worked to keep it up.

"Come here," Gavin said abruptly.

His voice sounded a little strange, a little hoarse. It sent a shiver through me. Ignoring the reluctance tugging at me, I moved toward him. He reached to set his bottle on the table beside him without even glancing in that direction as I reached him, missing the table almost completely. To give him credit, his reflexes were amazing. He caught it even as it began to topple from the edge, righted the bottle, and set it carefully in the center the second time.

He didn't touch me. In fact, he shifted back in his seat, as if to lounge more comfortably, but I saw, as I looked down at him, that he had a raging erection. It was no small thing and it occurred to me that he might've shifted to give it more room in the jeans that were abruptly way too tight in that particular area.

My nipples, already semi-erect just from undressing, grew to hard peaks as he studied my breasts.

I hoped to hell he couldn't see the stretch marks from my pregnancy. I'd been fortunate enough I hadn't gotten many, and they'd faded, thankfully, over the years, but I was still keenly aware that my skin was far from flawless. Since I'd been so young when I'd gotten pregnant, I hadn't even actually gotten the chance to reach adulthood with pretty skin. At least my breasts were still fairly firm. Considering my penchant for going braless whenever I could, I was *really* lucky.

"Turn around," he said finally.

Feeling more and more uncomfortable, I turned and put my back to him.

"Take your hair down," he ordered after a prolonged silence.

Reaching up, I started pulling the pins out. As old fashioned as the 'do' was, I'd clung to it for years. My hair was exceptionally thick and grew twice as fast as anybody else's that I knew of—which I'd found to be both a blessing and a curse. It was just as well I liked to keep it long because I couldn't afford the upkeep on regular hair cuts. When I'd collected all of the pins, I pulled the elastic loop out that I used to confine it on top of my head and shook it to loosen it.

My hair fell to my hips. It was, and always had been, my only claim to beauty, which was why I liked to keep it long even though it wasn't fashionable anymore to do so.

Of course, as short as I was, it only made me look shorter, but I had a deep seated anxiety that I wasn't terribly feminine looking in the face and was afraid if I cut it short I'd either be mistaken for a lesbian or, worse, a male.

At least, I thought a little wryly, they seemed content enough for the moment just to look.

Jessie crooked a finger at me after a moment, summoning me to him, and examined me with the same thoroughness as Gavin had. When they'd all, apparently, looked their fill, Gavin told me to go 'freshen up' and put on the outfit that had been left on the bed for me.

And not to lock the door because they might want to watch.

And to shave my pussy, because they preferred it bare to *au naturale*.

So much for thinking they'd been appreciating the view, I thought irritably!

The 'outfit' brought me to an abrupt halt when I spied it.

Even though I was well aware, acutely aware, that I'd taken on the role of trollop for the next six months, it was still a jolt to discover I was expected to dress the part. The 'outfit' looked like something from a house of prostitution.

At least Hollywood's take on it.

Ignoring it for the moment, I stalked into the bathroom and defiantly locked the door to take care of private matters. I was tempted to leave it locked but decided that privacy, when they were around, for personal matters was probably about all I could hope for.

Maybe not even that if they were really weird and kinky.

I'd heard stories—from my son no less!—about people who liked to watch other people go potty and some even went a step further and wanted people to go potty on them. I was damned if I could see where the thrill in that was. We were definitely going to run into trouble, real fast, if they were that weird!

I wished I'd had enough backbone to demand that they list their preferences and quirks before I'd agreed. Jail might actually have been preferable.

Might still be.

* * * *

Gavin adjusted his dick in his jeans and lifted a shaking hand to scrub it over his face as soon as he heard the bedroom door shut behind Stephanie Bridges. He'd thought the first time he'd noticed her that she was an attractive woman—older than he had any interest in since he knew she was in her thirties even if she didn't look it—a little short and plump for his tastes for that matter, but she had a pretty face and pleasant smile that she was generous with. He hadn't especially liked the way she wore her hair all slicked back from her face in a ball on top of her head. He hadn't especially liked the fact that she hardly wore any makeup, not because he particularly liked women that did but because he'd suspected it meant she was some sort of religious freak—same with the hair, for that matter.

He'd begun to think he'd completely misjudged her from the moment they'd discovered the breach in their security and begun investigating her, not the usual background check, but a thorough, in depth investigation that had turned up all sorts of interesting information.

That hadn't prepared him for what he'd seen when she'd stripped for them, though.

After a moment, he glanced toward his brother, Luke, and his cousins, wondering what they thought about her. From the vacant looks on their faces he thought they'd probably been as stunned as he was. "What did you think, Luke?"

Luke flicked a glance at him, cleared his throat and abruptly grinned. "I think I'd like to watch her shave her pussy. If it's as pretty as the rest of her …."

Annoyance flickered through Gavin. The thought had crossed his mind, as well, but he couldn't see the five of them piling in to the bathroom to watch.

Jessie cleared his throat. "We're going to have to work out some kind of system."

Gavin glanced at him questioningly.

Jessie shrugged. "The woman's built like a fuck doll, Gav. I don't know about you, but I didn't figure there was going to be any real trouble taking turns at the trough. One week night for each of us and a toss on the weekends seemed reasonable enough when we talked about it before, when none of us actually knew what she looked like. I'm not sure I'm going to be satisfied with one night a week and, maybe, once on the weekend. In fact, I'm pretty fucking sure I won't. No. Make that, I'm *sure* I won't."

"As badly as I hate to agree with Jessie, on anything," Jared drawled, flicking his older brother a glance of wry amusement, "I could fuck her five times a day and not get tired of it in any hurry. God damn, that's a beautiful woman!"

Gavin's lips tightened. "She's all ours for the next six months."

Luke chuckled. "Which, at the current going rate, means twenty four shots at her tight little ass … with, maybe, a few extras, depending on who wins the toss on the weekends. That going to be enough to pacify you, big brother?"

Bret got to his feet abruptly. "Look, the only damned reason we came up with this to start with was because we were tired of having blue balls. I can get once a week from my ex-girlfriends."

Jared grinned at him. "Yeah, but you have to work for that. This'll just be waiting—like having a wife, except better."

Gavin gave him a look. "If you'd ever been married, you wouldn't be stupid enough to think that way. I was lucky to get it once a week after she got the ring on her finger."

"Except I won't be getting any more than I can now!" Bret retorted on the heels of Gavin's comment.

Gavin flicked him a look of annoyance. "We can't fuck her to death, Bret! There's five of us—one of her."

"So? We've got six months. We could split that up and each take her part of the time—all to ourselves."

"I don't think so," Luke growled. "I'm about to explode now."

"Fuck that shit!" Jared and Jessie both seconded him.

Gavin studied them. "Alright, so we'll have to think of some way to sort it out between us that won't convince her she'd be better off doing time in jail," he said dryly.

* * * *

The bathroom, I discovered, had a monster tub. Soaking wasn't something I usually had time for—I wasn't sure I did at the moment—but it was tempting. After rummaging around for what I needed, I studied the tub thoughtfully while I trimmed the old bush with a pair of scissors I'd found. I'd never shaved that area before, beyond a little hedge trimming for neatness, but I figured cutting it as short as possible before I attacked the problem with a razor was probably the best way to go about it.

They'd shaved me in the hospital when I'd had Jimmy without first trimming it short, but then I also needed to shave my legs and pits and I didn't figure the razor would hold up to that much use.

Although I wasn't in any huge hurry to dash right back out to the guys—I was, in point of fact, trying to focus on *anything* besides what might await me—I decided to wait on the bubble bath for another time since it occurred to me that the longer I lingered the more likely I was to have company.

Unless they got busy enjoying the beer and each other's company while I was otherwise occupied?

It seemed possible, but how likely was that, I wondered?

Ordinarily, men seemed to prefer each other's company, but there was pussy on the menu tonight. It might be a different story.

I wasn't certain I could handle becoming part of a peep show … yet. Too heavy a dose of reality too quickly and I might unravel. A sense of unreality had gotten me this far, and shock had heaped upon that and gotten me through the strip show.

Bathing was a chore. It was always a damned chore when I shaved. I had short legs but there was still plenty of area to cover. Adding an extremely sensitive area with all sorts of crevices that I couldn't actually see all that well made it *more* of a chore. I had to take care of a lot of it by feel and I didn't especially like having to do that considering where I was using the razor.

It occurred to me to hunt a mirror, but that was one area of my anatomy I wasn't actually that familiar with and I liked it that way.

I didn't want to know what *they* would be looking at.

Contrary creature that I was, in spite of everything, I couldn't dismiss my tightly wound nerves and erratic pulse as just anxiety about my situation. Humming beneath it was a teeny tiny bit of anticipation.

I supposed, if I hadn't been a complete moron, there wouldn't have been even a smidgen of anticipation threading my veins. I would've been building self-righteous indignation, hate for the men who'd put me in the position.

Unfortunately, although I did feel some resentment, I was too honest with myself and too fair-minded to slough the blame off on them. Granted, their choice of restitution bordered on the bizarre as far as I was concerned, but I realized I did owe it to them. Whatever their motivations, they'd saved my son from his actions. I was grateful.

I wasn't sure I was grateful enough that I would've been even vaguely excited if they'd been twice my age, saggy, and balding, but I was pretty sure I would've been willing to try to close my eyes and my mind and do what I had to do, regardless.

There wasn't much I wasn't willing to do to protect my idiot son.

I was resolved to beat the snot out of him if he ever even looked at a computer again, but I knew in my heart that I would've taken on Satan if I'd had to.

Good thing for me, the five devil's waiting for me in the living room weren't Satan.

I hoped they weren't, anyway.

When I'd finished bathing, I discovered I didn't have any make up.

I shrugged it off. I never wore much and I doubted they'd waste a lot of time looking at my face.

Blotting dry, I went back into the bedroom and sat down on the bed, studying the outrageous costume they'd gotten for me, wondering if it would actually fit or if I could tell, given the skimpiness, if it didn't.

They'd forgotten to include panties, I discovered.

An oversight? Or was I not supposed to wear any?

When I'd thoroughly searched the area for panties, I finally concluded that that was a no. Alrighty, then. A corset that left most of my boobs hanging out, a garter belt and hosiery—and let us not forget the beautiful wrap to go over it that I could've read newsprint through.

I moved to survey myself in the mirror when I'd gotten in to the slutty outfit, wondering how I could look and feel *more* naked with it on than I'd felt before I put it on.

Ok, so part of it was the fact that it was designed specifically to frame points of interest—boobs and pussy—without cluttering the view by showing anything else. The rest of it was the fact that my pussy was airish now that it was completely denuded.

Narrowing my eyes, I studied the lips of my sex, wondering if they'd always looked like that, or if they were swollen, or maybe it was because they suddenly looked so white? White always looked bigger, I reminded myself.

I hadn't realized my pussy lips were fat, though. I didn't like that.

I was sorry I'd decided to examine them in the damned mirror. Now I was going to be self-conscious about *that*!

Girding myself, I finally decided I really didn't have any choice but to go out, even though I was actually tempted to just sprawl out on the bed, hook my heels behind my head, and wait.

I discovered a cookout was in progress when I left the bedroom. My stomach growled at the delectable scent wafting through the French doors, which opened onto a wide screened-in back porch.

And I was certainly dressed for a good old-fashioned barbeque, I thought wryly, wondering if there was any way I could actually eat and still breathe with the corset I was wearing ... and eat without dribbling grease down between my boobs and/or pussy lips.

Despite the sarcasm and irritation behind the thoughts, my mind leapt to an image of them licking the juices off of me and I abruptly felt really warm for someone mostly naked.

Chapter Four

Gavin, heading in through the screen door, glanced in my direction, did a double take when he caught sight of me, and put on brakes. If I hadn't been looking straight at him when he did, I would never have known it. He collected himself after a pause that was little more than a hesitation and headed toward the dining table with the platter of steaks he was carrying where most of the others seemed to have gathered.

I discovered when I'd followed him with my gaze to the table that the others had suddenly become aware of me, as well.

They were all staring but I couldn't decide whether it was with approval or not.

The sound of a bottle hitting the floor and a curse, snatched my attention away from the men at the table and I saw Luke had followed Gavin in and had dropped one of the bottles of beer he'd been carrying.

I was barefoot. Heading toward the area of disaster where broken glass littered the floor didn't seem like a good idea, but he looked like he could use some help. "I'll get something to help you clean up," I volunteered, turning away and heading toward what I assumed was the kitchen. It transpired that I was right. A small closet yielded up a dust pan and broom.

Luke had collected a handful of glass by the time I returned. He glanced up at me when I paused just outside the puddle. His gaze flickered over me, lingering—surprise! Surprise!—on the serving of tits and pussy the outfit displayed. Frowning, he looked away again. "Just hand me that," he muttered somewhat irritably. "You're barefooted."

He had amazing powers of observation to have noticed I was barefooted when, as far as I could tell, his gaze hadn't dropped below my crotch, but I supposed that was one of the reasons he was head of security. He had an eye for details.

I couldn't decide whether to crouch down and hand them to him or to bend over.

Shrugging internally, I bent over. My boobs promptly fell completely out of the corset. He looked up at me. His gaze snagged on my bobbing boobies as he groped blindly for the dust pan. I shoved it into his hand.

"If you'll hold that, I'll sweep up what I can."

He was still staring at my boobs. I think it took him a moment to realize I was talking about the dust pan. A faint flush suffused his cheeks.

"That's alright. Just go sit down before you step on the glass."

Yielding up the broom, I adjusted my boobs and headed for the table.

Gavin, Jessie, Bret, and Jared leapt up from their seats so fast they almost turned their chairs over. I politely pretended I hadn't noticed because I could see the moment they realized what they'd done and that they'd suddenly encountered a situation they weren't certain how to react to. Good manners had obviously been so ingrained in them that they automatically leapt up when a woman approached the table. Now they were wondering if they should give me the same courtesy as they would a lady.

I could see the debate in their expressions.

Gavin ended it by stepping around to pull a chair out for me.

The glance he sent the others was speaking, but I couldn't tell what he was saying.

I looked down at my lap uncomfortably. My appetite had mysteriously vanished and the ugliness of my situation hit home in a way it hadn't before. It didn't matter what they thought of me, I told myself fiercely. It wasn't as if they'd thought highly of me *before* they'd propositioned me. Being looked upon as a common thief was just as disreputable as being looked upon as a slut.

Alright, maybe not, but it still didn't matter. If not for what had happened none of the five would ever have known I lived and breathed. *Maybe* they would've treated me with the courtesy of a lady if they'd noticed me, but that would only have been because it was ingrained in them to behave like gentlemen, not because they'd given any thought to whether or not I deserved respect.

I wasn't going to think about that, I decided. I was here for one reason only. If I could tolerate it, that would be great. If I actually liked and/or enjoyed some of it, that would be even better, but the bottom line was this was restitution and when it was over with I didn't have to see them again.

So it didn't matter what they thought.

To be fair, they tried politely to gloss over the awkward moment. As soon as they'd settled in their seats again they began to pass the platter of meat, the bread, the salad bowl, and everyone was so occupied with helping their plates that the uncomfortable silence passed quickly, hardly noticeable, really. Luke, now reeking of beer, finally made it to the table with enough bottles to go around. Settling beside me, he passed them around.

"Sorry," he murmured as he handed me one. "I hope you drink beer. Nobody thought to get anything else."

Why the hell not, I thought, although I'd never had one?

It tasted worse than it smelled and that was saying something. I made a face and shuttered.

Bret, seated across from me, choked on his swallow of beer and nearly spit it in his plate.

"I guess that means you don't like it?" Luke murmured, amusement threading his voice.

I looked at him. "It's actually … well, no," I finished, deciding there was no point in lying.

"It tastes better as you go along," Jessie murmured.

I saw amusement and something a lot warmer glittering in his eyes. I'd been debating heading to the kitchen for water, but I decided being a little tipsy might be just the thing. I needed a little bottled courage.

I needed *something*!

The discomfort I'd felt from the time I'd arrived had only deepened with the preparations and the outfit. I was excruciatingly aware of the seat of the chair against my bare ass. The corset, hard to breathe in when I was standing, squeezed me even more sitting, and my boobs kept threatening to spill out and land in my plate every time I leaned in to take a bite of food.

Beyond that, I could see the guys were a lot more interested in staring at me than eating. They made a pretense of it, but they drank more beer than they ate of the steak and fixings, and even though I only actually caught them staring at me a few times, it was enough to assure me that I wasn't just imagining it.

It was a shame, really, because the steaks were fabulous and cooked to perfection. They deserved a lot more appreciation than they got.

I *tried* to appreciate the food, but the corset, as it turned out, was the best diet invention ever conceived. It was impossible to stuff yourself while wearing one, I discovered, no matter how badly you wanted to. I hadn't taken more than three bites before I was so full I thought I might pass out. Of course, it was possible that the three gulps of beer I chased it with were at least partially responsible for the dizziness.

It was certainly responsible for the 'don't give a damn' that began to infiltrate my brain. I was tempted to pursue it, but Luke removed temptation from my reach, replacing it with water.

I sent him a resentful look. He encountered it with one of cool censure and put me in my place. Grimacing, I pushed my plate away and sipped at the water, hoping the slight buzz I'd gotten would sustain me through the evening ahead of me.

It was the unknown, I knew, that was the source of most of my anxiety. If I could just get through the first little bit, acclimate to the situation, it wouldn't be so nerve wracking anymore.

When they'd finished their meal, everyone got up and headed to the kitchen with their scraps. I got up and followed them, discovering when I arrived that they'd formed a line by the trash to rake plates. The line flowed from there to the sink and the dishwasher.

I'd hardly touched mine. I broke ranks and headed to the refrigerator to squirrel it away for later. They watched me as I turned and headed back to the great room. I didn't look, but I knew.

I was beginning to wonder, in fact, if they were just watchers—not that I'd object to that—I didn't think. Obviously there were a lot of men who just loved to look at naked women or there wouldn't be so many magazines of naked women.

I wondered, as I reached the great room again, if I should try 'posing'. After considering it for several moments, I realized I didn't actually have it in me to pose—not with the audience I had. One—maybe—that was debatable because I didn't know a single one of them well enough to be comfortable.

I wasn't an exhibitionist at heart, but I wasn't shy either, not especially. When at home, comfortable to me was half naked anyway. To spare my son's blushes, I covered everything up, but ditching everything that confined—bra, shoes, any clothes that actually touched me—that was comfortable—and, unless I was doing anything outside of the house, I frequently spent half of the day in a big, roomy t-shirt and panties and nothing else.

This getup was a little exposed, even for me, though, and it made me blush just to think about fanning coochie for their inspection. I didn't have enough of a buzz from the beer for *that*!

Waiting was driving me crazy, though! Admittedly, I was a little stirred up. They were a good looking bunch of young, healthy males and I sure as hell wasn't immune. Beyond that, the sensitive skin bared by my outfit was tingling almost constantly, which prevented me from 'settling' even though it wasn't nearly arousing enough to appease me. Mostly, though, I was just tired of being anxious.

I looked at them a little expectantly when the five trooped back in to the great room, but except for glancing at me, more as if to make certain I hadn't flown the coop, they proceeded to ignore me. Settling at the table, Gavin produced a deck of cards and began to shuffle them.

Trying to ignore the sense of deflation that washed through me, I perched on the couch for a little while, allowing my gaze to wander around the room curiously while I listened to the conversation bouncing back and forth between them. I was tired, but I wasn't used to doing nothing. Being a single mother, idleness wasn't something I was very familiar with. There was always something that needed to be done.

I got up after a little bit and decided to explore the house more thoroughly. The place was neat, but there were enough personal items scattered about here and there that I felt sure that the house wasn't just a 'love nest' they'd leased specifically for sex. There also didn't seem to be enough to indicate permanent residence, though, so I decided that it must be sort of a hangout for the young Thornes.

I found three additional bedrooms on the opposite end of the house—obviously the one where I'd been installed was the master bedroom. These shared a bath. None of them were very large, but two had a pair of single beds. The third—at first glance it looked like some sort of medieval torture chamber. I nearly passed out with fright right there.

The temptation instantly assailed me to head for the nearest exit and run. As I stared at it bug eyed, unable to move in any direction, however, it finally dawned on me that it was sex toys. The handcuffs were fur lined for comfort. The whips weren't leather, but something that looked much softer.

Mostly everything had been piled in—as if they'd made a shopping trip to some adult store and bought up anything that caught their eye.

Oh, they were planning on experimentation!

I couldn't decide how I felt about it—almost indulgent, I thought. The enthusiasm it seemed to indicate not only appeared to point to the fact that they hadn't done it before, but also to their youth. They were such serious minded and responsible young men that it was hard to remember that they were so young.

Tangled in that sense of fond amusement was a mixture of uneasiness since I was going to get to experiment with kinky, too, and I wasn't sure I wanted to, and a little bit of curiosity.

I closed the door when I heard sounds in the living room indicating that they were stirring. The door hadn't been locked, so I didn't think they were particularly worried about me finding it, but I decided finding me in the room might be too much temptation for them. They might decide to just jump right in.

I discovered the game had broken up. I might've been surprised to discover this since I knew a little bit about men and their habits, except Gavin completely distracted me. He was laying in wait for me at the end of the short hallway that connected the bedrooms and bath on that side of the house, propped causally against the wall, and yet there was tension in every line of his body.

The impression rolled over me that he was ready to pounce.

My heart instantly leapt and commenced to pounding in double time. A wave of weakness washed over me. I hesitated for a brief moment, feeling the 'flight' instinct grip me, then battled it to the back of my mind and approached him.

He snagged my waist as I drew near enough, dragging me closer.

I hadn't expected a kiss. Did men actually kiss women they considered prostitutes, I wondered vaguely? I'd always had the impression they didn't. They didn't want to waste their dime on anything superfluous, and anything that didn't pertain to their own pleasure was definitely unnecessary. They were paying to *be* pleasured, not give it.

Since I hadn't expected it, I wasn't prepared. I flinched instinctively, but I was wide open, defenseless.

He was aroused before he even touched me, his breath already rapid, faintly ragged, nearly unnoticeable tremors traveling through him and into me by way of his hand. My reaction was instantaneous and stunningly powerful. Gavin's heated breath puffed against my lips, setting them to tingling before his mouth even made contact with mine.

The moist flesh of his hard mouth settled over mine, clung. He swiped his tongue along my lips as if commanding me to open for him, thrusting into me before I even had time to obey. The tang of beer assaulted me first as his tongue rubbed along the keenly sensitive surface of mine and then his own taste and the faint roughness of his tongue took precedence, overwhelming me with a barrage of sensation that delighted, made me as drunk as if I'd ingested the beer I'd first tasted instead of him.

Briefly, it flickered through my mind to wonder if I could 'catch' his intoxication in that way, but I knew I couldn't blame it on that. *He* made me drunk with the taste and feel of him.

He'd settled one hand on my breast as he'd pulled me against him. His hand tightened almost reflexively as he pulled my taste into himself, explored the slick surface of my inner lips and cheeks all too briefly and broke away.

I felt myself sway, opened my eyes to try to orient myself.

It was as well I did.

He turned, pulling me with him, his hand sliding from my waist to my exposed buttocks as he did so. He stroked the bare skin as he guided me across the living room. I got a brief impression of the others—watching—but it was all I could do to focus on walking.

Without bothering to close the door when he'd pulled me into the bedroom, he waltzed me to the bed and down on the mattress, barely breaking contact between us. I was too dizzy with the fall to figure out how he'd managed it, but we collapsed in a tangle of arms and legs, his weight pinning me to the surface.

I didn't know if my breasts had spilled from the top upon impact with the bed or if he'd scooped them out. I felt his fingers close on one turgid tip, though, as he took my mouth beneath his again, forcing my lips to part from the pressure of his and instantly reclaiming the territory he'd briefly yielded to get me to the bed. He reclaimed it all, sending my senses into a fresh riot, submerging me again into a swirling, intoxicated bundle of nerve endings where no thought emerged. I was at once aware of every throbbing pulse point in my body, every keen nerve ending, the blood pounding through my veins and in my ears and little else—no sense of self—just feelings.

He broke the kiss abruptly, just as I was sinking into oblivion, rearing up and peeling his shirt off over his head with jerky impatience, tossing it aside. I managed to lift my eyelids in time to catch a glimpse of his broad chest—surprisingly well sculpted with muscle, lightly furred across his male breasts and the center of his chest with dark hair.

I got to feel it in the next moment as Gavin dropped over me, moving restlessly against me as he explored my throat with his mouth. The faintly rough texture of his hair against the ultra sensitive, turgid tips of my breasts, the hardness of his muscles, sent another shaft of excitement curling through me. My mouth dried with my mostly ineffectual efforts to drag enough air into my lungs.

Every gasped breath brought more of him into me—his scent possessing me as surely from the inside as his heat and touch did from without, until I felt not just surrounded by him, but part of him.

He slid downward, tilting his head to latch onto one nipple and tug at it with vigor. The force of the fiery jolt that shot through me to melt my core was powerful enough to knock the breath from me. For a handful of seconds I thought I might actually faint. The electrifying sizzle along my nerve endings seemed the only thing preventing it, the heat scoring me so intensely I couldn't completely lose touch with awareness.

He dragged his knee up—the one he'd wedged between my thighs. The rough brush of his jeans against my nether lips abruptly split my focus between the tug at my breast and my quaking sex. My clit throbbed in a whining demand for a little of the attention. The pressure of his knee against me, like the pull of his mouth on my nipples and the flick of his tongue was almost more of a torment that pleasure.

My cup runneth over. My sex, I realized, had reached maximum saturation. I could feel the lips of my sex slipping against each other. It discomfited me. I couldn't recall a time when I'd gotten so wet—so fast.

But then it was Gavin. A glimpse of him was enough to make weak and wet. Having him touch me, caress me, was like heaven.

Almost as if my thoughts had redirected his attention to that area, he released his grip on my breast and slid his hand over my mound, parting the lips of my sex. I nearly went off when his finger rubbed over my clit as he reached to 'test' the waters, found my hole and shoved his finger inside of me. Uttering a choked groan, I arched against him mindlessly.

"Jesus, baby!" he muttered, sounding almost as mindless as I felt. "You're so wet."

I hadn't particularly wanted him to notice that, but it seemed to set him on fire. Breaking off his exploration before he'd even gotten started good, he began to fumble with his jeans, heaving over me as he fought to pull his cock out and shove his jeans and shorts down his hips.

I thought I'd pass out when I felt the object of my desires butting against my cleft. Truly mindless now, I bucked against him, trying to help him ring the hole. He ignored my determination to engulf his flesh, guiding his cock back forth along my cleft to gather moisture on the head.

I felt like biting him. I might have. I was never afterwards sure of anything I'd done beyond fight for breath, groan, and pull at him with frantic fingers. I murmured a moan of pleasure when he finally made the connection and I could feel the sweet pleasure-pain of his entry, feel my aching flesh stretching to accommodate his girth. A momentary panic seized me when he continued to stretch me without making any real progress toward filling the aching emptiness until pain began to take the upper hand.

"God damn!" he growled.

I couldn't tell if pleasure or pain or impatience had inspired his swearing. He got a better grip on me. I spread my thighs wider as I felt the pressure increase. He began to shake. Abruptly, he eased off, sucked in a couple of gulps of air like a drowning man coming up for breath and thrust again. It was like trying to shove a piano through a keyhole. I'd begun to entertain grave doubts about the entire situation when his determination and my moisture finally worked together. He sank so deeply inside of me I thought I might've split in two if not for the corset preventing it.

"God!" he muttered through gritted teeth, pausing for breath. "I'm going to come. God damn it!"

Oh no! I thought as Gavin withdrew shakily and thrust again. *Not yet!* He began to pound into me with the frantic pace of someone racing toward culmination, however. I wrapped my legs around him, tilting my hips. Three hard jabs in just the right spot sent me flying toward my own release. I arched my back, quivering with it, groaning mindlessly with the first deep climax I'd had in forever. It hit a ten on the Richter scale and kept climbing, threatening to shake me apart. I was hardly even conscious when he jolted to a stop, ground himself against me and came.

He sagged heavily against me when his body ceased to pump his seed into me, still shuddering with an occasional aftershock. The heavier he got, the more difficulty I had in trying to stabilize my own heart rate and breathing. Finally, thankfully, he shifted a little to one side and I managed to drag in a decent breath of air.

One big hand settled heavily on one of my breasts, massaging it.

I groaned inwardly, but he merely nuzzled his face against my neck for a moment and finally lifted his head to kiss me briefly, gustily, and rolled away.

I uttered a sigh of relief, too content and too weak to move.

The bed dipped. I managed to drag my eyes open enough to see if Gavin had departed and caught a glimpse of Luke's face and then the top of his dark head in descent. My nipples were still far too sensitive for me to ignore the play of Luke's mouth and tongue. I struggled to do so anyway ... for all the good it did.

Heat flashed through me. I was still wavering between renewed desire and reluctance when Luke lifted his head to study my face. His expression was taut, his eyes glittering with heat. My body responded to his desire completely without permission.

Angling his head, he dipped toward me, engulfing my already kiss swollen lips beneath his. I was vaguely amazed that Luke's mouth felt nothing like Gavin's, not his touch, not his taste—and it still sent me spiraling off in a drunken haze of pleasure.

He'd undressed, I discovered the moment I gripped him.

I wasn't certain if I'd explored Gavin as I did Luke. I'd been too caught up in the fever. I was now, but not so mindless that I wasn't aware of the feel of his skin beneath my palms and fingers.

I could feel his struggle for control in the tremors wracking him—as they had Gavin. I didn't know why they were so impatient—it seemed totally against character for either one of them—but Luke's trembling need turned up the fire inside me until I was almost as anxious as I had been before I'd come. I pushed at his fragile control, intentionally trying to drive it from his grip.

I succeeded. His kisses and caresses rapidly became filled with desperation. He settled his narrow hips between my thighs, nestled his cock against my cleft and arched against me, nipping almost painfully at my nipples and the sensitive flesh between my breasts and face, sucking hard enough to make the skin tingle. Moving restlessly from my mouth to my breasts to my throat, almost as if he was trying to distract himself, he abruptly gave up the effort to prolong the pleasure—or yielded to the greater need to feel my body engulfing his. Reaching between us, Luke grasped his cock and guided it to the mouth of my sex. Poised with no more than the head inside of me, he coiled his arms around me, curling his hips and thrusting.

I grunted as if I'd been speared by a lance.

Actually, something a good bit thicker.

I couldn't decide if I'd encountered a family trait of monster cocks, or if it had just been so long since I'd had one in me I'd forgotten what dick felt like.

He struggled as mightily to claim my channel as Gavin had. We were both panting for breath and slick with sweat by the time he'd managed it. He didn't move for many moments afterward, breathing gustily against my neck, obviously trying to divert his mind to prolong the pleasure.

The thought made my kegels clench around him.

He grunted, shuddered, and began to arch his hips rhythmically, holding me tightly and using only the motion of his hips to drag his cock back and forth along my channel in slow, measured thrusts. The angle teased me maddeningly. I could feel just enough friction across the patch of nerve endings that made up my g-spot to increase my desperation and keep me seesawing between hope and doubt that I was actually going to make it to bliss before he did. My sex kept giving off warning quakes of imminent eruption and yet not quite making it to full explosion.

Abruptly, he shifted his grip on me lower, tilting my hips to just the right angle so that he could grind against me with each deep thrust. The grinding motion against my clit lit the fuse, sending sharp jolts through me that ignited the smoldering fire inside me and triggered an explosion to rival my first climax. I sucked in a keening breath as my entire body went rigid, hovered for an endless moment, and then flew apart with shattering convulsions.

Dimly, at some point during the fireworks, I realized Luke reached his peak, as well, but I was too wrapped up in the pleasure threatening to shake me apart to notice it more than peripherally. I might not have noticed at all except that he stopped thrusting at some point and his dead weight, in his weakened state of post coitus, began to feel as if it was pushing me through the mattress. Luckily, the mattress had enough give to keep him from flattening me. I was as near unconscious as I could ever recall when he finally rolled off, allowing me to drag air into my starved lungs. I was so thoroughly, blissfully sated, however, I was far more interested in simply lying semi-comatose and enjoying it than rousing myself to see if I had anything—or anyone—else coming at me.

Either I didn't or I looked too close to dead at the moment to entice the others. I was left in peace to drift lazily, trying to decide whether I had enough energy to roll over and go to sleep or if I could rouse myself enough to go wash the stickiness off. By the time I decided I just couldn't sleep with my thighs sticking together, I'd roused enough for wariness to creep in. Prying one eyelid up, I surveyed the room. Relieved to discover I'd been left alone and they weren't just waiting for me to come to, I managed to lift my head enough to look at the door.

It was still open.

Damn it!

I allowed my head to hit the mattress again, wondering if I could creep to the bathroom without alerting them. I was only two down with over half the herd still, no doubt, champing at the bit.

I examined that thought, wondering if the others were as eager to sample as Gavin and Luke had been. Maybe they weren't, I thought a little hopefully? It seemed obvious to me once I'd roused enough for a little thought that Gavin and Luke must have hit a dry spell. Nothing else, to my way of thinking, would explain the fact that they'd lost control so quickly.

Unless I'd completely misjudged them and they were always fast off the mark?

Not that I was complaining.

I dismissed that conclusion. Everything I'd observed about the two before led me to believe they were cool, calm, and collected under any situation. They hadn't even lost control over the eight million dollars they'd believed they'd nearly lost.

They'd calmly tracked down the culprits 'playing' hide and seek with their money.

As little as I knew Luke and Gavin, I'd at least had a good bit of time to observe, and lust over, both of them from afar. I knew much less about Jessie, and his brothers, Jared and Bret, but I'd gotten the impression these apples had all fallen close to the trees.

It seemed unlikely, in any case, that they could be cooler than Gavin and Luke.

So, I finally, concluded, dry spell.

Could I also conclude, I wondered, that the first rush was finished?

I decided not to take a chance on it. When I'd revived enough to regain some use of my muscles, I eased off the bed carefully and tiptoed into the bathroom to wash up. It was still relatively early in the evening, but I'd put in a full day at work and the two climaxes I'd experienced had really sapped me. I was more inclined to go to bed than to encourage more sexual activity for the night.

Just about the time I patted Miss Puss dry, I discovered Jared standing in the bathroom doorway. I jumped all over. Amusement entered his eyes. A slow smile curled his lips, drawing my gaze.

I hadn't gotten more than a glimpse of Jared before—previously. Since I worked at the main bank, there was the occasional meeting of the board there … when all of the tellers got the chance to ogle the beautiful Thornes. I'd never gotten the chance to catch more than a brief view of them as they strode purposefully through the bank, though, and I'd been a little too preoccupied since I'd arrived to actually check him out.

I discovered the family resemblance between the Thornes was strong. Despite the fact that he was fair haired, his features certainly pegged him as a close relative and, although his complexion wasn't quite as swarthy as the 'dark' Thornes, he was tan.

The darker skin tones, I saw, went amazingly well with his golden brown hair and pale blue eyes.

Saw it up close … because he straightened away from the doorframe as soon as he had my attention and moved toward me. I eyed him a little warily as he grasped my waist, more than a little disconcerted when his hands tightened and he lifted me straight up and plunked me down on the vanity.

It was wet. My dry ass reacted to the wet countertop like a rubber tipped dart. I didn't have time to do more than briefly register the discomfort, however. He grasped my knees, pushed them wide enough to accommodate his hips and leaned in to me. For a space of a couple of heartbeats, we studied one another eye to eye.

Then he tilted his head to one side and locked his lips to mine.

Oh hell!

Chapter Five

Either the Thorne men were just like catnip to me, or my body was locked into fuck mode. By rights, I shouldn't have felt any interest whatsoever—I was sure I shouldn't have. The feel of his lips on mine, the caress of his tongue, stirred the caldron again, though, breathed life into a body I'd been sure five seconds ago was now dead to feeling.

Even Miss Puss clapped happily—damn her hide!

Actually, I had reason to be relieved. Jared didn't seem any more inclined to spend a lot of time in foreplay than Gavin or Luke had. Almost the moment his mouth locked over mine, he scooped a hand around my hips and dragged me close enough to spear me with the raging erection he'd dragged out.

My ass tingled when he ripped it loose from its lock down on the countertop. Miss Puss reacted by clamping down on the head of his cock and refusing to let go. He battered at the opening a couple of times and finally lifted me clear of the countertop and began trying to shove me down over the dick, gaining about another inch of ground.

He broke the kiss. "I think we need lubrication."

He didn't sound very happy about it, but what could I say? I was about juiced out after two rounds, damn it. I'd had enough come inside of me before I'd washed off that probably wouldn't have been noticeable, but it was too late to worry about it now. "Maybe a shoehorn?" I muttered.

Amusement, to my surprise, flashed in his eyes. He settled me on the countertop again. Instead of looking for lubrication or a shoehorn, though, he bent down and began to tease my nipples, suckling at first one and then the other until I felt the response he'd been aiming for. He shoved a thick finger inside of me to test the 'waters', grunted appreciatively, and replaced his finger with his cock. It was still an uphill battle. After jogging me up and down on his shaft a couple of times, though, he managed to coat his cock with enough moisture to make the gliding easier.

Thankfully! I'd begun to think I was going to get a knee lift out of it.

Apparently, he wasn't completely satisfied that he'd hit bottom even when he had, he kept pressing down on my hips. I thought, maybe, he was just giving me a moment to adjust. The expression on his face said otherwise, however. When I lifted my head, I saw that his face was contorted in the throes of agony/ecstasy. He dragged in a harsh breath after a moment and opened his eyes.

When he saw that I was studying him, he studied me back for a long moment. "Hold on, baby," he muttered. "This ride might be a little rough."

Rough? My heart skipped a couple of beats. Miss Puss reacted by trying to squeeze him out, however, and that appeared to be a turning point for him. He gritted his teeth, ground them together, and then let out a harsh breath. Squeezing his eyes closed, he gripped me tightly and began to drive into me like a pile driver.

He was right. It *was* rough.

I hit my third climax. My body quaked sluggishly at first, as if it just didn't have the oomph to complete the cycle, but it gained ground as he continued to slam into me until I was groaning incessantly with the waves of glory pounding through me, nearly screaming. I probably would have if I could've drawn in enough breath to manage it. As it was, it was like someone trying to scream while somebody beat the breath out of them at the same time, more a series of yips.

Jared reached his crisis about the time I hit the blackout point, holding me in a bone-crushing embrace as his body jerked with his release.

Finally, he eased me on to the countertop again, leaning weakly against me and puffing gustily into my ear while he gathered himself. He uttered a breathless grunt when he finally pulled his flaccid member from me.

He paused, nuzzling his face against the side of my neck. "I wouldn't wash off," he muttered. "You'll need the extra lube. Jessie's hung like a fucking horse and Bret isn't more than a shade behind him."

I almost fell off the counter when he leaned away from me. He steadied me, looking me over with an expression that almost seemed like genuine concern. "If you can't handle it, say the word. I'll tell them they'll have to give you a little time."

I stared at him dully, wondering what 'a little time' would constitute. A week? A month?

Somehow I doubted it.

I let out a gusty breath, wondering if I was up to it.

So good of him to 'warn' me that I hadn't seen nothin' yet!

"They may have to settle for me lying there like a dead thing," I muttered, realizing I might just as well take my 'medicine' and get it over with. At least then, maybe, they'd let me sleep.

He chuckled huskily. "I doubt that'll be anything new to either one of them."

I didn't take his advice so much as I realized that it was pointless to try to clean up when I still had two more raring to go. Wobbling back into the bedroom, I discovered Jessie was already waiting—in the process of stripping actually.

It must have been some family joke, I decided when I'd collapsed on the bed again and got my first good look at what Jessie was packing. I thought for a handful of seconds that the poor man was just deformed and had a third, slightly atrophied leg. Crouching on his knees between my thighs, he slicked it down with both hands and a half a tube of lubrication. When it dawned on me that he fully intended to try shoving that thing up me, I would've become *extremely* lively if I'd been in any state to do it—as in leaping from the bed and racing around until I found a way of escape.

It didn't seem to occur to him that it wouldn't fit, or that I might not be able to stretch to fit.

Or maybe it did. He grabbed my hand and pulled me upright. "This is going to have to go," he said decisively, working at the catches on the corset.

I managed to drag in my first deep breath since I'd put the damned thing on when it fell free. It was a good thing, too, because I'd no sooner fully expanded my lungs to scream like a banshee than he bore me backwards on the bed, attempting to plug both holes at the same time. He succeeded in the first, shoving his tongue in my mouth before I could voice an objection.

Maybe it just *seemed* really big, I thought a little hopefully?

Then again, it only took a couple of seconds to realize that wasn't his knee he was prodding me with.

He didn't manage to kiss me into submission or drunken lust to divert me. He *did* manage to warm me up enough, though, damn it, to wedge the head of his cock into the mouth of my sex far enough I couldn't dislodge it or escape. The muscles along my channel promptly clamped down on it, but even I wasn't certain if it was reluctance and a determination to shove him out again or an insane, mindless urge to pull him in.

I was beginning to have serious doubts about Miss Puss' intelligence.

My reaction didn't seem to matter a great deal one way or the other, however. In fact, I was pretty sure he was too focused on his problem to really notice anything else. He was grimly determined to conquer the Stephanie Channel, digging furrows in the sheets with his toes in a Herculean push he countered by trying to pull me down over it at the same time.

The lube worked a lot better than I'd thought/hoped it would. Clearly he'd had more experience with that battering ram than I'd supposed.

Given the size of it I'd thought it likely he'd had much more practice dragging it out of his pants than he'd had putting it in a female—at least of the human variety.

The excessive lube, I realized, wasn't nearly as excessive as I'd first concluded. It seemed, with enough lube, one *could* shove a piano through a keyhole!

Once I realized he wasn't going to shred Miss Puss, I got a lot more enthusiastic. It became a mountain I was determined to climb. It occurred to me that I might have to put a drawstring in poor Miss Puss when he got done with her, but I figured, what the hell? Miss Puss hadn't seen any action at all in so long she was raring to go. I might as well enjoy it while the getting was good. Who knew when the guys would get tired of their toy?

And it was for damned sure they were going to get tired of it in a hurry if they couldn't play with it.

Gasping hoarsely, sweating profusely with exertion, Jessie stopped to rest and catch his breath when he'd finally managed to wedge that third leg of his in the hole. I was having a little trouble catching my breath, too, but it hurt so good all I could think about was how it would feel moving. I lifted my legs and dug the heel of one of my feet into his ass to get him going. He shuddered, dragging in a deep breath and holding it, but he didn't move.

Tightening my legs around him, I lifted my hips from the bed, grinding against him. Jessie groaned. Burying his face against the bed just above my right shoulder, he pumped his hips slowly a couple of times. It wasn't much but it didn't take much effort on his part to stir some wonderful currents. There wasn't a millimeter of flesh from the mouth of my sex to my womb that he wasn't touching, pressing tightly against until the muscles were quivering with anticipation, my body ready to explode with exquisite sensation. I undulated against him out of sync, pressuring him to pick up the rhythm a little. Uttering a choked breath, he complied, but it was unwilling, more as if he'd lost grip of his control than a voluntary reaction.

I knew that for an absolute fact when I felt his cock twitch inside of me and realized explosion was imminent. Hoping his balls weren't comparable to his cock and he wasn't about to launch me into orbit, I focused on reaching my own goal. It was a near miss. I hadn't even felt the first tremors when I felt him come, but it sent a thrill through me when he did that pushed me over the top. I managed to maintain a grip on him until I'd rode my climax to the end then, my arms and legs feeling totally boneless, I allowed them to fall uselessly to the bed.

He lifted his head, studying me intently for a moment—checking for signs of life, I didn't doubt. I managed to lift one eyelid high enough to peer at him. He looked for several moments as if he would say something and then instead he pushed downward enough to align his mouth with mine and kissed my swollen lips lightly, almost lingeringly.

I was still wondering about that kiss when he left.

Struggling for a few moments, I finally managed to roll over on to my stomach. I was too washed out to try to get up, however, and, in any case, the opening door reminded me that I still had one more mountain to climb before I was done for the night.

Actually, I was already pretty well done for the night—for the year. Not that I figured I had anything to complain about—besides being tired. I'd had a climax every time. I was long overdue, of course, since I hadn't had sex with anything but myself for years and that was never quite as much fun, but ... well, four climaxes in one night was a bit more than I'd bargained for.

Bret didn't seem to mind the fact that I was lying flat of my belly. He simply climbed over me, gnawed a path up my spine that sent tingling shivers all over me and then explored the side of my neck and my ear. I groaned in response, but he didn't seem to notice that it wasn't altogether from happy anticipation. Slipping a hand beneath my belly, he lifted my hips up and plugged in to the still dripping hole.

It was a good thing there wasn't a hair's worth of difference between him and Jessie. I was pretty sure there was enough lubrication by now for him to fall in and get lost otherwise. It appeared, though, that it was just enough to help him fit that monster in the holster. He had almost as hard a time as Jessie had had, but that was fine by me. I was in no shape to really enjoy it and Miss Puss was hot enough and tight enough that, like Jessie, he was almost ready to ejaculate by the time he was firmly seated.

It still felt surprisingly good. In fact, I was just starting to really enjoy it when he finished.

I took it with a grain of salt. Obviously, four climaxes in a row was my limit.

Although ...

I was just conscious enough when he finally collapsed spent on the bed to realize that there was trouble in paradise. I lifted my head with an effort and discovered he was staring at the ceiling.

Uh oh!

Man thinking post coitus was a bad thing!

I managed a gusty sigh. "God that felt good!" I muttered a little drunkenly.

He perked up immediately, but he looked damned suspicious when he glanced at me. His lips tightened. "You didn't come."

"Like hell!" I lied. "Did, too!"

Some of the angry suspicion left his expression. "Did you?"

I managed to curl one corner of my mouth into a semblance of a smile, although, truth to tell, I could hardly feel my lips anymore. Instead of replying, I struggled to wiggle close enough to nuzzle my face against his shoulder in appreciation of his efforts. It seemed to satisfy him.

Thank god!

I passed from conscious on the thought, certain I'd averted a 'problem'.

* * * *

Bret had mixed feelings as he left the bedroom. He was still high on the rush he'd gotten from fucking Steph and yet not entirely satisfied. He wasn't sure if that was because he'd come so fast or if it was because it had felt so damned good that he'd wanted to fuck her again the minute he caught his breath. He just knew that he was damned reluctant to put his pants on and leave, that he felt like he just wasn't finished.

He was also uncomfortably aware that part of his reluctance was due to the persistent uneasiness that he hadn't satisfied Steph, regardless of what she'd claimed, and the uncomfortable feeling that he'd been so quick that the others would know the minute he returned to the living room that he'd shot his load before he'd barely gotten started good.

He discovered the last was a worry he could dismiss. The others had gathered at the table to play another hand of cards. They looked up as he came out, but none of them actually looked at him. Instead, they stared hard at the bedroom door for several moments, as if they could see through it, and then turned to frown at the cards in their hands.

He knew the look. They wanted to go right back in as badly as he did.

He had mixed feelings about that, too, he discovered. On the one hand, it made him feel a little better since he could see they were in the same boat he was—just as edgy to go back for another round—which meant they'd basically done nothing more than wet their appetite just as he had.

That probably also meant they had been as quick on the draw, or damned near it, as he had been. They wouldn't be so antsy if they'd managed to work off more of their hunger.

That didn't make him feel a hell of a lot better, but some better, definitely. At least he wouldn't have to put up with listening to their humorous quips about being quick draw.

At the same time, he felt himself tense with possessiveness—completely misplaced, but easily recognizable. He knew he didn't have any more claim to Steph than they did—not as much if he was honest. They'd all stood to lose a lot more money than he had in the little game Stephanie's son had played with them.

He still felt possessive. He didn't like it. It made him a hell of a lot more uncomfortable than his anxiety about his prowess and his dissatisfaction with the limited time he'd had with her, but he couldn't help it.

Gavin dealt him a hand when he'd grabbed a beer and joined the others at the table, eyeing him speculatively. "She too tired to go another round?" he asked almost casually as Bret settled in the chair and picked up his cards.

Bret immediately felt a flush rise to his cheeks. It irritated the shit out of him. "She is now," he growled, daring Gavin to comment on it further.

Gavin lifted his dark brows, but his expression hardened. Bret didn't particularly care for the speculation he saw in his cousin's eyes.

"We already agreed that we wouldn't push it," Luke said, the hint of a growl in his voice. "I think it would be safe to say we'd all like another turn—tonight—which means it isn't going to happen."

Gavin transferred his attention to his brother. "I was merely asking after her welfare," he said coolly.

Luke sent him a derisive glance. "Bull shit, Gav!"

Gavin glared at him a moment but finally, reluctantly, grinned, uttering a sardonic snort that fell short of actual amusement. "Fuck you! Don't hand me any bullshit about not wanting another chance at her yourself because I'm not buying it."

"Did I say that?" Luke muttered. "I went off so fucking fast I don't feel like I even got a damned piece of ass."

"I guess that makes it unanimous then," Jessie said dryly. "Shit! I thought I was going to lose it before I even got in."

Bret relaxed fractionally. It had seemed to him that it took a hell of a long time for his turn to come around, but if they were willing to admit that they'd shot their load as fast as he had it must have been his imagination—combined with his impatience.

"I'm not sure this was such a great idea after all," Gavin said after a short silence while they played their hands. "It's already starting to feel more hellish than my marriage and that's saying something. Maybe we should reconsider Bret's idea—draw straws or something and divide her time up that way? It would be a little over a month for each of us to work her out of our systems."

"Great idea—except some of us would have a hell of a wait!" Bret snapped.

"It was your idea to start with," Gavin pointed out irritably.

"And if we'd agreed to it before we all screwed her, it might have worked! I don't know about the rest of you, but I felt like I'd just gotten started good when it was all over. I'm hornier now than I was *before* I fucked her. Well—not hornier, I don't guess, but I'm sure as hell not satisfied. Maybe we should just draw straws on who's going to spend the night with her—tonight—and then tomorrow and so forth?"

"Jesus fucking Christ, Bret!" Luke growled. "We *all* just fucked her! When was the last time your girlfriend—any one of them—let you fuck her five times in a row? She's going to be sore as hell as it is. You want her to run screaming to the cops the minute we let her go and beg them to lock her up? That'll make for a damned short party!"

Bret felt a little sick to his stomach. "You think she'd do that?"

"I think we can't push her too damned hard if we want her to cooperate," Luke said tightly. "Otherwise jail might start to look better."

"That isn't very flattering," Gavin said dryly. "You don't honestly believe that?"

Luke glared at him. "I don't honestly want to find out the hard way. Aside from the fact that I still think we want to keep this on the quiet—all of it—and I'll admit I had my doubts about it—Now that we've set it in motion I like it a hell of a lot better than I'd expected to. I'm not keen on having it cut short. In fact, I'd like it better if we'd bargained for a year—at least. If we made a mistake, I'd say it was in limiting the time. Six months sounded like plenty of time, I'll admit, but we weren't considering the fact that we were going to have to share time and *her* limitations. Maybe she'll get used to it and it won't be as rough on her. Hell, women can and do. Prostitutes fuck a half dozen johns a night, or more, right?"

"I don't think I fucking like you comparing her to one," Jared growled. "In fact, I know I don't! *We* put her in this position, damn it!"

"I agree with Jared ... to an extent," Jessie said tightly. "Although *we* didn't put her in this position. Her son did."

"No, he didn't," Bret disputed. "We did. He just put her in the position of having to bail his irresponsible ass out of trouble. *We* took advantage of it."

Luke glared at them. "I wasn't comparing her to a prostitute, damn it! I was only trying to point out that a woman could get used to having multiple lovers in one night—and that *she* isn't used to that kind of thing because she isn't a whore."

"So … you're saying we took unfair advantage and we should just let her go?" Gavin asked coolly.

The question gave them all pause. Luke, Jessie, Bret, and Jared all exchanged uncomfortable glances and then focused their gazes on their cards.

Gavin threw his hand of cards on the table. "I'm not shouldering any damned guilt you feel about this just because I went along with it. It wasn't even my idea to start with. Anybody who wants to bow out, speak now, or shut the hell up!"

An uncomfortable silence gripped them for several minutes. "I'm in," Bret mumbled finally. "I just think we need to consider if there isn't a better way to work out her time."

"I'm in," Luke agreed, "I'm just saying there isn't going to be a better way to work it out. She'll have to get used to having the five of us constantly trying to mount her because I'm damned well not giving up any opportunity that arises."

Jessie and Jared exchanged a questioning look and finally nodded. "Luke's right. We'll just have to try to go easy on her at first. We should've thought about that before we all had a go at her tonight."

"At the rate we're going, she isn't going to get used to it fast enough to keep us from going off the deep end," Gavin said dryly. "Speaking for myself, I barely took the edge off. I think it's the situation that's got us so frisky, though. It's a fantasy none of us have ever gotten the chance at. I imagine it'll get old before too long and then she can cruise through the rest of her 'time served'. As long as we don't abuse her, there's no reason for her to figure she'd be better off confessing to the cops. I damned well don't consider fucking us that much of a hardship."

* * * *

Sunlight was streaming into the room when I woke, but I had no clue of what time it might be and discovered I really didn't care. I felt like I'd been run over by a Mac truck. I didn't have to search too hard to discover the reason for it. The Thornes had twisted me into a pretzel the night before, fucked me every which way but loose, and that wasn't something I was used to.

I was rubbing my belly, trying to decide if the reason it was so sore was from all the prodding the night before or from the four mighty climaxes I'd had or maybe a combination of the two when the door opened and Luke poked his head in. "You up for breakfast?"

I peered at him through sleep-blurred eyes, doing an internal search. Ordinarily, I never ate. I just drank my breakfast in the form of coffee, heavy on the cream and sugar, but not only did I not have my fixings with me, I was actually starving. I nodded. "I just need to get cleaned up," I grunted as I pushed myself upright with an effort.

"Rough night?"

I sent a startled glance at him, saw his eyes were dancing with teasing amusement, and was torn between equally opposing urges to glare at him and laugh. The impulse to chuckle at his quip died by the time I finally managed to get off the bed. I was *really* sore!

"Take a hot soak in the tub," he advised. "It'll ease the sore muscles. You've got time."

I nodded instead of answering, gritting my teeth to keep from groaning as I struggled to ignore complaining muscles and walk with some appearance of ease toward the bathroom. Thankfully, I discovered once I'd reached the door that he'd disappeared.

Closing the door behind me, I adjusted the water, and left the tub to fill while I took care of morning needs. I wasn't actually in the mood for a soak in the tub, but I knew he was right and I didn't particularly want to be creeping around the place like an old woman.

I *felt* every one of my thirty something years—actually about twice that.

That would show me for romping around with five younger men like I was a teenager!

Of course I hadn't actually volunteered to do all that romping.

Then again, despite the soreness, I couldn't deny I'd thoroughly enjoyed getting old and decrepit overnight. In some ways, the night before all seemed to run together and yet I discovered when I settled in the tub and closed my eyes that it wasn't just a blur. I distinctly recalled every kiss and every touch from each of them individually, and with equal pleasure.

I supposed I should've felt misused over the situation. Even though I did feel responsible for Jimmy's actions and guilty about it, they'd taken advantage in a way that wasn't the least bit gentlemanly—which clearly indicated they thought very poorly of me. I'd decided I wasn't going to dwell on that, though. If they considered it restitution, then so be it. All the better for me that it was a hell of a lot more pleasant form of compensation for my part in the robbery than prison would've been.

I'd just begun to drowse when the door opened. I repressed a groan when I saw that Luke had obviously decided to join me.

So much for thoughtfulness!

I watched him shed his clothing with mixed feelings. I was still too sore from the exercise the night before, and had been too thoroughly satisfied, to be greatly interested in more sexual play. On the other hand, there was no getting around the fact that the man was a beautiful specimen of manhood.

I hadn't had the chance to properly appreciate that the night before, but I was almost dismayed to realize that he was far more beautiful even than I'd imagined when I'd fantasized about him before. It made me uncomfortable in an indescribable way, reminded me that he was several years younger than me and looked it to my mind.

He let out a hiss as he stepped into the tub. "Fuck! I didn't mean boil yourself."

"It is a little hot," I agreed. "It didn't seem this hot when I turned the water on."

He turned off the hot water and turned the cold wide open, mixing the water with his hand for a moment and finally eased carefully down into the water with me. When he'd settled facing me, he caught one of my ankles and pulled me across the tub to him. I made a grab for his shoulders to steady myself and keep from going under completely.

Draping my legs over his thighs, he settled one arm along my back and the other around my hips and pulled me closer until his genitals were nestled against mine. I studied his cock as it went from semi-erect to fully erect right before my eyes, trying to ignore the pull of sore muscles along my inner thighs and finally lifted my head to meet his gaze questioningly when he made no attempt to do anything else.

I discovered he was studying my face.

I wasn't particularly happy about that, wondering if the morning sun left any of the fine lines I knew to be there unrevealed to his gaze.

He surprised me.

"You're prettier up close," he said almost thoughtfully. "I think it's the hair."

I wasn't sure how to take that.

"And the clothes."

I frowned. "I'm not wearing any."

He chuckled. "I meant when I noticed you before."

I *was* surprised then. "When did you notice me before?" I asked curiously.

He almost seemed to shrug. "When you started working at the bank."

The comment made my heart pitter patter, sent a flush of pleasure through me. I hadn't had a clue that he'd ever noticed me at all. "Oh."

I wanted more, but I decided not to fish for it. I was certain I would be doomed to disappointment. He'd noticed. As nice as it was to realize I wasn't invisible to him like I'd thought I was, he was a man after all. No doubt he noticed all of the women.

He lifted his hands and pulled the scrungy out that I'd used to gather the mop on the top of my head with.

"Now it'll get wet and it'll take forever to dry."

"I like it better down. You have beautiful hair."

The compliment warmed me. "Thank you."

"Why do you always keep it all balled up on top of your head?" he asked curiously.

I shrugged, grimacing. "I'm a little old to wear it loose, don't you think? It would be a little too girlish for a woman my age."

He frowned. Obviously that wasn't the answer he'd expected.

"What did you think?" I asked curiously, wondering if I even wanted to know.

"I thought, maybe, you just didn't want to attract attention."

I thought about that. "Maybe—mostly I was just trying for a more professional look … in the bank, you know."

He slipped his hands to my thighs. I flinched even though I tried not to.

"Sore?"

I felt my face redden. "Contrary to what you obviously think, I'm not used to … spreading them," I said a little defensively.

His lips tightened. "I don't think you know what I think. Turn around."

I lifted my brows at him in surprise, both at the command and the anger threading his voice, but struggled to turn around. He pulled me back to rest against his chest once I had. Lifting my legs, he draped them over his again and grasped my thighs, kneading the strained muscles. I couldn't help but gasp in pain.

"Too hard?"

"A little."

He eased his grip, stroking his hands along my inner thighs and then slowly and more gently kneading the flesh. The tightness began to ease but there was a building tension in my lower belly that was getting harder and harder to ignore.

Regardless, the heat of the water and the stroke of his hands relaxed me almost to the point of bonelessness. I finally dropped my head back against his shoulder. He lifted a hand to brush the hair away from my neck. The touch, or the contrast from the heat of his hand and the warm water that quickly cooled in the air sent a shiver through me, made my nipples pucker to hard points.

He nibbled a trail along the side of my neck with his lips, sucking at my ear and lifting more gooseflesh.

A sound near the door he'd left open caught our attention. Luke lifted his head. I opened my eyes with an effort.

Gavin was standing in the doorway. When we looked up, he casually propped one shoulder against the frame. "The food's done," he said when he saw he had our attention.

Luke skimmed his hands up to cup my breasts and teased the hardened nipples with his fingers. "I think I'd rather have this for breakfast," he murmured huskily, amusement threading his voice.

"I wouldn't mind nibbling on her myself," Gavin agreed.

I couldn't quite grasp what passed between the two of them—it seemed almost a warning—but Luke released me and gripped my waist, helping me up. "I guess we should focus on the food."

Gavin stepped forward as I stood, grasped my waist and helped me from the tub. My legs felt like cooked noodles. I wasn't sure if it was from the heat of the water or the internal heat Luke had generated, but it made standing damned hard. The water my hair had soaked up cascaded down my backside, forming a huge puddle on the floor. I turned away as soon as Gavin released me, leaning over the tub to wring out my hair.

He took the opportunity to slide a hand over my ass, which brought me upright with a jerk.

He smiled faintly when I whirled to look at him and handed me a towel.

Luke was frowning when he got out of the tub, but he didn't say anything. Pulling the lever to empty the tub, he grabbed a towel for himself and began to dry off with brisk efficiency.

It occurred to me as I dried my hair the best I could and then focused on drying off that I had no idea what they expected me to wear. They hadn't given me the chance to pack anything of my own. "What should I wear?" I asked a little uncertainly as I watched Luke pull his own clothes on.

He paused in the act of zipping his jeans up, studying me. "I don't think what we brought you is a good idea," he finally said dryly. "You'll be spread eagle on the table." He smiled wryly. "Not that I'm against the idea. Wait here. I'll get you something."

Chapter Six

I didn't know what to think about the way Luke had behaved—or what he'd said for that matter. It was almost ... flirtatious.

Dangerous thinking.

Trying to put it from my mind, I finished drying and went into the bedroom to see what, if anything, had been furnished for me to wear besides the corset I'd been given the day before. Most of the drawers were empty. One held a stockpile of 'fuck me' lingerie similar to what I'd already been given.

I wasn't too prudish to appreciate the lingerie. In point of fact I so rarely had money to squander on such things that it was something of a thrill to examine all of the beautiful, new, sexy under-things.

I certainly saw Luke's point, though. Appearing at the breakfast table in any of these outfits was guaranteed to get a rise out of any red blooded male, I was sure, and obviously they didn't especially want the distraction at breakfast.

Luke didn't anyway.

The closest thing I could find to panties was a pair of crotch-less bikinis.

Shrugging inwardly, I put them on. Luke reappeared at the bedroom door as I adjusted them. I discovered he was holding a t-shirt. Thanking him, I took it and pulled it over my head.

Pleasure warmed me when I discovered that it was roomy enough for comfort and long enough that it might almost have been a mini-dress. He looked me over critically once I'd put it on and finally nodded. "I guess that'll do. Come on before it's cold."

I would've preferred to brush my hair first, but he had a point. It wasn't as if my situation warranted a great deal of time devoted to grooming, I reminded myself. This was basically my prison and they my jailers, however strange it felt to think of my situation that way. I was serving time, not socializing.

I had to keep reminding myself of that as I joined them at the table for breakfast.

It wasn't terribly hard. Unlike the night before, there wasn't a lot of talk or jibes passing between them. Either they weren't morning people, or they were nursing at least a touch of hangover from the beer consumed the night before. Except for the fact that I'd been intimate with all of them the night before and it had completely changed my perception of them in that respect, they were all still virtual strangers and there wasn't a lot of small talk either to allow me to get to know them a little better or completely relax.

I hadn't been given any particular guidelines or had rules lain out for me beyond the vague description Gavin had given me, I realized uncomfortably as the meal ended. They didn't seem to expect me to cook. Was I supposed to just remain in the room on call, I wondered?

They hadn't objected when I'd wandered around the house the night before, though, so I supposed I had the run of the house.

Trying to shrug off the discomfort the uncertainty of my limitations gave me, I got up when we'd finished eating and helped with clean up as I had the night before. Someone came up behind me as I was finishing up, startling me as he slipped his arms around me and cupped my breasts. I glanced up and saw that it was Bret. Instantly recalling that he hadn't been particularly happy about the way things had turned out the night before, I studied him a little warily.

Some men took it as a personal affront if a woman didn't seem to enjoy their efforts enough to come. I couldn't see anything in his expression, though, to suggest I needed to be particularly worried about it and relaxed fractionally.

That still left me with the confusion as to just how I was expected to react.

I looked away again, shut the water off and reached for a towel to dry my hands.

He grasped my wrist before I'd finished drying them good and tugged me off toward the bedroom. My belly instantly clenched, but it wasn't exactly reluctance.

It wasn't exactly enthusiasm, either, after the night I'd had, but I discovered I was definitely warm and willing. This was so unlike me, I wondered at it. I supposed it was enough that I was surrounded by the Thornes and the entire pack was scrumptious, not to mention that I'd had a good deal of interest in them even before I'd experienced intimacy with them. Maybe the experiences of the night before still had me primed. The episode in the bath with Luke had certainly done some priming.

Then, too, I was the next thing to naked. Although that usually didn't heighten my sexual awareness, I also didn't usually run about in crotch-less panties and those made it pretty impossible to completely ignore Miss Puss.

The one thing I didn't attribute it to was a lack of satisfaction from the night before. I hadn't quite gotten there with Bret, which I could understand might ordinarily have left me in the mood, but I'd already had more climaxes before that than I'd had in as many years prior. It didn't seem reasonable to be revved for action only because I hadn't quite gotten there the last time around.

Whatever the reason—maybe all of it together—by the time Bret escorted me to the bedroom, anticipation was already pounding through my blood. He tugged me to a halt when we reached the bed and released his hold on my wrist to grasp the hem of the t-shirt. When he'd pulled it off, he dropped it on the floor and hooked his thumbs in the top band of the panties, pushing them down my thighs. I finished wiggling out of them while he focused on studying my breasts.

Unlike the night before, he didn't seem to be in a rush. I wasn't sure what his mood was, in all honesty. For several long moments, he simply stared down at me. I couldn't tell if my breasts were his focus or lower. Finally, he lifted both hands and lightly touched my nipples. They immediately reacted by standing erect, growing harder the more he stroked them with his fingertips until I could feel my pulse pounding there and tension began to coil in my belly.

He dropped his hands to his own t-shirt, catching the hem and peeling it upward. I stood watching the belly and chest he revealed in the act, the play of muscles from his movements, feeling the warmth inside me gain ground, and finally climbed onto the bed.

Watching my every movement, he pushed his shoes off with his toes and unfastened his belt, then his jeans snap. Instead of pushing his jeans off once he'd unzipped them, though, he climbed on the bed on his knees. Grasping my ankles, he made me bend my knees. Planting my feet on the bed, he pushed until I spread my thighs wide in response.

I sat up in surprise when, instead of moving over me as I'd expected, he flopped onto his belly between my thighs, propping the upper half of his body on his elbows.

That was when I discovered he'd left the door wide.

I wasn't sure whether it was intentional or he'd been too focused on his intentions to think about it. I was still wondering if I should point it out when he caught my attention by stroking a finger lightly over the outer the lips of my sex.

This was disconcerting. I hadn't expected to be inspected at close range and I felt my face heat with discomfort. The urge hit me at once to clamp my thighs together. Unfortunately he'd blocked that possibility. His shoulders were firmly wedged between my legs by the time I realized his intention.

I flopped back on the bed and dragged a pillow over my head, hiding my face since I couldn't hide what I wanted to.

I heard a low chuckle and made a grab for the pillow when I felt him tug at it.

Too late, he snatched it away and tossed it onto the floor.

I grabbed the other pillow. He snatched that away from me, too, but instead of tossing it to the floor as he had the first, he shoved it under my ass—the better to 'display' me, I supposed, struggling with both irritation and embarrassment.

I forgot both when Jared strolled into the room. He paused beside the bed, staring at the 'display' for a long moment and then met Bret's gaze. Almost as if a silent communication had passed between the two of them, Jared pulled his own shirt off.

My belly clenched. I wasn't sure of what they had in mind or if it was anything I wanted any part of, but I wasn't left in suspense long. After pushing his own shoes off, Jared climbed onto the bed behind me. Urging me to sit up—no easy feat when Bret already had my pelvis elevated, my thighs spread as far as he could push them and my heels against my ass. He settled me in the V of his thighs. I could feel his erection butting against my lower spine even through his jeans.

The uneasiness mounted, but my belly was doing the jitterbug by now and the warmth rising off of me wasn't from embarrassment. When he'd settled my back against his chest, he reached around to cup my breasts, massaging them and plucking at my nipples. They'd calmed somewhat since Bret had teased them but it took no more than a light touch to have the blood pounding almost painfully in the tips.

For several moments, I was totally focused on Jared's play, but after watching for a long moment, Bret settled on his elbows again and lightly, almost carefully, stroked the lips of my sex until the moist petals parted for him. I felt cool air waft along my cleft. Blood rushed to my clit, making it pound almost as hard as my nipples were pounding and he hadn't even touched it.

The anticipation alone had my heart hammering so hard I was panting for breath as he shifted closer and I felt his warm breath coast over the keenly sensitive flesh he'd exposed. He settled a hand on either side of my cleft, using his thumbs to curl the inner and outer lips of my sex wider and then, with no more than his lips, caught my clit. The pressure of his lips on the blood-engorged nub sent a hard, almost electric, bolt through me. I made an instinctive grab for his head, although I had no idea myself whether my intention was to push him away or merely grab him.

Jared had undoubtedly anticipated the move, either that or he was just that quick. He caught both wrists. For a moment, I struggled to exert my own will. The minute I allowed the tension of resistance to slacken, he began to slowly, inexorably, guide my arms behind my back. Overlapping my wrists, he curled a hand around both.

Almost as if Bret had merely been waiting for Jared to subdue me, he released his hold on my clit with his lips and opened his mouth over it instead, sucking on it. Fire shot through me that was so sharp I wasn't certain whether it was pain or pleasure knifing through me. I bucked instinctively, but discovered I was pinned fairly effectively. I tried pushing with my legs instead when the fiery sensations continued to pour in to me.

Jared pinned my hands between his crouch and my buttocks and reached around me, catching my legs just beneath the knees and lifting them high enough I couldn't get leverage. I managed to free my hands but discovered his arms were blocking me from grabbing Bret's hair and either shoving him away or pulling him closer.

I was already mindless enough by that time I wasn't sure which I wanted to do. The steady tug of Bret's mouth on my clit was driving me crazy. I twisted my head, gasping for breath, but I was too breathless, I discovered, from what he was doing to continue struggling. The tension fell from my arms, legs, and torso as I gave up on trying to evade but there was an explosive tension rapidly coiling inside of me. I found myself spiraling toward climax so fast it made me drunk, but reluctance to give up the pleasure so quickly had me struggling to ignore the call.

Abruptly, I sensed a presence where no one should be. Prying my eyes open a slit, I discovered that Jessie, Gavin, and Luke had come to watch. Luke had settled his hands on the mattress beside me and leaned close. My heart skipped several beats when I realized his intent.

I groaned when he covered the tip of one breast and began tugging at it as Bret was teasing my clit. For a handful of seconds, I came close to losing it right then, but greedy determination made me hold on. Just a few moments more, I promised myself. The pull of Luke's mouth on my breast and Bret's on my clit was like nothing I'd ever felt before, sending hard, almost painful rushes of pleasure through me to collide in my belly.

I was almost disappointed when Luke lifted his head, but it gave me a chance to suck in one decent breath of air before he knocked it from my lungs by catching my other nipple between his teeth. It was so swollen by now that it was almost more painful than pleasurable—at least to my mind. My body reacted otherwise. The moment he scraped his teeth along my nipple, I came, shatteringly. I tensed, bucked, screamed with the intensity of the climax that tore through me.

It rocked me until I began to think I'd pass out.

I'd begun to beg them to stop before I passed out before they finally did. I sagged limply against Jared in relief when they moved away from me, but I discovered there was no rest for the wicked. As soon as Jared released his grip on my thighs, Bret—I thought—began to urge me to turn over. Pretty thoroughly disoriented and mindless still, I managed to comply, getting on my hands and knees since that seemed to be what he had in mind.

I discovered Jared hadn't moved. The sound of a zipper made me open eyes and I saw that he'd pushed his jeans wide enough to allow his cock free. He caught it with one hand, nudging my chin with the head.

As mindless as I was, I understood that, too. Still panting for breath, I opened my mouth and took the head of his cock inside, sucking on it a little experimentally. I suppose I shouldn't have been too surprised to discover I liked the taste of him. I had his scent and taste memorized already as a treat. When he settled a hand on the back of my head, urging me to take him deeper, I did so with enthusiasm.

He grunted with appreciation as I settled on my elbows to free my hands to stroke him. I'd just begun to get a rhythm going when I felt Bret's hands on my nether regions, pushing on my thighs to position me.

I'd had a dim idea, I realized, from the time the two of them had climbed into bed with me that this was going to be a three way. I hadn't actually done one before, but it wasn't hard to grasp.

I hadn't reckoned on the size of Bret's cock, although how I could've forgotten beat me. He shoved me face down in Jared's lap with his first push and I nearly strangled on Jared's cock. He didn't seem to take my gag reflex as a turn off, however. Even so, I was careful to remove my mouth for the next push.

Jared helped, gripping my shoulders to keep Bret from shoving me into him again. Despite the lubrication I could feel as Bret slowly entered me, I also felt a slight burn. It eased as he withdrew a little and then pushed again. He pushed my legs wider until it was all I could do to balance with my ass in the air but he managed to plow deeper with the next thrust. Instead of withdrawing again, he merely paused a handful of moments and pushed again. I was gasping for breath by the time he'd driven as far into me as he could.

I held perfectly still while he sawed in and out of me a couple of times. When he seemed to settle on a rhythm, I returned my attention to Jared's cock.

I discovered the double penetration was far more wildly exciting than

I would've thought it would be. Despite the mind-blowing climax I'd already had, I felt my body gathering to take another leap. It was hard to concentrate on giving Jared pleasure and focus on my own, but I discovered my enthusiastic stroking and sucking on his cock was all he needed. He began to pant for breath, to rise slightly to meet me each time I went down on him. The realization that he was nearing climax shot me closer to reaching my own.

Almost as if Bret had been fired by the rising excitement in the two of us, he began to thrust faster, forcing me to stroke Jared that much faster and deeper. His hands fisted in my hair abruptly as his cock bucked in my mouth. "I'm going to come," he growled warningly, pulling at my hair as if he meant to thrust me away. I wasn't having any of that, however. I was determined to come with him in my mouth. I could handle it if he came. I thought I might actually relish it.

I clamped my mouth more tightly around his cock, sucking hard.

He uttered a choked grunt. I hit my climax and sucked at him a little frantically as the waves pelted me. I groaned around his cock. His seed jetted into my mouth. I swallowed and sucked more greedily, feeling Bret stiffen and then begin to pound into me harder as he came. He nearly buckled my spine but it drove my climax to a peak I hadn't achieved before. The climax had only just begun to dissipate when Bret leaned weakly against my back.

Discovering Jared's cock had gone flaccid in my mouth, I finally let go of it and dragged in a deep breath, shuddering with the aftermath of my climax. We toppled like a row of falling dominos, Bret beside me, Jared onto his back, and then I collapsed half on top of Bret.

Bret curled his arms around me, nuzzling his face along my neck and sending shivers through me. "Now I know you came," he murmured in supreme satisfaction into my ear.

His heated breath lifted gooseflesh along my neck and arm.

His comment both amused me and warmed me in an indescribable way. I felt a tired smile tug at my lips. He released me a moment later and rolled off the bed. I rolled to my back to watch him straighten his jeans, which he hadn't discarded, and pull on his t-shirt.

When he noticed I was watching him, he leaned down, bracing a hand on either of me and staring into my eyes for a moment, then moved close enough to drop a brief peck to one side of my mouth and straightened.

Bemused, I watched him stride out the door. It occurred to me after a moment that I'd had Jared's cock in my mouth, though, and that might be why he hadn't kissed me on the lips.

I struggled with the urge to laugh.

Jared, who'd rolled off the opposite side of the bed shortly behind Bret, waggled his eyebrows at me on the way out the door.

Discovering I had the room to myself—I wasn't certain at what point the others had departed—I rolled onto my stomach to stifle the snickers I couldn't completely contain.

Someone smacked me on the ass, effectively distracting me from my amusement. I reared up to see who it was and discovered Gavin had returned. I studied him uncertainly, wondering if the pat had been playful or reproving of my amusement at his cousins' expense. I couldn't tell from his expression.

I could clearly see desire in his eyes, though.

Evidently, he'd enjoyed the show.

"That deserves a shower," he murmured, jerking his head slightly, either to indicate the departing brothers or to urge me off the bed toward the shower.

I could certainly see his point, but that didn't stop me from feeling as if I'd just been castigated for being 'nasty'. How unfair was that?

Stifling the sense of resentment that rose in me with an effort and the pique of hurt that rose with it even though it irritated me to feel it at all, I got off of the bed. He followed me into the bathroom, undressing while I adjusted the water in the shower.

Most of the sense of resentment and injury I'd been feeling evaporated when I realized I'd undoubtedly completely, or at least mostly, misread his motives. I couldn't completely dismiss it. Of the five Thornes, Gavin was the hardest to read. Luke and Jessie ran him a close second, but Gavin was definitely the most enigmatic.

I thought I had Jared and Bret pretty well pegged. Neither of the two had shown nearly as much suspicion or animosity toward me at any point as the others had. To my mind that either meant they didn't really believe that I'd tried to rob them, or the stakes hadn't been quite as high for them, maybe both. Any maybe they were more inclined to think all was well that ended well—Jimmy had returned the money so they'd 'forgiven' the scare it had given them to see all of their money vanish and realize how easily they could be left destitute.

Due entirely to the kinky sex we'd just had, I also thought this entire situation was more of a game to them than an attempt to punish me for having a hand in, or at least breeding, the villain that could just as easily have left them flat broke and run with the money. They seemed far more interested in taking advantage of the situation that had landed their lap to explore some fantasies they hadn't had an opportunity to try before.

It was possible the elder Thornes were similarly inclined, but I also thought they harbored more animosity toward me and were more focused on the punishment.

Maybe I was wrong. Maybe a lot of my thoughts were colored by the fact that I'd already had a 'thing' about both Gavin and Luke before all of this had happened and was therefore more emotionally sensitive where they were concerned. Maybe it just felt more like a punishment because I'd allowed myself to dream one of them might actually notice me and become interested in me.

And maybe, for my own sake, I should put forth an effort to flush those thoughts from my mind?

If there'd ever been that possibility, and I knew it was extremely doubtful given the vast chasm between our classes and economic situations, that had definitely vanished when Jimmy decided to prove his 'superior intelligence'. I'd caught their attention alright, but it wasn't going to turn out well for me—not now—not if I couldn't dismiss my own fantasies. I was just going to get hurt when they finished and discarded me like last week's trash.

It wasn't even safe to enjoy the attention I had. It was a lot easier for men to thoroughly enjoy intimacy without becoming emotionally involved than it was for women—certainly for me.

There was really no bracing myself, though, I discovered when I'd stepped into the shower and Gavin followed me a few minutes later. I'd figured I might as well wash my hair. Just about the time I got it good and soapy and had shampoo in my eyes—and was at a complete disadvantage—Gavin decided to bathe me. I should, by rights, have been totally desensitized by now, I thought irritably. After not having been intimate with any man at all in years and years, I'd spent the night before being gang banged by five—and thoroughly enjoyed it. I'd hardly even had time to settle down from the last double hitter.

Maybe that accounted for it, though?

Or maybe it was just because I was particularly susceptible to Gavin?

I didn't know but I wasn't particularly happy about the fact that my engines started revving the moment Gavin began to glide the soapy cloth over my breasts. I shouldn't have been. This was going to be a hellish situation for certain if I couldn't enjoy the intimacy I couldn't avoid, but it was still fresh in my mind just how easily I could fall for Gavin if I wasn't very, very careful.

He didn't linger overlong at my breasts. He seemed intent on actually bathing me, not more focused on foreplay, and I didn't know how to feel about that.

Actually, I did. The disturbing thought that he looked upon me as something nasty rose in my mind again as he turned me and scrubbed my back and buttocks and the crevice between. I focused on rinsing the soap from my hair until he turned me again where I could tip my head back and rinse the roots and my scalp.

He pushed at my legs in a silent command to spread them. Sloughing the water from my face and eyes, I looked down even as I obeyed and discovered he'd knelt in front of me. The soap stung when he stroked the soapy bath cloth along my cleft and I let out an involuntary hiss of pain.

He flicked a look up at me, studied me assessingly a moment, and then returned his attention to thoroughly washing the nasty thing. His touch was gentle enough I didn't think I would've had any complaints ordinarily, but obviously I'd either nicked myself with the razor or poor Miss Puss had just had too many poundings too closely together.

Straightening, Gavin commanded me to rinse and focused on bathing himself. His expression was more thoughtful than angry when I turned to face him again and moved away from the spray to allow him to rinse.

I discovered we had an audience when I moved around Gavin. Luke, still damp from his own shower and wearing nothing but a towel around his waist, was leaning against the vanity watching. He beckoned with a gesture as he caught my eye, holding out a towel when I stepped from the shower and onto the bath mat. Instead of simply handing me the towel, though, he flipped it around my shoulders like a shawl.

I caught the ends, looking at him questioningly as he settled his hands at my waist and guided me around until my back was to the vanity. He lifted me to the counter then.

"Put your feet on the counter."

I blinked at him, trying to figure out how I was going to do that. He grasped my calves and helped me lift my legs until I could hook my heels on the edge. It was narrow and the position awkward. I let go of the towel and braced myself with my hands on either side and slightly behind me.

Gavin turned the shower off and grabbed a towel to dry off as Luke crouched in front of me, placed a thumb on either lip of my sex and pushed them back. Alerted by his demeanor to the fact that this was more of an examination than sexual interest, I studied his face while he studied my sex.

Looking for cooties, I wondered somewhat irritably?

The doctor had thoroughly checked me out. No way had I developed anything since then ... unless they thought one of them had given me something, I thought, feeling an uncomfortable stab of uneasiness. The hardness of Luke's expression made me more uneasy. I tried to lean forward far enough to examine it myself.

Gavin very calmly shoved me back, bending to look Miss Puss over, as well.

I glared at him, but he missed it since his attention was way south of my face.

He crouched beside Luke.

Now I was really starting to get uneasy. Lifting his hand, he very gently stroked one finger along my nether lips. The moment his finger touched I realized I had a tender spot. His stroking it didn't make it feel a lot better either.

"What is it?" I asked, unable to bear the suspense any longer.

Luke and Gavin both flicked a look at me, but returned their attention to my pussy almost immediately without responding.

Gavin rose. Luke moved closer and dragged his tongue along my cleft from the mouth of my sex to my clit. My skin pebbled all over, became abruptly acutely sensitive to my surroundings as if microscopic antennas had popped out all over the place. My mind was instantly diverted to better things. I stared down at Luke's dark head, mesmerized as much by watching his face as he explored my cleft with his tongue as I was by the feel of his tongue.

Images flooded my mind of the unapproachable man I'd so often caught a glimpse of at work, watched surreptitiously with a mixture of lust, awe, and uneasiness, superimposed over the image I saw now. It was hard to reconcile the two and yet oddly erotic by itself. My heart sped up until it was hammering at a rate of about ninety miles an hour as he ceased to tease the bud at the front by circling it with his tongue and began to alternately flick the tip of his tongue over my clit and pull at it with his lips. The goose bumps covering me got goose bumps. My skin suddenly felt way too small for me.

I watched him until my mind had descended so far into the dark, swirling, heated mists of lustful intoxication that my eyelids slid to half mast of their own accord. Luke's mouth felt so good on my tender flesh that I wanted it to last forever, struggled to ignore the rising tide inside me that spelled an end to it.

Gavin nudged Luke's shoulder, dragging his attention from me. Vaguely miffed by the distraction when I'd really, really begun to enjoy myself, I glanced at the tube he had in his hand without comprehension. Lifting his head, Luke took it, squeezing some of the contents onto his fingers.

I saw then that Gavin was stroking the glistening salve over his cock and my heart leapt with the thrill of excitement that rushed through me.

It contracted painfully when Luke touched me. I hadn't realize how heated my entire cleft was until he'd touched me with the chilling salve.

It warmed as he stroked it all along my cleft from my rectum to the mouth of my sex, even delving into the mouth and coating it before he straightened and reached for me. I lifted my hands and settled them on his shoulders to steady myself as he dropped his hands to my buttocks. Instead of merely scooping me off of the vanity, however, he lifted me up, bringing me against him. Instinctively, I lifted my legs and wrapped them around his waist when I realized he didn't intend to set me on my feet, but I was still a little confused about what was about to happen.

Gavin moved up behind me as Luke turned with me. I felt the stroke of Gavin's fingers over my rectum then and my heart stuttered to another halt.

I wasn't unfamiliar with rectal penetration, although I hadn't had sex of any kind in years. In point of fact, although it had taken some getting used to, I discovered that the bundle of nerves that made up my g-spot was just as accessible from that channel as the other.

I was still confused. I'd never tried it standing.

It became clear almost immediately, though, that he fully intended to penetrate me here and now. Tightening my arms around Luke's neck, I focused on relaxing when I felt the probe of Gavin's cock. For a few moments, the burn of penetration threatened to overwhelm my anticipation, but when he paused to allow me a moment to adjust and then began to ease slowly inside, I relaxed, focused on the thrill of feeling him inside of me.

It sank into me abruptly even as I felt him sinking deeply inside of me, that nothing was ever going to thrill me more than knowing I had Gavin inside of me, that it wasn't something that would ever grow old for me. When he could go no deeper, he wrapped his arms around me, cupping my breasts and pulling.

Luke allowed him to take part of my weight, but caught my thighs before I could uncoil my legs from around him.

I discovered he'd dropped his towel at some point. When I glanced down the space that had opened between us, I saw that he had coated his own cock with the lubricant. After stroking the residue on his fingers over the mouth of my sex again, he guided the head of his cock into me.

I held my breath as Gavin and Luke shifted closer, pinning me between them, and Luke penetrated me as Gavin had. I was almost ready to come before Luke had fully plumbed my depths. The only thing that could possibly be more thrilling than having Gavin inside of me was Luke, and the only thing better than that was both of them at the same time.

It would've been heaven if they hadn't done anything else. When they began to move, awkwardly at first, I thought I'd lose my mind. By the time they'd mastered the rhythm they both needed, I was already gasping and moaning like someone dying, too caught up in the sensations pounding through me to spare much thought for them. The heat that rose between the three of us was evidence enough, though, that they found it as erotic as I did even if not for their harsh breaths and the tremors I could feel running through both of them as they struggled to prolong the connection.

It seemed to go on forever and still not nearly enough. I held out as long as I could, but nothing had ever felt as wondrous. It needed only the realization that it was Luke and Gavin both pounding into me to send me flying over the top. I didn't make any attempt to stifle the urge to voice my extreme pleasure. I wasn't sure I could've contained it if I'd tried. The cries of ecstasy seemed to be forced from me, seemed necessary to keep me from shattering.

When I began to convulse with the throes of ecstasy and utter sharp cries, it seemed to push both of them beyond their limits. Gavin's arms tightened almost crushingly as he burrowed hilt deep and spewed his hot seed in my nether channel. I felt the scalding tide, felt his cock jerking within me and it sent a fresh rush through me. Luke uttered a choked groan and began to come on the heels of Gavin's climax.

The force of it sapped the strength from all of us. Gavin and Luke both swayed. It was all I could do to continue to cling to Luke, who was primarily supporting me.

Dragging in a shaky breath, hissing with the intense sensations the move stirred, Gavin withdrew. Luke held me a moment longer and finally pulled out, allowing me to slide down until my feet were on the floor.

It was just as well he didn't completely release me. My legs were so weak it took focus to lock my knees. Holding me with one arm, he braced a hand against the lavatory to hold us both up.

Gavin recovered first, edging the two of us away from the sink to wash up. When he'd finished, he moved away, collected his towel and then moved past us, headed toward the bedroom.

Luke, apparently satisfied that I could stand without help, stepped away from me and took Gavin's place at the sink to wash up.

Gavin paused in the door. "When you've cleaned up, you should get dressed. Luke will take you back."

Chapter Seven

I tried to convince myself as Luke drove me home that Gavin's dismissal hadn't been as cold as it had seemed to me. I was just hypersensitive, I assured myself.

And it was really stupid to let it bother me under the circumstances.

I should be glad they hadn't considered it necessary to keep me there the entire weekend. I'd come off lightly, all things considered.

I was too wrapped up in my misery even to be overly dismayed by Luke's driving, which, if possible, was worse than the trip out to the 'playpen'.

He seemed to be in a much fouler mood, for that matter. The few times I glanced at him, his expression was as dark as a thundercloud.

I hadn't actually expected him to walk me to the door. We hadn't been out on a date, after all, but it still bothered me when he merely pulled up at the curb and sat glaring out the windshield, waiting for me to get out.

I should be relieved he hadn't just driven by and shoved me out of the door without stopping, I told myself angrily as I got out and stomped around the car.

"Steph…."

I paused, turning to look at Luke questioningly, feeling a surge of hopefulness that only made me angrier with myself.

He stared back at me tightlipped for a moment and finally shook his head. "Rest," he finally said flatly. "You'll need it."

I blinked at him, feeling my jaw go slack that he'd thought it necessary to remind me that we weren't finished. Finally, I merely nodded, turned, and headed for my front door, forcing myself to walk, struggling with the urge to flee the censure I was certain he'd aimed at me.

He pulled away before I'd reached the front door. I was glad. I didn't have to try to maintain a pose of indifference anymore. My shoulders slumped.

I was tired, I realized without any great surprise, totally sapped of energy, but I knew it was only partly because of the unaccustomed 'exercise'.

The house was so quiet it was almost eerie, another absurdity brought on by my chaotic emotions. Jimmy spent most of his time in his room when he was home and he was no rambunctious toddler. The most I ever heard was music wafting down the stairs.

The place smelled stale, too, as if it had been locked up tightly for weeks, not just a couple of days.

I *felt* as if I'd been gone for weeks.

When I'd locked the door behind me, I simply stood where I was, staring at nothing in particular and trying to decide what I wanted to do, or what I should do.

I hadn't done any of my weekend chores and I shouldn't ignore them. They weren't going to just go away. Instead, I shoved away from the door and went into the living room, flopping down on the couch and staring at the black screen of my TV.

I realized after a while that all I really wanted to do was cry my eyes out but the moment it occurred to me I stubbornly refused to give in to it.

I was hurt and disappointed ... and too stupid to live!

Despite the fact that I'd known going in to this that it was punishment, restitution for crimes against the Thorne family, the intimacy had more totally fucked with my mind than *they* had fucked me.

I could've blamed it all on them. I wanted to, but I realized that they hadn't tried to mislead me. They'd been very upfront about the entire thing. The behavior I'd subconsciously interpreted as flirtation hadn't been anything but enthusiasm for the sex they were going to get without any effort on their part beyond commanding it.

And innate good manners that had been bred and no doubt drummed into them, as well, until they 'wore' them at all times, in every situation.

It was the kisses, I finally decided. That, I realized, more than anything else had spelled 'romance' to my mind. I didn't suppose I could blame them for that either. It was obviously a built-in behavioral pattern. They were predisposed to seduction and romancing a woman and that came first.

It would still have benefited me if they'd refrained. I wouldn't have gotten caught up in the fantasy and forgotten that this was just a transaction if they'd treated me like a whore and simply told me what they wanted and commanded me to perform. I wouldn't have lost sight of what my situation was.

I suppose I shouldn't have anyway.

It was my own fault. I'd done it to myself.

How was I going to manage to remain emotionally detached for months, though, when I was already in trouble?

By constantly reminding myself that I was 'doing time', I thought angrily. I was going to have to focus on reminding myself every time I experienced a little thrill at their attention that it wasn't romance. They weren't flirting. They just wanted to be paid back for the peace of mind I'd ripped away—or Jimmy had.

But I couldn't lay all of it on Jimmy either. He was addicted to computers in general and mind games in particular. Giving him another computer was the equivalent of handing a case of beer to a drunk and expecting them to ignore the temptation of drinking any.

Not that he was blameless either, but I had to accept that part of the guilt was mine.

He was paying and I would pay, too.

I wondered how he was doing. Now that I was home again, I felt a sudden stab of guilt that I hadn't thought about him when I was getting my brains fucked out. I realized I missed him and he hadn't even been gone but a week.

I'd promised my brother I wouldn't call him for the first couple of months, that I'd give Buddy time to establish his control. I was sorry now that I had. I'd never felt so alone in my life—not that I could remember, but then I'd been so young when Jimmy was born it seemed like he'd been there my entire life.

I should get used to it, I thought morosely. Jimmy was nearly grown and already talking about going away to college. By the time the two of us got through 'doing time' I was going to be looking at losing him forever not far down the road.

It occurred to me that I'd never looked into the future. It hadn't been easy being a single parent and I'd been focused almost entirely on keeping afloat—when I wasn't focused on Jimmy. I hadn't thought about my own needs or desires—ever—not since I'd become a mother, anyway.

What was I going to do with myself when I was truly alone? I'd made Jimmy my entire world, but I couldn't *be* his world once he became an adult. He loved me. I knew he wouldn't entirely abandon me, but he would be focused on his life—as he should be.

Shaking that thought off, because I just couldn't deal with it at the moment, I pushed to my feet and forced myself to concentrate on housework and laundry. After a while, I didn't have to force it. I fell into my routine and my mind began to wander again.

It was mid-afternoon before I even thought about eating. After glancing at the clock, I finally decided I might as well just wait and have an early supper.

Maybe I should treat myself and go out?

It didn't especially appeal to me, but then eating alone at home wasn't a lot more appealing.

I wasn't allowed to date while I was doing my time. Gavin had made that crystal clear, but there was no reason that I could think of not to go out. *That* wasn't forbidden … that I knew of, anyway.

Deciding I needed something to distract me, I called the theater to find out what was showing and settled on a movie and dinner. It was Saturday. It had been forever and day since I'd gone out at all.

It was better than staying home and dwelling on the fact that I was at the beck and call of five beautiful men and I couldn't really have any of them.

When I'd finished my chores, I went upstairs to take a leisurely bath to relax. Reminded when I'd undressed of the tenderness in my nether regions, I searched for a small hand mirror and sat down on my bed to examine Miss Puss. Without a lot of surprise, I saw that there were a couple of tiny fractures in the thin skin. It had been a while since I'd had sex, but it didn't take a lot of thinking to figure out it was from the gargantuan dicks I'd been 'playing' with. All things considered—Jessie and Bret in particular, not than any of the five had anything to worry about—I decided I was more surprised there wasn't more damage than a few tiny tears. There wasn't enough lubrication in the world to prevent a little tearing. It would heal.

I wasn't so sure about my emotions.

Pushing that depressing thought aside, I set the mirror down and decided to go all out and pamper myself. Instead of the shower, I opted for a bubble bath with oils. I'd always loved the rose scent, but the bath products were so expensive I didn't indulge very often. When I'd soaked until I was nearing the prune stage, I let the water out. Grabbing my exfoliating pad, I scrubbed until my skin was pink all over and then took a quick shower and washed my hair since I'd only half finished the job I'd started earlier in the day and it was dry and hard to comb from the lack of conditioner. Since I was being decadent, I used the rose scented shampoo and conditioner.

The smell of roses was nearly overpowering by the time I emerged from the bathroom. I felt a little lightheaded, but I couldn't decide if it was from the fumes or the long, hot soak.

Then again, I thought wryly when I glanced outside and discovered it was dusk, maybe it was a lack of sustenance coupled with a lot more exercise than I was used to.

I trotted downstairs naked to grab a cool drink from the fridge and then headed up again to dress. Someone knocked at the front door before I'd gotten even halfway up. Startled, I jumped and whirled to look at the door as if I could see through it.

"Who is it?" I called when a second knock followed closely on the heels of the first.

A deep male voice answered, but I couldn't really tell what his response was. After a brief debate, I trotted down the stairs again. "Who is it?" I asked again.

"Jared."

My heart instantly began to gallop a little wildly. I debated whether to leave him standing while I dashed up to get something on, but I was certain it couldn't be anything that would require that kind of dashing around.

And I wasn't up to it. The cold drink hadn't revived me that much.

I unlocked the door and peered at him through the crack. "I'm not dressed ...."

He caught the edge of the door and pushed. "Good."

Startled, I leapt back as he pushed the door wide enough to enter, staring at him with my mouth open in surprise when he shut the door behind him and locked it. His gaze swept over me, taking in everything at once. Something flickered in his eyes. He settled a hand at my waist and reeled me closer. "Expecting someone?"

His voice was laced with angry suspicion. I noted it peripherally, but I was too surprised, and dismayed if it came to that, to react to it. "No. I was getting ready to go out to eat," I responded distractedly. "You weren't supposed to come to my house."

He shrugged. "It's dark out, and I parked down the block. Who were you going out with?"

I gaped at him. That time I didn't miss the accusation in his voice. "I was going out alone," I said tightly.

He threaded a hand through my still damp hair. There was a warning in his gaze that I didn't particularly like even though I acknowledged the fact that I'd agreed I was theirs completely. "Like this?"

Irritation flickered through me. "Not like this! I'd just come down to get something to drink when you knocked."

He skated a hand down to my buttocks and yanked my pelvis tightly against his. He was hard. His erection dug into my belly almost brusingly. "I wasn't talking naked, Steph," he growled, dragging in a deep breath of the cloud of roses that I suddenly realized still clung to my skin and hair.

"I just took a bath," I responded, feeling dismay begin to usurp my irritation as it dawned on me that I couldn't afford for any of them to get the idea that I wasn't living up to my end of the bargain.

He studied my face for a long moment. "Good," he growled finally. "It's bad enough I fucking have to share you with the others."

My lips parted in surprise at that comment.

He moved his head closer, nipping at my upper lip and then the lower before he covered my mouth and thrust his tongue inside. My skin instantly erupted with sensation, my belly clenching with the excitement that spiraled through me as he alternately gnawed hungrily at my lips and tongue fucked my mouth. "Where's the bed?" he asked hoarsely when he finally drew away.

It took me a moment to remember. "Upstairs."

"I don't think I can wait that long," he muttered, waltzing me back toward the stairs, but throwing a glance around as if he expected a bed to magically appear. My heels made contact with the riser of the stair and I felt my center of gravity shift. He lowered me in a controlled fall.

It occurred to me as I felt the grit on the stair I landed on with my bare ass that I'd forgotten to vacuum the stairs when I was cleaning and then that the stair digging into my back wasn't softened in the least by the carpet covering it.

He seemed too dedicated to exploring me to spare a lot of thought for my comfort or his, but he broke off after a moment, leaning away from me. His gaze skimmed me, but he rose and pulled me up. "You'll have bruises all over you if we do it here."

My sentiments exactly!

He turned me on the stair and gave my ass a pat to get me moving, following me up closely enough to stroke my ass all the way and put a little quickness in my step. He stopped just inside my room and began pulling his clothes off. Knowing the drill, I moved to the bed and lay down to wait for him.

He didn't turn off the light.

Instead, as soon as he'd stripped, he moved to the bed, grabbed my legs and shoved them up, leaning down to examine Miss Puss.

Well, really!

I knew guys were 'in' to visuals but it was more than a little embarrassing to have my pussy constantly examined.

To my surprise, he looked equal parts aroused and disturbed. "Poor baby," he murmured as he settled beside me on the bed, grasping me and rolling me onto my side to face him. Sliding a hand to my leg, he lifted it and draped it across his hips, and then slid his hand between my thighs, lightly stroking my cleft.

I wasn't sure of whether he was talking about my pussy or me. I guess it showed.

He removed his hand from my pussy and stroked my cheek lightly. "I'll be careful, baby. I don't think I can take a week, though," he said gruffly.

I wasn't sure what he meant by that, either, but he distracted me. Curling his hand around the back of my neck and drawing me closer, he settled his mouth over mine again. His kiss was surprisingly gentle, more coaxing, it seemed to me, than demanding.

Despite my earlier resolve to close my mind and not react as if I was actually being courted, I couldn't seem to stop myself from responding. I kissed him back, found myself caressing and exploring his body even as he did mine. He made no attempt to hold anything back. The moment I responded, his entire demeanor changed. Hunger and possessiveness crept into his touch and his kiss.

Rolling me onto my back, he broke the kiss and targeted my neck and then my breasts, moving over me restlessly as if he couldn't decide what part of me he wanted to taste more. The brush of his bare skin against mine, the nibbling kisses he bestowed, the kneading caress of his hands, lifted me on a cloud of sublime pleasure until I was intoxicated and fevered with need.

He seemed in no great rush despite his initial behavior. He continued to tease me until I was ready to start begging him to enter me and then shifted downward and focused on teasing my breasts. I clung to his head, arching my back as he tugged and sucked at my nipples until the muscles along my channel were clenching a little frantically and I was soaking wet.

"Jared!" I finally gasped a little frantically. I'm ready! More than ready!

He seemed to grasp what I was too mindless to voice. Slipping a hand between us, he stroked a finger along my cleft and pushed it slowly inside of me. I lifted my hips, pushing in counter. Apparently satisfied that he'd coaxed enough natural lubricant from me, he removed his finger and shifted upward enough to press his cock into me.

It felt wonderful!

Anxious for more, I lifted my legs and curled them around his hips. "More!" I gasped a little desperately when he merely sawed shallowly in and out a couple of times, licking my fever dried lips.

"Easy, baby," Jared said raggedly. "I don't want to hurt you."

I felt like grabbing him by the ears and screaming at him. "Please?" I whispered instead.

A shudder went through him. He pressed deeper. Holding perfectly still, he adjusted his position and weight, breathing heavily against the side of my neck as if gathering himself. I coiled my arms around him, reaching down to grasp his buttocks to urge him to finish what he'd started.

I was so close! And too impatient to wait.

"You aren't going to get slow and easy that way, baby," he growled against my neck.

"I need deep," I countered.

He released a pent up breath and slid his hands beneath my hips, tilting them up to receive as he withdrew slowly and drove deeply again. "Oh god!" I gasped, feeling the muscles along my channel quake with imminent release.

"Jesus, baby!" Jared muttered breathlessly.

I felt his cock jerk inside of me in response. He began to stroke me a little faster, grinding against me with each thrust and sending shockwaves through my clit to my sex. I dug my fingers into his buttocks mindlessly, dropping my feet to the bed so that I could counter his thrusts.

I wasn't certain if we came together or if he came and it triggered my climax or the other way around, but we seemed to reach our peak together, to soar the heights of ecstasy together and plummet back to earth at the same time.

We lay gasping for breath almost in sync for several moments.

And then my stomach growled.

He was ungentlemanly enough to utter a snort of a laugh against my neck.

"I told you I was hungry," I muttered a little crossly.

He bit my neck, but I could tell he was grinning. "I thought you were hungry for me."

I considered whether I should answer that honestly or not.

"Anyway, you didn't say you were hungry. You said you were going out."

"I said I was going out to eat," I reminded him.

"I'd rather stay in bed and eat you," he growled.

My stomach grumbled again.

"Alright!" he said with mock testiness, rolling off of me. "Get dressed. I'll take you out and feed you before I breed you again."

I looked at him in surprise and more than a little doubt. "You sure that's a good idea?" I finally said, albeit reluctantly. It wasn't as if I was particularly worried about being seen with him, but I had a feeling he didn't want to be seen in public with me. Besides, that was only going to make it harder for me to separate the illusion of a date from actuality.

He frowned. I had the feeling it wasn't entirely because of what I'd said. "Fuck it!" he retorted finally. "I know where we can go."

That didn't help my feelings. It sounded like I'd been right and he *was* worried about being seen with me. "I'm sure I could find something here, although … I haven't had the chance to get groceries."

"Well, that settles it," he said cheerfully, leaning down and sucking on one of my nipples with enough relish that my belly quivered. Heat gleamed in his pale eyes when he lifted his head again. "Don't look at me like that, woman, or you won't get fed … food."

I couldn't entirely grasp his mood … beyond the obvious. I also wasn't too keen about going with him when I was pretty sure he wanted to sneak me in to some dark dive where nobody knew him, but I was hungry, damn it!

I rolled out of the bed and went to the bathroom to wash up. My hair was wild since I hadn't gotten around to combing it after the shower, but it was mostly dried.

I was sure my bed was mostly wet now that it had soaked up the moisture from my hair. Jared, now wearing his jeans but still shirtless and barefoot, joined me. Encircling me with his arms, he grabbed a handful of breast and one handful of pussy. "Wet," he murmured, thoroughly examining Miss Puss and ramming one finger up my hole.

"Full of come," I pointed out a little dryly. "Don't act like you didn't expect to find it in that condition."

He chuckled, nuzzling my hair aside and sucking on my ear. "That's just the way I like you, baby. Full of my come."

It defied reason and I still felt warmth flutter through me.

Almost reluctantly, he withdrew his finger. "Get some clothes on before I change my mind," he said, slapping my ass before he turned and left.

"You need to wash that hand!" I called after him, turning on the faucet to clean up.

He poked his head around the doorframe again. This time he had his shirt on. His blond hair was still wildly tousled, however. He was grinning cockily. "It's just me and you, baby. You didn't mind when you were sucking my cock before."

I slid a look at him. "I didn't say I minded. I thoroughly enjoyed sucking your cock."

His cocky grin faded. "Keep that up, woman, and you won't get fed tonight."

I shook my head at my reflection when he departed again. What was I *thinking*? As if he needed any encouragement at all!

And that had bordered on flirting, I reminded myself. Bad Steph! No flirting!

Closing the door firmly, I relieved myself and then washed up and brushed the tangles from my hair. I was tempted to put on makeup. I'd planned to, but I decided not to push my luck. I'd already pushed the boundaries more than I should've. He'd think I was dumb enough to think of it as a date if I stayed in the bathroom primping.

Grabbing a scrungy, I gathered my hair back from my face into a ponytail as I left the bathroom. Jared parked himself on my bed and watched my every move as I dug through my chest of drawers for something to put on. He looked mildly disapproving when he'd looked my underwear over.

I wasn't surprised—nothing sexy about the bra or the panties, although I'd made sure I dug out under-things that were relatively new.

I debated inwardly on what to put on, briefly, but opted for jeans and a comfortable shirt. I doubted he was taking me anywhere fancy. In any case, he was wearing jeans and a casual shirt himself.

He bounded off the bed while I was trying to find a shirt. "Fuck! Forgot I left the car down the road. Wait here. I'll go get it."

I looked at him questioningly. "That's alright. It won't kill me to walk." I focused on putting the shirt on that I'd found. "It's dark. No one's likely to see us together. Anyway, I doubt it would attract as much attention as you driving up to the house."

I discovered when I looked at him that he was frowning. "I don't give a fuck if your neighbors do see us together," he said a little tightly. "You that worried about it?"

I stared at him blankly, feeling my face heat with discomfort. It hadn't occurred to me until that very moment that I'd spent most of the day thinking 'Woe is me! I'm a dirty little secret!' when I was no more anxious for the neighbors to know what I was up to than they were.

Because if the neighbors knew, Jimmy might hear about, and I *definitely* didn't want Jimmy to know.

I didn't have to say anything. He read it in my expression.

The playfulness that I realized had thoroughly charmed me vanished. Anger radiated from him as he took my arm and escorted me down the stairs and outside. He didn't touch me again after I paused to lock the door. I had the feeling that it was only good manners that prevented him from stalking off and leaving me.

He opened the car door for me when we finally reached his SUV, two blocks down and one north of my place.

Boy oh boy! He *really* didn't want anybody to know where he was, I thought when I'd gotten in and he shut the door. He fished his keys out of his jeans pocket as he moved around to the driver's side, got in and started the car without a word.

Actually, we made the entire trip to the restaurant cloaked in an uncomfortable silence that made me on edge and almost completely killed my appetite. I was too needy for sustenance for it to vanish entirely, but I began to feel vaguely nauseated and head achy by the time we arrived. The place looked more like a club than a restaurant and my stomach tightened even more with nerves when I saw how many cars were parked in the lot.

So much for discretion!

I didn't know whether to be more alarmed or less so when Jared had escorted me inside and I discovered that the crowd was really young. They didn't look *old* enough to be out partying, I thought with dismay, wondering uneasily if was possible that any of Jimmy's friends were there.

There seemed to be a mixture of barely legal age drinking adults and not quite legal wearing bands than indicated they weren't to be served alcoholic beverages.

The band was pounding away deafeningly and the lighting so low I could hardly see where I was going.

That was a relief, at any rate. There would be no point in even trying to carry on a conversation and I didn't think it nearly as likely that anyone would see me and recognize me.

Settling a hand at my waist, Jared guided me through the throng toward the back where I discovered they were actually serving food—of a sort. Wings seemed to be the only thing meat-wise on the menu—from hot to nuclear. I leaned close enough to Jared to speak into his ear over the music. "Do they have wings that aren't hot?"

He looked at me as if I'd grown another head. "You don't like hot wings?"

I swallowed against a wedge of dismay in my throat, wondering if he'd brought me here just to emphasize the age difference between us. Not that I hadn't spied a handful of 'old people' among the spring chickens, but this was clearly primarily a night spot for very young people because the few I spotted that, like me, looked to be early to mid-thirties seemed to stick out like a sore thumb.

"I haven't tried them," I said spinelessly instead of telling him I just didn't like spicy food.

"I'll get you the mild. They're hardly hot at all," he said, lifting a hand to catch the attention of one of the waitresses flitting around the place.

The waitress could hardly seem to tear her eyes off of me when she arrived. I wondered uncomfortably if it was because she recognized me or if she was just so appalled to see Jared with me that she'd completely forgotten her manners—and her job.

She nodded as Jared reeled off his order, though, and went off without writing a single thing down.

I tried to focus on the music—which I discovered I liked—while we waited, but I couldn't shrug off my discomfort. Jared hooked a hand behind my neck and pulled me closer. "Relax, baby. Nobody here's going to recognize you," he said gruffly.

I couldn't refrain from sending him a hopeful look when he pulled away to look at me. He shook his head, catching my chin and kissing me full on the lips right there in public! It was no comforting peck, either. He kissed me with a thoroughness that could leave absolutely no one that witnessed it in any doubt that we were intimately acquainted.

I decided I'd gone off the deep end, because it roused me—publicly!

When I finally managed to get my eyes open, I saw that it had aroused him, too. Grinning wryly, he shifted in his seat.

It made me warmer when I realized why.

The wings, though, set me on fire! I was so hungry by the time they arrived that I managed to eat two before the fire hit me. Jared grinned at me when I started huffing air to try to cool my mouth and handed me the drink the waitress had set on the table. I took a gulp to cool the fire that nearly choked me when I discovered it was a mixed drink. The alcohol burn was almost worst than the hot pepper. The minute it hit bottom a wave of dizziness swept over me. My head reeled.

Jared frowned at me, obviously concerned. "You alright? Is it too strong?"

I blinked at him owlishly. I wasn't alright. The alcohol on my empty stomach, particularly when I wasn't in the habit of consuming alcohol at all, nearly knocked me for a loop.

"What is it?" I asked a little hoarsely.

"Strawberry daiquiri. You don't like it? I'll get you something else."

I stopped him when he started to rise. "No, it's fine. I just … I thought it was a slush."

He looked amused. "You sure you don't want me to get something else?"

I shook my head. I wasn't up to any more surprises. I tried filling the void in my stomach with French fries, but discovered after a few more cautious sips of the daiquiri that I couldn't really taste the alcohol or the peppers anymore.

We didn't linger. When we'd finished eating, Jared paid the tab, tossed a tip on the table and helped me up. The room swam around me when he did. His grip tightened. Curling an arm around my shoulders, he walked me out. It was a good thing, too. I was sure I wouldn't have made it otherwise. As it was, he had to keep a firm grip on me and aim me toward his car.

I dropped my head back on the headrest with relief when I'd finally settled in the car again, but the world was still spinning.

Jared fastened my seatbelt. "You're drunk as a skunk, aren't you, baby?"

"I've got a definite buzz," I murmured in a slurred voice without opening my eyes.

Chuckling, he started the car. "Mental note—Steph can't handle hard liquor."

I shot him a bird. He grabbed my hand and sucked my bird finger until my belly was dancing.

He parked his SUV in my drive. It wasn't that I didn't notice, but I realized I was in no shape to walk three blocks and supposed he did, too.

Instead of walking me into the house, he swept me up into his arms and carried me to the front door. I looped my arms around his neck and dropped my head to his shoulder. "Nosey neighbors'll see," I objected.

"I'll move the car later," he responded, trying to juggle me and get the door key in the lock. "Although I'm damned if I can see the problem when they haven't seen a man at your house before. Do they think you're a nun?"

I don't know why I found that funny, but I snickered at that. "That's it—I don't get none."

Having finally managed to get the door open, he stepped through with me and kicked it shut behind him.

"I can walk," I said quickly when I saw the stairs looming before us.

"You can't walk a straight line. You'll bust your ass on the stairs."

"You'll drop me and we'll both bust our ass—asses."

"No, I won't," he said, starting up the stairs.

"You're not going to be in any condition to do anything when you get me in bed, though."

"Don't count on it, lady. You'd be wrong."

Chapter Eight

I hadn't actually thought that Jared was serious, but he proved me wrong. When we reached my room, he set me on my feet and proceeded to help me undress and into the bed. My head still swimming, I closed my eyes and snuggled against the pillows, ready for sleep.

Jared had other ideas. When he'd skimmed out of his own clothes, he joined me and picked up where we'd left off. I passed from consciousness of the world when he'd brought me to climax again, sleeping deeply until he woke me sometime in the wee hours and made love to me again.

I felt like I'd just gone to sleep when a pounding from somewhere nearby woke me. I struggled for a few moments to get my eyes open and finally gave up the effort.

Whoever it was pounding on whatever they were beating on started up again just about the time I started to drift off.

"Someone's at the door," Jared muttered, his voice roughened with sleep.

"Oh." I thought hard about getting up and finally decided I just wasn't up to it. "They'll go away."

They didn't. After a short pause, the knocking started again.

"Fuck!" Jared snarled, bounding out of the bed. "I'll get it."

I knew there was some reason why he shouldn't be answering my door, but I couldn't think of what that reason was at the moment.

"Hold on!"

The moment I heard Jared yell out to whoever was beating on my door I recalled exactly why he shouldn't be answering my door. My eyes popped open and filled with tears at the burning. Blinking to see, I half climbed half fell out of the bed and looked around a little frantically for something to put on.

Jared's abandoned shirt caught my eye and I grabbed it and dove into it even as I stumbled toward the door. I discovered even as I reached the upper landing that it was too late. Jared—thankfully he'd at least grabbed his jeans and pulled them on—snatched the door open. When he did a horde of men poured through. I blinked, trying to adjust my blurred vision, and discovered it was the Thornes.

All of them looked seriously pissed off, too.

"What the hell?" Jared growled.

"That's what I'd liked to know," Gavin said coldly.

"So would I," Luke said tightly. "We agreed to leave Steph alone for a few days."

"You mean you two ordered it. I didn't agree to a damned thing," Jared retorted. "How did you find me?"

Luke sent him a look. "You mean aside from the fact that your fucking SUV is parked in her front yard? You know the place is under surveillance. They spotted your SUV around the corner last night and in her driveway this morning. Unfortunately, they didn't think it was worth mentioning until this morning—which is why that bastard Sloan will be looking for a new job Monday morning."

"What the hell have you got a tail on me for?" Jared demanded.

"Not you, numb nuts, Steph!" Bret growled. "I feel like kicking your fucking ass."

"This isn't the place for that," Luke said sharply.

I was just considering tiptoeing quietly back to my room before they noticed me when Gavin pinned me with a sharp look, raking me from head to toe—which was when I remembered I was wearing Jared's shirt and nothing else. "I think it's a little late to worry about putting on a show for Steph, don't you, Ms. Bridges?"

I gaped at him blankly, too stunned to discover I'd come under fire to even figure out what he was implying.

"Of all the manipulating little …"

He didn't finish the sentence, but he didn't have to. Despite the shock and the residual sluggishness from having been dragged from a deep sleep, I knew what he'd meant to say and exactly what was running through his mind. It was untrue and completely unfair. It should've made me angry. Instead, I felt a wave of hurt wash over me.

"Don't say anything you'll live to regret," Luke said sharply, obviously trying to head Gavin off before he could finish.

"Too late," Jared said angrily. "You are a total asshole, Gav. This is between us. It's got nothing to do with Steph."

"Right. And just when was the last time we nearly came to blows over anything?" Jessie asked coldly.

"Nobody almost came to blows," Jared said disgustedly. "Bret's always threatening to kick my ass."

I'd already turned to head to my bedroom before I heard the last comments, but it didn't make me feel any better that Jessie was of a similar frame of mind to Gavin.

Not that I gave a damn what either of them thought!

Any of them!

I nearly slammed the bedroom door behind me before it dawned on me that I was behaving as if I was an equal when I knew damned well I wasn't. Closing the door more gently than I'd intended, I stood staring at nothing in particular for a moment and finally moved to the bed, flopping on the edge and staring at my feet.

I couldn't decide if the argument had arisen from Jared breaking ranks and ignoring orders from his elder cousins or if the five of them were merely squabbling over usage of their plaything, but it wasn't my fault, whatever Gavin thought. It wasn't as if I'd asked Jared to come or even as if I was in any position to turn him away when he had shown up.

How dare the man accuse me of trying to manipulate them into fighting among themselves!

For that damned matter, I couldn't think of any reason why they should. It wasn't as if they weren't all getting a piece of me, damn it!

Alright, so I could see why Jessie might feel as if he wasn't getting his fair share. We'd only had sex once, but the others damned well had no room to complain!

I heard the front door close and then footsteps coming up the stairs. I was tempted to rush to the door and lock it, but it dawned on me that I was wearing Jared's shirt and that he hadn't put on his shoes when he'd gone downstairs.

He surprised me by tapping on the door instead of barging right in. Sniffing, mopping my cheeks off with my hands when I realized they were damp with tears, I told him to come in.

He'd walked right up to me before I realized it wasn't Jared. I stared down at the toes of shoes for a moment while that sank in and then lifted my head. A jolt went through me when I saw that it was Gavin.

His expression was as hard as I'd ever seen it. There was a muscle working in his jaw as if he was grinding his teeth.

I felt a wave of cold wash over me. I shot up from the bed. Although I had no clear idea of what I intended, retreat sounded loudly in my head. He caught my upper arms, preventing the retreat my instincts had urged me to. "I came to apologize," he said irritably. "Damn it, Steph. Don't look at me like that."

What look? The cornered rabbit? A dizzying wave of relief went through me, though.

"I know what I said was uncalled for and untrue. It's not your fault. At least . . . ." He grimaced. "It is, but not the way I said it."

I didn't know what to say. I couldn't actually think of anything to say because my mind had gone blank when I felt threatened and I couldn't seem to get it going again. I looked away.

He caught my face in the crook of his hand and tipped it up again, searching my face. "I can't quite figure you out, Stephanie Bridges," he murmured.

I swallowed a little convulsively, discovering it was really hard to swallow with my head tipped at that angle. "You can't?" I asked, mesmerized by the look on his face.

One corner of his mouth crooked upward faintly. "I can't ... and I can't tell you how deeply disturbing I find that."

That sounded deeply intriguing. "You do?"

The faint smile became a little more pronounced. He gathered me closer. "How much did you drink last night?" he asked, amusement flickering in his eyes.

I frowned, wondering what that had to do with anything. "One."

His dark brows rose. "Only one? I think I need to try one of those," he murmured, lowering his head until he could brush his lips across mine.

To my vast disappointment, that was as far as he took it. He teased me with the promise of a kiss for a handful of moments and then lifted his head. "They'll be back in here in five minutes, wondering what I'm up to."

I fell back against the bed weakly when he released me and turned away, striding through the door and out of it.

I listened to his footsteps as he took the stairs at a brisk pace and then the front door opened and closed again. As tempted as I was to go to the window and peer out when I heard the cars start up, I resisted, mostly because I felt too weak to attempt it. Feeling curiously blank, I climbed into the bed and collapsed face down against the pillow. Despite the chaotic thoughts rambling through my mind, I was out like a light before I knew it.

* * * *

Despite the fact that I spent most of the day in bed, asleep, I'd had a very long, rough weekend and I felt like it when I headed to work Monday morning. Thankfully, I was sluggish enough and distracted enough that the one thing that I'd worried about before I'd spent the weekend with the Thornes didn't come to pass.

I'd thought I might have trouble behaving as if nothing was any different, as if my entire world hadn't been turned upside down, but I didn't even see Luke or Gavin. I didn't look for them, didn't think to, although I generally did when I arrived at work, just for the thrill of it. Even coffee failed to get my engines revved like a glimpse of Luke or Gavin could.

My nosey next-door neighbor had noticed the Thornes. It was just too much to hope that she'd gone off for the weekend and hadn't had her damned nose pressed to the window facing my house when they'd arrived.

She'd greeted me as I left the house for work by asking me why all those men had been at my house the morning before. "They were looking for Jared," I mumbled, more irritated with myself for not having anticipated the question and come up with a believable lie than I was with her.

"Oh? He must be that nice looking young man you went out with Saturday?"

I felt my face redden. Clearly she knew he'd still been there the next morning. "Have a nice day, Ms. Nose ... Mrs. Niece," I said instead of answering the question.

I wasn't overly worried about her noticing that Jared had spent the night. I was pretty sure she had no idea who he was and it would be months before Jimmy came back. I was convinced she'd find something else to gossip about in the mean time.

I didn't think she could've failed to recognize Luke or Gavin.

That was the part that worried me, because their being at my house was probably just too juicy and fraught with possibilities for her to give up on it very easily.

I was still trying to jog my sluggish brain into providing me with a believable story to cover their presence at my house when I arrived at work.

Anything but the truth!

The Thornes would have my hide if the scandal got out. I was completely sure that the only reason they'd come up with the bizarre plan they had was because of their reluctance for it get out that their bank wasn't safe—and an equal reluctance to let me and Jimmy off with just a slap on the wrist. I didn't think it would actually have looked as bad if the bank had been held up. Even I could see that it would seriously undermine the confidence of their customers if they discovered a sixteen year old had hacked in and transferred eight million dollars to the Caymans and back.

When I'd put my purse away and collected my cash drawer, I headed to my window, settled on my stool, and began to sort the cash. I didn't glance up when I noticed the security guard head for the door to open it. I was sure it wasn't Luke. He was rarely the one who opened the door in the mornings. Instead, I glanced at the clock. Uttering a deep sigh as the day yawned before me, I quickly finished up and braced myself for the first customers.

That was when I discovered it actually was Luke who'd opened up.

He sent me an enigmatic look as he welcomed the first customers in and then headed back towards his office.

"What was that about?" Phyllis whispered.

I glanced at the clerk next to me guiltily. "What?" I asked, striving for a pose of confusion.

She smiled thinly. "Mr. Thorne looked right at you."

I felt my face heat but doggedly pursued mystification. "Really? I didn't notice."

"Mmmhmm. You didn't notice when he walked by and looked you over either."

I stared at her in dismay, checking my appearance with my hands self-consciously.

"He gave you a ride home Friday, didn't he?"

Thankfully, a customer stepped up to her window before she could pursue the interrogation. It gave me a few moments to think of a reply, but unfortunately I was too agitated to come up with anything.

"I have to go," I said quickly when the customer left and she turned to me again, striding away before she could question me any further.

I ducked into the bathroom since I'd used that as my excuse for leaving, but it was a waste of time. I was too upset to think.

Why hadn't it occurred to me that I needed some sort of cover story, I thought unhappily. It was all very well to say we'd keep everything hush hush, but what was I supposed to say when nosey people noticed anyway and started pumping me for information? I couldn't tell them the truth and I couldn't claim that I was dating. What the hell was I supposed to say?

Realizing I needed to ask what was permissible, I debated between Luke and Gavin and finally decided to ask Gavin since he was clearly the 'big boss'. His secretary looked down her nose at me when I entered the reception and asked if I could speak with him. "Did you have an appointment?"

She knew damned well I didn't since she was the one who made them. I cleared my throat. "No."

She sniffed dismissively. "I'll ask him if he can see you, but I'm sure he's busy."

She looked surprised and not at all pleased when he told her to send me in. Instead of doing so, she walked me to the door and opened it.

Gavin gave her a cool look when she opened the door. "I don't want to be disturbed."

Me and the receptionist both halted in our tracks. "I thought you said …?"

His lips tightened. "Have a seat, Ms. Bridges," he said pointedly.

Red faced, the secretary nodded and retreated, closing the door.

I crossed to the chair he'd indicated, but I was too agitated to sit down.

He lifted his brows at me questioningly, leaning back in his chair. "You needed to talk to me?"

I let out a pent up breath. "It's just that ... Well, you didn't say what I should tell anybody if they asked me anything and I didn't want to say anything until I knew what you wanted me to say."

He stared me blankly when I stopped babbling, a slow frown gathering his black brows together. "Run that by me again ... a little slower."

I took a deep breath, looked at the chair and then decided against it when it occurred to me that his secretary might have her ear to the door. Instead, I moved around the desk and crouched in front of him so that I could speak more quietly. "My neighbor saw all of you when you were at my house yesterday morning and now the teller next to me is asking me about Luke driving me Friday. I know you don't want gossip going around, but I don't know what I'm supposed to say."

He studied me when I stopped speaking, rocking slightly in his chair. "This isn't something you've come up with to get out of your obligations?" he finally asked coolly.

I gaped at him. It dawned on me abruptly that I didn't particular *want* to get out of my obligations. With sudden clarity I knew it was the fear that discovery might end it that was the main reason I was so upset. I was so stunned by that realization that I couldn't think of anything to at all to say for several moments. "I'm sorry," I said finally. "I shouldn't have bothered you with this. It's my problem."

He leaned forward abruptly, grasping my upper arms before I could rise. I found myself caged by his knees. "Speaking of problems," he murmured lazily. "I have one I think you can help me with."

It took me a moment to figure out what he was suggesting, but a movement in his dress pants drew my attention and gave me my first clue. I could see the outline of his erection through the fine, loose fitting material. I stared at it a long moment, feeling my mouth go dry, and then met his gaze. "Here? Now?" I croaked weakly.

"Right here. Right now," he responded implacably.

I threw a glance toward the door. "What if ...?"

"If she comes in we won't have to worry about what to tell the gossips, will we?" he murmured, releasing his grip on my arms and leaning back to unfasten his belt and the waist of his pants. I watched his hands as he lowered the zipper.

Clearly, he was dead serious, although I'd more than half suspected it was a joke or a dare. I still wasn't sure it wasn't a dare, but I felt my pulse pick up.

I wasn't sure if it was from excitement or nerves, but I decided it didn't matter. He'd commanded a performance. If he didn't really want me to, he'd stop me.

Settling on my knees, I reached to push his trousers back and slipped a hand through the opening of his shorts. His cock almost seemed to leap into my hand. It was hot to the touch, felt like iron sheathed in silk. I pulled it free of his shorts, studied it a moment and flicked a look at his face. His expression was taut, his eyes glittering with heat. He covered my hand with his, slowly guiding my hand up and down his shaft.

It flickered through my mind that I should feel belittled to be commanded to perform for him. I realized I didn't. Gavin was the most powerful man I knew or ever had ever known. The taut look of need in his expression made me feel powerful.

I returned my attention to his cock. As cocks went, his was beautiful—no great surprise. I didn't think anything on the man wasn't. A bead of pre-cum formed on the tip as I studied it. He shifted restlessly in his chair. I leaned forward and licked the slit at the tip of his cock. When I glanced up at him again, I saw that he was watching every move I made. Holding his gaze, I opened my mouth and sucked at the head. He swallowed convulsively. His hands, which he'd settled on the arms of his chair, tightened.

Dragging in a deep breath, I went down on him, trying to take all of him into my mouth. It wasn't possible, but it pleased me that it wasn't. I didn't realize that I was humming with pleasure until he speared his hands in my hair. "I won't last long if you keep that up," he said hoarsely.

The realization that he was near to coming sent a thrill through me. I wrapped both hands tightly around his shaft, alternately stroking him with my hands and sucking at the part of him that I could fit into my mouth. He began to lift toward me with each stroke, uttering choked sounds of pleasure that made my own pleasure skyrocket. Abruptly, he stilled, his hand tightening almost crushingly on my skull. I moved faster, knowing it was what he needed to bring him off. I came when I felt his cock jerk in my mouth and the first of his seed hit the back of my throat. Shuddering, I sucked frantically at his cock until I couldn't get more out of him and finally released his flaccid member, resting my head in his lap and struggling to catch my breath.

He kneaded my scalp, stroking my hair and the side of my face.

"I've made a fucking mess of your hair," he murmured wryly.

I lifted my head at that, feeling the rat's nest he'd made of my carefully neat hairdo. Catching my arms, he pulled me to my feet and onto his chest. "I think I'll have that for breakfast tomorrow," he murmured.

I chuckled at the teasing note in his voice, glancing up at him in surprise.

He was smiling faintly. It was amazing how handsome he was when he smiled.

He dragged on my hair, tipping my face up, and kissed me lingeringly, uttering a deep sigh when he broke the kiss. "I owe you one. Unfortunately, I think it'll have to wait till the weekend ... unless I can figure out a way to get into your house and still avoid your neighbors."

I didn't understand, at first, what he was talking about. I felt my face heat when it dawned on me that he didn't realize I'd come when I brought him off, but I decided not to tell him that. He'd think I was weird.

He studied my face for a moment. "Tell them to mind their own business," he said almost gently.

I lifted my brows questioningly. "You think that'll shut them up?" I asked doubtfully.

His lips twisted wryly. "*Nothing* will stop a wagging tongue, but you're under no obligation to answer interrogations by your co-workers or your neighbors."

Realizing I'd been dismissed, I straightened. Pulling the pins from my hair, I finger combed it then coiled it again and pushed the pins back in. "I look ok?"

He stood up. Lifting a finger, he traced lightly around my mouth and grinned abruptly. "You look like you've been sucking my cock."

He drew me up and kissed me until I was breathless and dizzy, then leaned away and studied my mouth again. "Nope. That didn't do it. Your lips are still red and swollen."

I rolled my eyes. "Now I won't be self-conscious."

He surprised me by walking me to the door. "Thank you, Ms. Bridges," he said politely when he'd opened the door. "I'll check into that."

Nodding, I walked as briskly across the reception area as I could without giving the appearance of running. Fortunately, the secretary seemed more focused on Gavin than me.

I sincerely hoped he'd remembered to zip his pants after he fastened them up again.

Despite the length of time I'd been gone, I ducked into the lady's room again and checked my appearance in the mirror. I was dismayed when I had. My hair was pinned neatly enough, but definitely lopsided and he hadn't exaggerated about my mouth. It was red all the way around my lips. I didn't want to spare the time to retrieve my purse, so I straightened my hair the best I could and then cupped cool water over my lips until they didn't seem quite so red and swollen.

Phyllis eyed me speculatively when I returned to my window. "That was a long bathroom break."

I decided to ignore her. No doubt she would go straight to the supervisor at the first opportunity, always assuming she hadn't noticed herself, but I decided not to devise a lie to pacify her.

I should've realized there was no way I could completely avoid talk, but I never paid the least attention to my neighbors. It hadn't occurred to me that they would be so interested in my life. I'd thought as long as I didn't do anything blatant—like having Jared over for the night—no one would notice.

I supposed leaving his vehicle in my drive hadn't been very bright. Then again, I hadn't really been in any condition for a long stroll by the time I'd finished that daiquiri and of course Jared deciding to stay the night had also brought the others around the following morning and that wasn't something easily overlooked or explained away either.

So far I was batting a thousand for 'things guaranteed to arouse the curiosity of my neighbors'.

I was single, I thought a little resentfully. It wasn't as if I *was* a nun, for god's sake!

Jimmy wasn't going to be happy if he got back and discovered I was the talk of the town, I thought glumly, wondering if there was any chance the interest would die down before he returned.

The worst of it was that I was going to be stuck with whatever horrible reputation I picked up. I couldn't even move away, although that did occur to me briefly. Gavin and the others had specifically demanded that Jimmy work for the bank as a consultant when he got back and ferret out any other weaknesses in their security. That wouldn't stop me from moving, of course—once Jimmy was old enough to live on his own, but it also wouldn't do me any good if Jimmy had to be here because I didn't care what anybody else thought. I only cared what Jimmy thought of me.

There was no way to escape the situation, I realized. The best I could do was try to preserve an outward appearance of respectability and hope that the Thornes wouldn't prove difficult.

They were bound to get tired of me before long, I decided, even though it didn't make me particularly happy to acknowledge it. I was sure it was the novelty of having their own, living fuck doll that was creating such a flurry. It wasn't that *I* was such a great hit with them. It was Miss Puss, and fifty percent of the population had one. In a few weeks, a couple of months at the outside, they'd decide they were bored or they'd find a new interest and decide to let me out of my obligations early for good behavior.

Gavin had even suggested as much at the time.

Of course, he'd said six months and *then* they'd consider good behavior, but I was sure—I hoped—it wasn't going to be even half that long. I was enjoying it way more than I should and beyond that I didn't think I could continue to be intimate with them for months on end and come out of the situation without a *lot* emotional baggage. I'd been ripe to fall for Luke and Gavin before any of this. I wasn't any less drawn to them now and worse, I could see I wouldn't have any trouble at falling for the others. Jared and Bret *should* have been too much younger than me for that to be a problem, but their boyish charm was already getting under my skin.

Contrary to my hopes that I could count on Gavin and Luke, at least, to behave with discretion, I discovered that they were almost worse than Jared. He, at least, had made a stab at keeping things quiet and waited until dark, left his car several blocks away and walked to my house, even though he'd ended up blowing the whole discretion thing by parking in my drive and staying the night.

Then again, maybe it was at least partly my fault.

Although I generally wore slacks to work, I made the mistake on Thursday of wearing a skirt and apparently that was just too much of a temptation.

Luke waylaid me at the lady's room when I took my morning break. I was both surprised and happy to see him, though, naturally, I did my best to hide the last. It didn't occur to me until he grabbed my hand and dragged me into the lady's room that it was too much of a coincidence to be a coincidence. It actually didn't dawn on me, though, that he'd been keeping tabs on me via the bank's security cameras until he parked me on the vanity and dragged a tube of lubrication from his pocket.

Unless that was the case, though, he wouldn't have been in just the right place at just the right time and armed with lube, would he?

I couldn't decide how I felt about that, but I didn't have a lot of time to dwell on it. The moment he plopped my ass on the vanity, he shoved his hands beneath my skirt and dragged my panties off. He unbuttoned my blouse far enough to reach through the opening and caress my breasts while he distracted me with a heated kiss.

The fear of someone walking in on us kept me on edge and off kilter, but he'd managed to get me thoroughly stirred up when he heard approaching footsteps. Yanking me from the counter, he carried me into the last stall at the end and locked the door behind us. He didn't merely wait until they'd left, however. As soon as he'd wedged me between himself and the door, he slipped the head of his lube-slicked cock into the mouth of my sex.

My eyes widened. I'd been holding my breath, waiting for the unknown woman to finish and leave. I'd thought he meant to wait. The door rattled behind me as he struggled to drive deeper and he paused.

Apparently the woman had only come in to check her hair and makeup. She left after just a few thundering heartbeats.

Either that or she spied the legs of Luke's trousers beneath the stall door.

I hoped that wasn't the case.

The door hadn't even closed behind the woman when Luke shifted his hold on me and curled his hips to seat his cock completely inside of me. I couldn't find purchase to counter his thrusts, but he didn't seem to need help. He'd braced me at an angle that allowed him to pump into me as smoothly as a piston, and he did. I forgot all about the need to be quiet when I felt myself racing toward climax. Fortunately, Luke didn't. He clamped his mouth over mine just as I reached fever pitch and my low moans and gasps began to build in volume. I came with his tongue in my mouth, sucking frantically on it since I had no other outlet for the pounding waves of pleasure jolting through me. He managed three more deep strokes before he joined me in bliss.

For a few moments we leaned together fighting for breath. Finally, he eased his hold and allowed my feet to drop to the floor. He kept me braced between himself and the door until I finally managed to open my eyes. Leaning down, he kissed me briefly and then stepped back to adjust his pants.

A few moments later, he left the stall and, after pausing at the door, slipped out.

Thoroughly rattled, I spent most of my break in the lady's room cleaning up, repairing the 'wear' on my toilet, and trying to nerve myself to leave the room.

Mid-afternoon, Gavin called me to his office. As soon as I entered, he got up and locked the door. Even if not for that clear indication that he wasn't taking any chances on an interruption, the look of intent on his face was a definite clue when he turned and strode back to me. He caught my shoulders when he reached me and dragged me against his frame, kissing me until I was dizzy and then turned me and bent me over his desk. Dragging my panties off, he moved up behind me, stroking my buttocks before he stroked my cleft.

I got a minimum of foreplay, but I wasn't about to complain when the secretary no doubt had her ear plastered to the other side of the door. Producing a tube of lubrication, he prepared both of us and then speared me with his cock, driving into me with such force that I had to grip the edge of his desk to keep from being shoved over it. He was either conscious of the passing time or he'd built up a lot of horniness in two days. As soon as he'd sunk root deep inside of me, he set a jolting pace that should've been way too fast for me, but wasn't. I certainly wasn't 'needy', not when Luke had already pounded the hell out of me earlier that day. Or maybe it was only because I'd come so fast before?

I didn't examine it too closely. I was aroused by his kiss and panting with excitement by the time he'd filled me with his wonderfully thick flesh. The moment he began to drive into me I felt my body gathering toward orgasm and kept pace with him, coming almost the moment I felt him begin to shudder in climax.

It was a mixed blessing. I'd thoroughly enjoyed it, but not only did I have a hell of a time containing my tendency to 'yodel' when I hit my peak, I managed to lay down on an ink pen on his desk that was leaking and picked up a dark stain the size of my fist. Gavin 'fixed' it by dragging my shirt out of the waist of skirt and using the tails of the shirt to 'cover' it, but it not only didn't completely cover the stain, the fact that I'd left with my shirt tucked and come back with it out raised brows.

I began to suspect the element of 'danger' of getting caught was part of what turned them on to catching me at work—mostly because I found it somewhat titillating myself—scary as hell, but there was no getting around the fact that it added an element of excitement.

I would still have preferred not to take the chances they did, but I wasn't in charge.

Obviously, the workweek was a little too much for them. Bret climbed over the six-foot fence surrounding my backyard that evening and came face to face with Jessie, who'd already scaled it, nearly precipitating a fistfight in my backyard.

I hadn't exactly had a quiet first week, but in spite of that I was keyed up when Friday rolled around and Luke drove me to the house in the woods.

Chapter Nine

Luke surprised me on the drive out. Instead of driving like a bat out of hell as he had when we'd made the trip the first time, he kept the speedometer within five to ten miles of the speed limit the entire time. I relaxed after the first twenty minutes or so and peeled my fingers loose from the doorframe and the dashboard.

I was still keyed up, but this time there was no thread of uneasiness as there had been the first time. I discovered I was looking forward to the weekend with them with nothing but pleasurable anticipation.

I subdued it the best I could, reminding myself that my enjoying the situation was just a pleasant side effect. I couldn't afford to allow myself to sink too deeply into the fancy. I had to keep my head straight.

It was harder than I'd expected it to be. The Thornes were more relaxed, as well. I hadn't noticed, before, that they had been battling with doubts as much as I had been, but the difference in them made that abundantly clear.

They were better prepared. As soon as the grilled steaks hit the table, they produced a soft drink for me. Evidently they'd decided I didn't hold my liquor very well, I thought wryly.

I didn't actually feel a need for bottled courage anyway and I'd never been much for drinking. I wasn't particularly against it on principle, but I didn't socialize—hadn't in years—and I did disapprove of drinking when there was no socializing going on. Drinking alone was the surest road to alcoholism.

I'd headed in to the bedroom I'd occupied the weekend before as soon as I'd arrived and took my time unwinding with a hot shower. Leaving my hair down to dry and also because they'd made it clear they preferred it when I wore it loose, I dressed in the naughty lingerie they'd bought for me before I joined them.

It pleased me that they seemed just as bowled over by it as they had the first time. I knew familiarity was going to breed contempt at some point, but at least they were still appreciative.

When we'd finished eating and cleaned up, the guys settled to play cards as they had the weekend before. Deciding it must be a long-standing custom, I wandered around a while until I found a book that held enough appeal I thought I might be able to get in to it and settled on the couch to read while I waited for the real game to begin.

I discovered that although the book was interesting enough, I couldn't really concentrate on it enough to really get in to it. Anticipation had already been threading my veins from the time I'd left work and it wasn't abating the least little bit with me sitting virtually naked on the couch in full view of five of the hottest males ever created. I was more keenly aware of my erogenous zones with them exposed to air currents and the many accidental brushes of contact with my surroundings. No matter what position I chose to sit in, I was supremely conscious of my bare pussy—ditto my breasts. I hadn't realized how hard it was to do anything without brushing my breasts against things. The hungry gazes I encountered from time to time from first one and then another of the men only added to the building heat inside of me.

It didn't occur to me until I overheard Luke comment with disgust that it looked like Jessie had won the first round that it dawned on me that they were playing for me—or at least the order.

Actually, I didn't tumble to it until Jessie dropped his cards on the table, got up and moved to the couch. I set the book aside and got up when he paused in front of me, looking down at me. To my surprise, although he helped me to my feet, he took my place and pulled me down on his lap.

A little disconcerted, I allowed him to shift me around on his lap until he'd positioned me the way he wanted me—and I was more mystified. I leaned back against his chest when he urged me to, not totally relaxed because I wasn't entirely sure of what was going on, but I discovered soon enough that he had it mind to play. What I wasn't sure of was his intentions. I didn't know if it was merely that he enjoyed the idea of being watched—although that seemed a strong possibility considering the tendency I'd noticed in them—or if he was doing it to annoy and/or distract the others.

When I'd settled, he grasped my legs and guided them over his own thighs. Using his legs, he pushed against mine until he'd spread my legs so wide I could feel the strain along my inner thighs and the moist inner petals of my sex separated. Cool air brushed along my cleft.

We had the full attention of everyone left at the table. Even Bret, who'd had his back mostly angled toward the couch, changed positions so that he could divide his attention between the cards in his hand and what was transpiring on the couch.

The show didn't officially start, in fact, until he'd taken the seat Jessie had vacated. As soon as Bret settled and flicked a glance in our direction, Jessie slid the hands he'd settled on my thighs toward my cleft and began to stroke me. Warmth immediately began to filter through me at his touch. My belly tightened. My heart and respiration accelerated.

Pushing the thick index finger of one hand inside of me, he plucked at my clit with the other. Within moments, a heated languor had stolen over me. I was finding it harder and harder to remain perfectly still in spite Jessie's order for me to do just that. I dropped my head to his shoulder when I reached a point of weakness where it began to feel too heavy for my neck to hold it upright. The moment I did, he turned his head and lightly bit my neck, sucking at it.

My skin pebbled all over in reaction, my nipples standing tightly erect as the blood surged into them.

For a time, I merely luxuriated in the sensations he was creating but when it came to me that I was climbing perilously close to climax, I began to struggle with it. I knew I was going to be supremely disappointed if he brought me off like this, particularly when I could feel his monster cock digging into my back.

Images began to fill my mind of straddling his lap and trying to force that thick shaft inside of me. I remembered, with sharp clarity, how it felt when he'd forced that huge, swollen member inside of me before, the burn as he stretched me beyond my limits, the devastating combination of pain and pleasure as he'd driven deep. The ache had felt so good I hadn't wanted it to end. I hadn't wanted to climax. I'd wanted to him to keep plowing into me on and on.

A rush of moisture flooded my channel at the thoughts I'd allowed myself. I felt myself rushing closer to peaking and struggled against it.

Jessie lifted his hand from my clit and plucked at one aching nipple. The jolt that went through me was so hard I thought for a moment I'd climaxed. It had merely set off a wave of frantic convulsions within my sex, though. The more he plucked, the harder they got until I couldn't be still anymore.

Jessie covered my ear with his mouth, sucked at it. "Turn around and face me," he whispered hoarsely when he'd lifted his mouth from my ear.

I was more than willing. I was eager. Unfortunately, I was also weak and dizzy with need. He helped me to turn around. I stared down at him hungrily while he unfastened his jeans, lifting up on my knees when he had to lift up to push his jeans and shorts down.

He coated his member thoroughly with the lubrication he'd palmed from his jeans pocket.

I watched, mesmerized, feeling my throat close with need, feeling a wave of disappointment that he was using the lubrication. I thought I'd produced plenty of my own and, in any case, I wanted the full experience of that enormous cock. I wanted to feel him stretching me until I felt like I couldn't take any more.

I discovered there was no escaping that. Even with the lubrication, it took force and determination for me to conquer that mountain of flesh. The moment I settled on the head and began trying to lower myself onto it I realized that. The head of his cock was slightly smaller than the shaft and I was still panting for breath by the time I'd managed to envelope the head.

Jessie halted me, steadied me and reached around me to unfasten the restricting corset. I hadn't realized just how restricting it was until it fell away. When he grasped my waist again and pulled, his cock slid a little deeper. I panted for breath, gripping his shoulders frantically.

He paused again, studying my face.

For a moment, I was worried he'd decided he was too much for me. Before I could remind him that we'd managed it before, he began bearing down on my hips again. My eyes rolled back in my head at the sheer thrill of feeling the enormity of hard flesh slowly filling me almost beyond capacity. I discovered I was groaning almost incessantly by the time he'd gone as deep as he could.

He paused again. I dropped my head to his shoulder, panting for breath, fighting the urge to come right then. "That feels so good," I murmured breathlessly.

His arms tightened around me. He curled his hips, grinding against me.

I sucked in a harsh breath, feeling the threatening tremors of imminent climax. I knew I couldn't move a hair's breadth without coming immediately, but when he urged me to rise I struggled up, clinging tenaciously to the precipice.

He caught one of my nipples in his mouth when I'd lifted high enough for him to reach my breasts, suckling it with such enthusiasm that I lost my grip on my control. I tensed all over with the first convulsion. Either he realized I'd hit maximum overload, or he reached his limit at the same time. He pressed down on my hips. I managed three strokes before my electrical impulses went haywire and

I lost all ability to function.

He took control, jogging me up and down on that log of flesh until I was screaming with the explosion of ecstasy wracking me. I wilted against him gratefully when the spasms finally began to peter off, shuddering with the after quakes.

It was a while before I realized he was stroking my back soothingly, nuzzling his face against my neck, nibbling light kisses there. "I didn't hurt you, baby?" he murmured near my ear.

I shook my head, still too weak to muster enough strength to talk. He drew back enough to study my face. With an effort, I managed to open my eyes when I sensed his interested gaze. For a long, long moment we simply gazed into each other's eyes. When he finally broke contact, allowing his gaze to move over my face, I studied his.

Jessie was the one Thorne I knew the least about—beyond his history and his pedigree. I hadn't even scratched the surface of Jessie the man. Like all the Thornes, he wasn't hurt for looks. He wasn't quite as handsome as Luke and Gavin, but he didn't miss it by much. I discovered that I thought his features were actually more pleasing individually even though the whole somehow 'missed'. I finally decided it was because I was drawn more to Luke and Gavin's personality.

Abruptly, I remembered his comment the weekend before.

He'd seemed to agree with Gavin's assessment that I was trying to drive a wedge between them by manipulating them. Unlike Gavin, he hadn't apologized or taken it back.

It seemed significant that the two most determined to think the worst of me were the only two who'd married and I realized there was a lot more to the story than just the brevity of their marriages and the nastiness of the divorces.

Like me, they'd had a close encounter of the nasty kind and they were no longer as trusting as they'd been before.

He frowned, apparently sensing my internal withdrawal, his gaze searching mine.

Something flickered in his eyes—dawning understanding.

He slipped a hand to my neck, capturing me even as I began to pull away physically. Titling his head, he covered my mouth, kissing me almost roughly. I felt his cock stir inside of me, begin to swell.

Apparently, he decided to ignore it. He broke the kiss and helped me to 'dismount'. I wavered a little dizzily when I'd gained my feet but managed to catch myself. Collecting the corset he'd discarded, I headed to the bathroom to wash up.

He surprised me by following me.

I'd opted to clean up at the lavatory rather than taking another shower. Too many of those and my skin was going to be as dry as ash. He caught me around the waist and lifted me, settling me on the vanity, and examined Miss Puss with frowning intensity before turning his attention to cleaning me up himself.

Nonplussed, I merely leaned back and let him, propping on my arms. I could see he was wrestling his thoughts, but he either decided against what he'd been thinking about saying or he couldn't find the words he wanted. In the end, he didn't say anything at all—not pertaining to the confrontation.

When he'd finished bathing the semen off of me, he moved closer. Curling an arm around my shoulders, he cupped my mound with his free hand, pushing his index finger slowly inside of me. "I could get addicted to this sweet spot," he murmured, holding my gaze, "too damned easily. It worries me, makes me wonder what the real Stephanie Bridges is like."

I could get addicted to the sweet meat between his legs if it came to that, and that worried me a lot more, I was sure, than he was worried. "A total bitch," I responded promptly.

My response surprised him. Amusement flickered in his eyes. "A total bitch? As in completely a bitch? Any chance I could fuck that out of you?"

I swallowed with an effort, completely unable to keep the visions from my mind that instantly arose. I was more tempted to suggest that he give it a try than I wanted to be. It damned near spilled out of my mouth before I could stop it. After due consideration, I threw caution to the wind. He could hardly think any more poorly of me, could he? "I don't know. I suppose you could mount me on that huge cock of yours and give it a try."

His eyes darkened. He shifted his hand from my shoulders to the back of my head. "I think I will," he murmured, leaning close enough to suck at my lips.

He disappointed me, though. After the brief kiss, he helped me down, cleaned up himself and left me standing with a 'hard on' and no place to put it.

I thrust it from my mind. It wasn't as if I was going to be left wanting. He had two randy brothers and two randy cousins waiting their turn.

And not very patiently.

I discovered when I left the bathroom what the activity was that I'd heard in the bedroom.

Jared, Bret, and Luke were busy setting up cameras.

Alright, there was kinky and then there was *really* kinky!

"You're not … planning on filming this?" I asked before I'd considered that it was tantamount to an objection and I'd already been warned that that wasn't allowed.

Luke flicked a glance at me.

Bret uttered a snort of amusement. "Nobody wants a record that might come back to haunt."

Relieved but more bemused, I watched them check the cameras and angles. When Luke moved into the other room, I followed him to see what was going on and discovered they'd set up a huge TV in the main room. When Luke turned it on, the screen filled with four images of the bedroom—more specially, the bed from four different angles. Only one of the four was a distance shot.

I felt my belly clench instantly.

Apparently, they'd decided standing around the room to watch just wasn't satisfactory.

Satisfied, Luke turned and strode back toward me. Catching my hand as he reached me, he dragged me into the bedroom and told me to get on the bed. When I'd settled, he studied me for a moment and then arranged me, pushing my knees up until my feet were flat on the bed and then spreading my legs wide. After studying me frowningly for a moment, he left the room again.

He was back in a few minutes, but he paused in the doorway, instructing Bret and Jared to adjust the angle of the cameras until he was satisfied. After glancing at me, Luke told me to stay put and he and Jared left.

I glanced at Bret and saw he was undressing.

My belly tightened with anticipation. My throat went dry.

Luke reappeared dragging a cord. He placed it on the bed between my legs. I lifted my head to look down at the cord, seeing it had a small light on the end. "What's that?"

"A camera," he said a little distractedly, moving to the door and glancing at the TV.

I could tell this was going to be fun.

Bret climbed on the bed beside me when Luke left, settling on his side and studying me. Acutely aware of the camera between my legs, I gazed back at him a little tensely.

He lifted a hand to cup and massage one of my breasts. "Forget about the cameras if it bothers you."

I took that to mean it either didn't bother him or it turned him on. Considering the erection he had, I was guessing the latter. Forgetting the cameras was easier said than done, but I was wide open to sexual play. I'd been wide open before I'd even left the bank. I'd been aroused since I'd arrived. As thoroughly as Jessie had satisfied me, he'd turned right around and gotten me stirred up again.

For whatever reason, Bret took the time to thoroughly arouse me with foreplay, massaging my breasts until the blood had pooled almost painfully in my nipples before he leaned close enough to take the first in his mouth. The slow building of pressure made his first touch exquisitely torturous. A blinding jolt went through me as he closed his teeth lightly over the bud, bearing down until it bordered pain and then pulling so that his teeth raked me. I gripped two handfuls of the sheet to keep from grabbing his head.

He leaned away, studied me a moment and finally caught one of my wrists. Lifting my arm above my head, he wrapped something cool and silky around my wrist.

I looked up, discovering with a mixture of surprise and uneasiness that they'd installed restraints on the bed when they'd been setting up that I hadn't even noticed. It wasn't tight, but I discovered when I pulled at it that I was thoroughly restrained.

He crawled across me and caught my other wrist. I resisted briefly, uncertainty tightening my belly, but I knew better than to try to fight him. I relaxed the tension in my arm with an effort as he pulled my arm up and tied my other wrist.

My uneasiness grew when he pulled out another length of material and wound it around my ankle as he had my wrist. When he returned to his original position, he pulled another out and tied my remaining ankle, tugging until he'd pulled my legs as far apart as they would go without breaking something.

I was more than airish down below now. I felt like I'd been spread until, not just the lips, but the mouth of my sex was gaping.

I had a horrible feeling it was, but I couldn't do anything about it.

Settling again, Bret leaned down and returned his attention to stripping my nipple with his teeth. Contrary to all logic, I hadn't cooled while he was tying me up to make sure I couldn't move. It almost seemed that the nipple was more sensitive than before. I jumped when he clamped his teeth on it, again biting down until it approached pain before he pulled away. As torturous as it seemed, I felt moisture gather in my sex until it was so saturated I felt like it was oozing from the mouth.

I was too focused on what Bret was doing to spare the time to be overly concerned about the camera between my legs, though. In point of fact, I forgot all about it. He teased me in the same manner until I was mindless, until my entire body had begun to feel as if it was pulsing. I almost came out of my skin when he ceased teasing the tip with his teeth and closed his mouth over it, sucking. I jerked at the restraints on my wrists mindlessly, bucking. He lifted his head after a moment and leaned over to catch the other nipple between his teeth as he had the first.

The explosion of sensation that shot through me forced a cry from my lungs, carried me to the edge of darkness. I didn't descend completely, however. I was excruciatingly aware of every wonderfully torturous scrape of his teeth and then the suction of his mouth. I panted until my mouth and throat felt like a desert. The tension had built inside me until I felt like I would come any second, and yet somehow, I couldn't reach it.

I realized I didn't want to. I wanted his cock inside of me when I came. His cock wasn't quite as big as Jessie's, but it didn't miss it by much. In fact, the head of his cock was larger, almost the same as the shaft. I began to want it desperately, feverishly, but he seemed more inclined to play, to hold off on giving me what I needed.

Leaving off teasing my breasts, he allowed his lips to crawl over my ribcage and down my belly. The feel of his lips and teeth as he nipped at me made my flesh pebble all over, increased my sensitivity when I was already pretty much mindless with the barrage of impulses through my brain.

He paused when he reached the lips of my sex, breathing raggedly, his hot breath brushing that sensitive area until I thought I'd lose my mind. I thought he'd decided to ignore that area and disappointment flooded me. After a long pause, though, he caught my clit in his mouth and sucked it.

I almost came. I was so close my stomach cramped miserably when he released my clit and began to gnaw a trail along my inner thighs, from my knee to groin. He paused when he reached my sex again. I held my breath, waiting. He moved to one side and gnawed a trail up to the opposite knee. And then down again, skipping the most important part to drive me crazy.

Sitting up, he returned to my breasts. I was nearly weeping with need when he finally stopped, babbling his name breathlessly in desperation. He slid a hand down my belly and pushed a finger up inside of me.

"I don't think you're ready."

"I am!"

He sawed his finger in and out a couple of times and then removed it. I managed to open my eyes enough to see if he was changing positions and discovered that he was sucking his finger. "Sweet. I think I'll eat you out instead."

I felt like weeping or screaming. I was torn by the realization that I needed relief, any kind of relief, and the certainty that I wasn't going to be satisfied with anything less than his cock.

He studied my face. "Just a taste then. Don't come, Steph. I want you to come when I'm inside of you."

I nodded, I thought, but despair filled me when he leaned down over me again. I wasn't sure I could keep from coming if my life depended on it. I gritted my teeth as his mouth closed on my clit, straining against the bonds that held me, struggling against the climax that threatened. In spite of all I could do when he continued to pull on my clit, I tensed all over with the first convulsion of release.

He let go of my clit immediately. Turning around he settled on his side, staring down at me. "I told you not to come."

I bit my lip. "I didn't ... not really." It wasn't a lie. The spasm died the minute he let go of my clit, leaving me hanging and more miserable than before.

"You did."

I swallowed with an effort, barely able to gather enough moisture into my mouth to attempt it. "Only a little," I whined.

He tsked. "Now I'll have to punish you."

Oh god! I wasn't sure I could take much more.

He started over. The pleasure/pain of his teeth on my nipples was enough to send minor shocks through my sex, but not enough to give me release. I hardly knew where I was any more by the time he began to gnaw a trail down my body toward my clit. "I can't hold it!" I gasped the moment I sensed his destination.

He paused. "You will."

"I can't, Bret! Please don't tease me anymore," I said, uttering a choked cry when he ignored my pleas and caught my clit between his lips, suckling it.

I bucked against him, fighting for all I was worth, holding on to his warning not to come since I couldn't seem to hold on to anything else. My body convulsed in spite of all I could do.

I couldn't help it. I whimpered piteously when he lifted his head to look at me.

I'd braced myself for more torture when he climbed over me to crouch between my thighs. Relief swamped me.

Grabbing a pillow, he shoved it beneath my hips to lift my pelvis higher. I managed to get my eyes open to look down to see if he was going to give me what I so desperately wanted and felt like weeping with relief when I saw that he was spreading lubrication over his cock. He looked up at me when he'd finished. Holding it with one hand, he spread the residue around the mouth of my sex, delving inside. I couldn't believe I needed it. I felt like every ounce of moisture in my body had pooled there.

Leaning toward me, he pressed the head of his cock against me. A mixture of relief and pain went through me but I was beside myself. I didn't care if he ripped me apart if he would just assuage the ache inside. He remained where he was until he'd pushed the head inside and then leaned over me.

I opened my eyes to look up at him, discovering his image was blurred with the tears I hadn't realized were seeping from eyes. His gaze flickered over my face. "This will make it better, baby."

It did. The first wave of convulsions hit me as he drove fully inside of me. I was fully in the throes of it by his third stroke. I couldn't seem to stop, though. His driving thrusts seemed to carry me higher and higher until I was screaming hoarsely. The hard spasms had just begun to taper off when drove into me as deeply as he could and shuddered with his own release.

I'd never felt more wrung out from a bout of sex in my life. I sank so deeply toward oblivion that I crossed the threshold. A tug at my ankles revived me. I groaned when I felt a hand straightening my legs, stretching them. He released my wrists next, rubbing my arms and hands.

The tingles of returning sensation were painful at first but it dissipated fairly quickly. Bret gathered me into his arms, nuzzling his face against my neck. "That was … wild."

Amusement flickered through me, although I was too weak and exhausted to manage more than an attempt at a chuckle. "It was amazing," I murmured drunkenly.

His arms tightened around me. "You had me worried when I saw you were crying," he said huskily.

Surprise flickered through me. I didn't even remember crying. "Did I?"

He smiled against my neck. "I thought I'd gone a little too far."

"I might have died if you'd gone any further. Miss Puss thanks you for the thorough reaming."

He chuckled, leaning away to stare at my face. "Who?"

I felt my face heat. "You know," I muttered uncomfortably.

He rolled me onto my back, settling over me on his elbows. "How about Ms Steph?" he asked, laughter threading his voice.

My lips seemed to curl of their own accord. "Ms Steph adores …."

I saw the amusement had left his features when my eyes flew open in dismay at what I'd nearly said. He was studying me quizzically. "Coward," he murmured after a long moment when he realized I wasn't going to finish.

" ..the way you fuck," I finished a little lamely.

His brows rose, but he merely grinned. "Watch the language, lady. My virgin ears are offended."

I uttered an inelegant snort. "If your ears are virgin, I'm sure that's the only virgin territory on you."

He gave me a look. "There's other virgin territory, I'll have you to know, and it will forever remain virginal."

I stared at him blankly until that sank in. I bit my lip. "That wasn't what I meant."

"Good. As long as we're clear on that."

I lay drowsing while he used the bathroom, trying to get up the energy to get up myself. Remembering the cameras abruptly, I glanced around and discovered Bret had tossed the one that had been positioned for a good view of Miss Puss toward the foot of the bed. The red dot on the other cameras was still glowing, but I didn't know if the others were still watching.

Bret had given them a hell of a show. I doubted very many porn videos could top it.

It made me wonder if they'd be satisfied with their own private porn or if I was due more performances.

I wasn't sure I could get up the necessary enthusiasm after what I'd just experienced. Bret had taken me to new heights. My pussy was still clapping enthusiastically.

Apparently, I thought wryly when I'd finished clean up and headed into bedroom again, Bret had merely put them on their toes. Gavin was waiting for me when I came out and one look at his face was enough to assure me he wasn't going to be satisfied with anything less out of me than Bret had gotten.

This proved to be prophetic intuition. By the time Luke and Jared had followed with their own performance I'd reached a state of exhaustion just of shy of actual death. I dropped into a coma when Jared was done with me and didn't come around until nearly noon the following day. Temporarily appeased, the men spent most of the day lying around on the living room furniture watching ball games on the new wide screen TV. I might've been bored stiff since I didn't care for sports of any kind, but they didn't completely ignore me.

They spent the day lazily playing with my boobs and my pussy until I was torn between frustration and anticipation for the evening events. I didn't even tumble to what the 'game' was at first. Jessie dragged me into his lap as he had the day before when I decided to join the guys in the living room for want of anything else to do. Unlike the night before, however, he merely toyed with me, pinching my nipples until they were throbbing and finger fucking me until I was squirming. Then, almost casually, he scooped me off his lap and deposited me on the couch.

I was too stunned to react for a moment, staring at him as he got up and headed into the kitchen. By the time he returned with a cold bottle of beer, I'd recovered enough to decide to ignore him.

It went right over his head. He settled down, propped his feet up, and stared at the TV as if nothing had happened.

Luke dragged me into his lap when I started to get up and leave. I actually thought I was going to get some action when he set me on his lap facing him and dragged me close enough to cover the tip of one breast with his mouth. I was really getting 'in' to it when one of the others abruptly yelled 'touch down!'

Luke released my breast and plopped me down on the couch so fast I wasn't certain what had happened just at first.

Well *really*, I thought indignantly!

They'd fucked me blind the night before and now they were just going to ignore me?

Apparently, but not completely.

Jared corralled me before I could escape. Dragging me back on his lap as Jessie had, he *teased* me as Jessie had, tweaking my nipples and my clit until I was throbbing uncomfortably.

I caught a ghost of a smile as he set me on feet, though, a flicker of amusement in his eyes. The 'game' seemed to be tease Steph and focus on the game on TV. I didn't particularly want to play, but I was out numbered.

I stalked toward the bedroom when Jared let me go, intent on sulking. Gavin intercepted me. A faint smile curled the corners of his hard mouth. "Going somewhere?"

I looked up at him, trying to decide whether he really intended to keep me in the living room so that they could entertain themselves by playing with me or if he was just trying to get a rise out of me.

He settled his big hands on my shoulders and spun me around. "Bret's turn," he murmured near my ear, giving me a swat on the ass to get me going in the right direction.

Bret dragged me onto his lap when I reached him, crossways. For nearly fifteen minutes he divided his attention between the TV screen and playing with me.

Gavin crooked a finger at me imperiously when Bret decided he'd played enough. My belly clenched. In a way, I was enjoying it. In another sense I wasn't. It felt good. There was no getting around that, but I'd realized by that time that they had no intention of doing any more. I wasn't going to get any cookies until they were ready to give them to me.

Swallowing a little convulsively, I went to Gavin. He pulled me down astride his lap and latched onto the same damned nipple Luke had teased. The other was beginning to feel seriously neglected. It throbbed plaintively while Gavin focused on driving me up the wall pulling on the other. His eyes were glittering with heat when he finally lifted his head.

Instead of appeasing my need to even things out, he set me off his lap and got up.

My indignation had waned. I stared after, him feeling seriously put out, however.

Jessie summoned me.

Feet dragging, I went to him and endured until I felt like screaming—hours of teasing while the damned football game went on forever.

I was so relieved when the damned thing ended, I felt like cheering for the first time.

The men got up, stretched, and left me by myself. Luke and Bret headed for the kitchen and I heard the distinct clinking that told me they were getting ready for supper. I wasn't particularly hungry—for food, but my heart leapt anyway because after supper ….

Jared disappeared outside, I supposed to get the grill started.

Gavin and Jessie disappeared down the hall that led to the other bedrooms.

After debating whether to offer to help in the kitchen or not, I finally decided to simply ignore it. They did fine without my help and I was peeved with them anyway.

I was flipping through the channels when Gavin and Jessie emerged from the hallway again. I didn't glance at them until they crossed the living room and disappeared down the hall once more.

Curious, I waited for them to come back. Just about the time I decided they weren't going to, the two of them reappeared carrying some unidentifiable things.

It dawned on me when they headed for the main bedroom that they were moving their toys from the room where I'd seen them before.

My belly tightened. My throat closed. Even I wasn't sure if it was from nerves or anticipation. Heat scored me when the image leapt my mind of what Bret had done the night before but it had been almost as torturous as it had been thrilling—actually make that *more* tortuous and then culminating in the most excitement I'd ever had to bear.

I wasn't sure I was going to like what they had in mind and that kept me bouncing between fear and anticipation on top of the fact that I was still buzzing from all the play during the game.

Deciding to try to ignore them, I stared at the TV, but I was keenly attuned to the traffic.

It seemed to take them a good bit of time and, the longer it took, the more uneasy I was.

They were still busy when Luke, Bret, and Jared brought the food to the table and called everyone to eat.

My stomach was tied into so many knots I could barely swallow a bite of food. Afraid they'd notice, I focused on trying to make a decent account of myself. When everyone had finished, Gavin informed me kitchen clean up was mine and the men headed into what I was beginning to envision as a torture chamber.

Chapter Ten

I wasn't sure I wanted to go into the room to see what was waiting for me, but Gavin came to collect me before I'd even finished clean up—because I'd been dragging my feet to stall for time.

Settling a hand at the small of my back, he escorted me to the room.

It had been transformed. Even the 'playroom' where I'd seen the stuff before hadn't looked like this—because, I realized, most of it hadn't actually been set up.

My uneasiness magnified but Gavin either didn't notice or it didn't weigh with him. He slipped his hand from my back to one arm and led me over to the contraption that was clearly the focus of events.

It looked like some sort of torture device—*serious* torture—particularly since I could see what looked like some sort of electric device sprouting cables was attached to it. I sent Gavin a scared look.

He caught my face in the crook of one hand and fixed me with his gaze. "There's nothing in here that'll hurt. Trust me."

I certainly wanted to. I wasn't so sure I did. I discovered I was too weak with the adrenalin rush that had abandoned me to protest or struggle, though.

Backing me up to it, he yielded his place to Jared, who secured a restraint around my waist. Bret, whom I discovered was behind me, caught my wrists and pulled my hands behind me. I felt the cold bite of metal click around my wrists and then he continued to pull downward until I had to arch backwards. I heard a click and then he released his grip on me, which was when I discovered I couldn't straighten. Something soft and pillowy was pressed against the back of my head and neck, which had begun to feel the strain. I relaxed fractionally when I realized it supported my head and neck without my having to and then tensed against with he pulled a strap across my forehead.

Someone wrapped something like a strap around one of my thighs, just above the knee, tightening it snugly. I heard the clink of metal chains and then they moved to the other thigh and secured the same sort of binding around it.

A jolt of surprise went through me when I felt the bands tighten and then felt my legs lifted until my feet weren't touching the floor anymore. Panic clawed at me as the pulling continued and I felt my legs lifted higher and higher.

Gavin's face came within view. He was holding one of the wires I'd noticed before. At the end of it was a tiny alligator clip similar to those at the end of jumper cables. My heart slammed almost painfully against my ribs as that popped into my mind. "It carries a very low volt," he said almost soothingly.

It didn't particularly soothe me, though. I was fighting panic by now as it sank in that I couldn't move at all. Gavin tugged at my nipples until both of them were standing fully erect. I jumped when I felt something cold take the place of his fingers, wincing slightly as it pinched my nipple.

He repeated the process with other.

"Turn it on."

Oh my god!

"Tell me if it gets uncomfortable."

That relieved me considerably, but I noticed by that time that there was a very definite tingle traveling through my nipples. I thought at first it was the clip itself, which was just tight enough to trap the blood in the tips of my nipples. I realized as it increased, though, that it was actually little jolts of electricity. It didn't just *seem* to be.

I wasn't ignorant of such things. I'd heard about bondage buffs playing with low voltage electricity, but it hadn't been anything that had drawn my curiosity.

I was getting to experience it now, though—plus extreme bondage.

I winced when a particularly sharp current bit me and Gavin, apparently watching my reaction, ordered whoever it was at the controls to turn it down again. Feeling less threatened, I relaxed.

As soon as I did, my focus shifted to the throbbing 'nibbles' of the current and I realized it felt like someone sucking on them, stirring warmth all through me. Knowing they were watching and uncomfortable with that, I tried to ignore it but it continued to build heat inside of me and I could feel moisture seeping from the walls of my sex.

A third clip was attached to my clit.

I tried to squirm and discovered I couldn't.

The pulsing began there, almost in sync with the other 'pulls'. My heart rate shot up and so did my heat index. I opened my eyes and looked up at the ceiling, trying to ignore the growing tension inside me and discovered that the men were adjusting the cameras.

That realization made my heart rev a little faster.

Apparently, they were far more interested in simply studying me at the moment. None of them touched me once they'd bound me and attached the clips. I searched my mind, trying to visualize what they were looking at. My back was arched, pushing my breasts out. I could feel air wafting across my buttocks and along my cleft and knew just from the strain of my thigh muscles that my sex was fully on display—certainly was if they had the camera aimed at it. Otherwise I was too low for them to have much of a view.

Almost on the thought, I heard mechanical sounds and felt myself rising. It stopped when I'd been lifted only a couple of feet as far as I could tell.

The lights above me dimmed. All sounds stopped and I discovered I no longer had anything to distract me from the steady pulse, the feeling of someone tugging at my nipples and my clit. The tension inside me began to climb rapidly then. I passed from mildly aroused to a level that made it hard to catch my breath, made me dizzy. I struggled against the rising tide, knowing I was going to peak before many more moments passed.

Typically, as soon as I felt myself nearing it the battle began in earnest, desire to reach it warring with an equal determination to hold off and enjoy as long as I could. I was fighting the fight when I suddenly sensed a presence. Someone had moved close enough I could heard their rapid breath despite my own, could feel their body heat even though mine had begun to feel like I was going to catch fire.

I felt the pressure of hard flesh against the mouth my sex. I was wet, slippery with the heat that had built inside me and still it was a delicious tug at my flesh as he slowly spread it and entered me. He settled his hands on my waist, tightened them as he drove deep and then began to pump into me in earnest.

I couldn't see who it was, but the fact that I hadn't felt the burn I'd grown accustomed to feeling when Bret or Jessie shoved their huge cocks into me eliminated them.

"Come for me, baby," Gavin whispered hoarsely. "I want to hear you scream."

A shudder went through me. I gave up the fight to stave off my climax and felt it sweep me up. The steady tugging at my clit and my nipples together with Gavin's pounding rhythm sent me into a shattering culmination that forced sharp cries from me. He drove into me faster and deeper and finally drove deep and held himself as his seed jetted into me.

My crisis passed and yet I discovered that I couldn't crash. The steady pulsing kept me so close to the peak that I was still shuddering with the quakes. Gavin withdrew after a moment and I heard him step away, but I was too busy struggling with the heat pounding through me to be more than vaguely aware. The ache was back almost as soon as it had left, worse.

I moaned feverishly, unable even to writhe with the fire coursing through me. My heart leapt when I felt the pressure of another cock. His hands settled on my waist, but I was too fevered to know or care who it was. I needed. I needed desperately. He drove into my slick cavern with little resistance beyond the clenching muscles. His pace was maddeningly slow and measured at first, making me more frantic. I needed deep. I needed hard. The itch was driving me crazy. Almost as if he sensed the desperation in me, he increased the tempo and depth of his thrusts jarringly. My second climax hit me with screaming intensity.

The duration was longer and harder than the first, I thought a little wildly, shaking with the force of it and the aftershocks that seemed to go on and on. I didn't come down the second time either. Instead, it seemed the ache inside magnified.

I lost track of everything but the fever inside me after the third had pumped into me and brought me to another climax. Dimly, it occurred to me to beg them to make it stop but by that time I was too hoarse and mindless to figure out how to put the words together.

I knew when I felt the pressure against my sex again that it was either Jessie or Bret. There was no such thing as enough lubrication to make it easy for either of them even though I was dripping with both come and lubrication by that time. I relished it, hopeful this time I'd finally feel total surcease. For a handful of moments, I thought I had, but the throbbing ache returned almost before he'd withdrawn.

I knew it was hopeless when I felt Jessie take Bret's place and plow along my channel with such exquisite pleasure/pain that I almost came at once. I was beyond searching for complete release by then, though. I just wanted to feel a steady pumping inside of me because it eased the ache.

I thought I'd blacked out when I came that time. I might have briefly. I felt my world tilt and thought that it was unconscious falling over me. After a moment, I discovered it wasn't dizziness or a faint. The thing holding me had been tilted forward. A cock brushed my lips. I opened my mouth, taking it in, sucking on it with all the desperation I felt by that time. At the same time, I felt a hand settle on the cheek of my ass, felt someone press into my rectum. The double penetration brought me off faster. Before I knew it I felt the convulsions rocking me. Groaning, I sucked a little harder at the dick in my mouth until he'd pumped every drop of his seed into me.

They moved away and two others took their place. My jaws felt as if they were going to come unhinged before I was done—mostly because of Bret and Jessie.

I slumped when they moved away, gasping for breath. I felt the clips pulled from my nipples and then my clit and dragged in a shaky breath of relief. The restraints were removed, but I was hardly conscious by then, barely knew anything until I felt someone carrying me and then felt the cool sheets of the bed as they settled me.

A shiver went through me at the icy feel against my overheated skin. Someone settled beside me, dragging me up against them. I shivered uncontrollably for a while but eventually the warmth of his body and the soothing stroke of his hand calmed the shudders and I descended toward neverland.

"Jesus, baby! Why didn't you tell us to stop if it was too much?"

Because it didn't occur to me that it would do any good? The brainless idiots, I thought sluggishly. They might have considered *telling* me to call a halt when I thought I'd had too much!

"Are you alright?"

I uttered a deep sigh. "Ask me tomorrow."

* * * *

I wasn't certain what I expected when I discovered everyone had gathered in the living room and was waiting for me, but it certainly wasn't what happened.

Gavin was the spokesperson for the group.

"We've decided it'll be better all the way around just to keep you here."

I stared at him blankly in shock.

"The cover is going to be that you've been transferred to one of the other branches. There isn't any traffic between the branch employees that we'll need to worry about—and you won't have to worry about trying to field uncomfortable questions. Jared will drive you back to your place to close up and collect whatever personal things you'll want to have for a few months. But don't worry about it. If you forget anything important, we can always take you there to get it. I'll make sure the security people keep an eye on your place."

Considering that I'd more than half expected the topic of conversation to revolve around the bondage event from hell the night before, I was completely thrown off kilter. It took me a few minutes to completely assimilate what he'd said and then another few to struggle with how I felt about it. "But … how am I going to work?" I finally asked blankly.

"Remotely. Luke will set it up. You won't be doing teller work, naturally, but there's plenty of work you *can* handle on the computer."

I stared at him, trying to figure out if there was anything he'd missed but soon realized that, except for my agreement to it, he hadn't.

And I wasn't in any position to disagree. To all intents and purposes, they owned me, and it was clear they thought so. "Alright," I said a little weakly. "When?"

Gavin nodded in obvious satisfaction, although he couldn't have been in any doubt of the outcome. I could see the others had relaxed, as well. "Now's as good a time as any—better than some others, actually. It's Sunday. It'll be fairly dead in town and there'll be fewer people to see the move."

I got up a little stiffly and headed back into the bedroom to change—or rather to dress.

Gavin followed me. Stopping me just inside the room, he looked me over critically. "Are you alright with this, Steph?"

I looked at him in surprise, but since he'd asked, I thought it over. "It sounds reasonable," I finally said tentatively.

He looked uncomfortable. "You aren't … concerned after last night?"

I felt my face heat up. The truth was, I was half-dead and sore all over. I wasn't sure I was up for anymore of the same but every time I thought about it I tingled all over.

I *was* a glutton for punishment! "You promised not to hurt me and you didn't," I said finally.

"It was too much too soon. We got carried away."

Oh boy did they ever get carried away! "I'll live … I think."

He placed a finger beneath my chin and forced it up, meeting my gaze. "Next time just tell us to stop when you've had enough, alright?"

I smiled at him tentatively, tempted to ask him if that applied to everything we did, but I knew it didn't and I didn't want to push it. "Alright."

His gaze moved to my lips and lingered. I thought for a moment he would kiss me but he dropped his hand and turned away.

I still felt immeasurably better. They might be more focused on playtime than me, but at least they weren't completely oblivious to my situation. It occurred to me as I dressed that they had been from the first. They'd all been eager to sample their prize and yet they'd been paying enough attention to notice I hadn't weathered the first storm unscathed. Of course, Luke and Gavin's well-meaning attempts to hold the others off of me for a few days and let me recover hadn't worked out as they'd planned, but they'd made the attempt.

I wasn't entirely sure if that was due to real concern for me or anxiety that I might use it against them, but I'd had to sign an agreement upfront relieving them of any responsibility so I didn't think it was that.

It probably wasn't concern for me in particular either, but rather a quirk of their nature. They could be hard, but they weren't cold.

Not by *any* stretch of the imagination!

I didn't really *need* anything from my house. The Thornes had very thoughtfully provided for everything, but I was glad for the chance to have some of my personal belongings. I packed clothes. Jared clearly disapproved, but he didn't say anything. He merely followed me from room to room and watched me pack and then took it from me and carried it out to his SUV.

My nosey neighbor was out in her yard when I finished up and headed out. "Hi, Mrs. Niece."

"You moving?"

I shrugged. "Sort of. I've been transferred to one of the other branches of the bank for the time being."

I could see she didn't really believe me. She eyed Jared speculatively, but apparently decided not to try to pump him for more information.

"I guess that was the nosey neighbor."

"The most nosey one. They all watch. She's the only one that has the brass to demand answers."

"You carried it off well."

I sent him a look at his tone. "Are you complaining? Gavin told me what to say, you know."

He shrugged. "Somehow I'd gotten the impression that you weren't that good at lying."

That was a backhanded compliment if I'd ever heard one. "Everybody lies … sometimes. I don't like to lie. I usually just don't say anything at all if I don't feel comfortable telling the truth or don't want to."

He didn't say anything else. I mulled his comment over for a while. "Why did you say I wasn't very good at it?"

He sent me a questioning look.

"Lying?" I prompted.

A wry smile curled his lips, but he merely shook his head.

"You aren't going to tell me?"

He flicked an amused glance at me. "Nope." Settling his hand on the back of my neck, he massaged it briefly.

It struck me that the gesture was purely affectionate. I felt it right down to my toes. It scared me. It wouldn't take much of that to thoroughly ensnare me.

****

Jared had barely parked his SUV in the drive at the house and switched it off when we heard the approach of another car. Both of us turned to stare at it.

"Holy shit!" Jared exclaimed abruptly. "That's Aunt Clara and Uncle Robert!"

The tone of his voice alone was enough to send the urge through me to duck for cover.

He grabbed the door handle on his side. "Get inside and warn the others," he said sharply even as he bailed out and headed toward the car pulling up in the front of the house at a brisk stride.

I was so weak kneed, I wasn't sure I could make inside, but I scrambled out and scurried toward the front door. I almost hit Gavin in the face with the door when I dashed inside. "It's … I think it's your mother and father!" I gasped, staring at him owl eyed.

"Fuck!" he growled, twisting around to look the house over.

I could see the wheels churning in his head as all the bondage paraphernalia raced through his mind. "Lock the door to the master bedroom," he hissed at Luke in a loud whisper. "It's Mom and Dad."

For a split second, everyone froze, and then they sprang into action, racing around the house, grabbing beer bottles and dishes, shoving things into cabinets. I'd never seen such scrambling in my life and it sent a fresh wave of terror through me to see the unflappable Thornes in such a panic.

I discovered Gavin was looking at me thoughtfully.

"I'll hide!" I exclaimed.

He caught my wrist as I tried to dash away, yanking me to a halt. "They already saw you," he said dryly. Reeling me in, he kissed me soundly on the mouth. "Just watch that mouth of yours. Mom'll haul you into the bathroom and wash your mouth out with soap if she hears any of your language."

I gaped at him a moment before indignation hit me. "You just said fuck!"

He grinned at me. "If a tree falls in the woods and my mother's not there to hear it …."

I don't think he actually intended to finish the sentence, but since we heard Jared just outside talking loudly, he grabbed my hand and hauled me over to the couch. We hit the seat just as the door opened.

"Mom! Dad!" Gavin exclaimed as if pleasantly surprised, getting up again. "What brings y'all out?"

"We haven't seen you boys in a month of Sundays," his mother responded tartly. "I made Robert bring me so I make sure you were still alive."

Gavin chuckled but it sounded a little forced even to me.

His mother looked me over frankly. "And who is this?"

Gavin draped his arm across my shoulders possessively. "Stephanie Bridges ... my mother and father, Clara and Robert Thorne."

His mother offered her hand and a pleasant smile, though I could see speculation in her eyes. "How do you do?"

"Fine, thank you! And you?" I responded, shaking her hand.

She glanced at Gavin. "Better now that I haven't found the boys' bodies," she responded scoldingly. "Don't I get a kiss?"

Gavin released me and embraced his mother, planting a kiss on the cheek she offered. His father held out a hand. When he took it, his father clapped him on the shoulder.

"I guess the telephone out here stopped working?"

Gavin released a long-suffering sigh. "I had Sunday dinner with the two of you only a couple of weeks ago," he said pointedly. "I've been busy."

"I see that," his father said, chuckling.

"Don't encourage her, Dad," Gavin said irritably.

"Are you going to invite us to sit down?"

Gavin reddened and gestured toward the chairs facing the couch.

When his mother and father had seated themselves, he glanced around the room a little desperately, I thought. Apparently, all of the others had disappeared—including Jared.

Clara looked around. "What happened to Jared? I thought he came in with us."

"He said something about washing his car," Gavin returned smoothly, urging me to sit down and then joining me on the couch.

I would've far preferred to disappear with the others, but it didn't look like escape was in the cards.

"Really? That's odd. I thought I saw him drive up just before we got here."

Gavin's face darkened. "He went to get the stuff to wash the car."

"Just now?"

"While ago."

Clara let him off the hook but instantly transferred her gaze to me. I could see where Gavin had gotten his eyes. Hers were so pale they were almost eerie. "So ... when did you two meet?"

"Don't start, Mom," Gavin said irritably.

"Start what?" she demanded, pinning him with her cool gaze.

"You know what. You'll scare her off."

She studied him speculatively. "Meaning you're thinking about keeping her around a while? Interesting. She doesn't look like the type to scare easily," she added, turning to study me again.

'She' was pretty petrified at the moment, however.

Gavin draped an arm across my shoulders, pulling me closer almost possessively. Or was that protectively? "She doesn't, but we haven't known each other long enough for her to be comfortable with the third degree from my mother. Give it a rest, Mom."

She shrugged. "Alright! Fine! I was just curious to know if we could be expecting grandchildren in the not too distant future."

"Hell, Clara! That's blunt, even for you!" Robert said, clearly exasperated.

She shrugged. "I don't suppose you've seen anything of Luke?"

"He works with me, Mom. I see him every day."

She gave him a look. "I meant socially. Is he around?"

"Probably hiding out back."

"In that case, I'll go look for him," she said, getting up.

Gavin leapt to his feet when she did and so did Robert. It caught me off guard. I'd been leaning against him and toppled over. He nearly sat on me before I could right myself.

He sent me a look that was one part discomfort and two parts harassed.

"So ... how long *have* you two known each other?" Robert asked the moment Clara disappeared out the back door.

Gavin released a deep sigh. He turned to study my face. "A little better than six months. We haven't been seeing each other but a couple of weeks, though."

I struggled to hide my surprise. I could see why he was more inclined to fabricate the story than to tell his parents the truth. I imagined they were the last people in the world he wanted to know his deep dark secret. And it wasn't a lie—per se. I'd begun working at the bank seven months earlier and we'd been 'seeing' each other for two weeks. The surprise arose from the fact that he seemed to remember about how long I'd been working at the bank.

I wouldn't have thought he'd noticed, certainly not enough to pinpoint the time so closely.

I supposed he was a micro-manager or he wouldn't have had a clue.

"Is she mute?" Robert Thorne asked abruptly.

I could see he was teasing. I smiled back at him. "She isn't. She's just listening."

He studied me piercingly a moment. "Smart. I've always liked that in a woman." He released a huff. "I guess I'll go round up Clara. She's had time to pump Luke for whatever information she was after."

Gavin and I got up to follow him. "We were going to cook out,"

Gavin said with obvious reluctance when they reached the back yard and it was clear preparations were in progress. "I don't suppose you and Mom would like to stay and eat with us?"

"We'd love to!" Clara exclaimed before Robert could say anything.

He sent her a hard look. "I thought we were going over to have dinner with John and Marsha?"

She shrugged. "It wasn't settled. I haven't had anything off the grill in a while. This will be fun."

It was just a barrel of fun! The Thorne men gathered around the table like a group of sulky schoolboys and struggled to field the probing questions Clara Thorne kept tossing out artlessly from time to time. After an excruciatingly uncomfortable dinner that gave everyone indigestion, she finally kissed her 'boys' and announced that they should probably go.

No one protested.

Draping his arm across my shoulders, Gavin dragged me with him to bid his parents good-bye. Luke sent him a glare when the pair had driven off. "What the fuck was that?" he growled.

Gavin sent him a cool look. "What?"

Luke flicked a glance at me and folded his lips, stalking inside.

"You think she's suspicious?" Jared asked when we'd reached the living room again.

Gavin sent him a look. "What do you think?"

"Don't tell me you didn't notice her trying the door to the master bedroom twice," Jessie said dryly. "She didn't believe the bathroom was out of order for minute and locking her out just fired her curiosity."

Gavin dropped onto the couch, dragging me with him. "I have to suppose we can expect a visit from Aunt Marsha and Uncle John sometime in the near future."

Luke sent him a cool look. "I don't know. You were pretty fucking convincing claiming Steph as yours."

"Is that what's griping your ass?" Gavin demanded irritably. "You ducked out the back. What the hell did you expect me to do with her?"

This was starting to get uncomfortable. I squirmed against Gavin, but his hand tightened around my shoulders.

"She arrived with Jared and they saw. Don't you think that might've looked a little strange?"

"She's older than Jared. Aunt Marsha would've had a cow when Mom reported it and then she'd damned sure be knocking at the door!"

"Don't even go there!" Jared said, his face flushed.

"She's older than you, if it comes to that," Luke shot back at him.

I threw up my hands. "She's older than all of you. Can we not discuss it anymore?"

Gavin sent me an amused look. "Touchy, aren't you?"

I glared at him crossly. "I am not."

He dragged me half across his lap, whispering in my ear. "Like fine wine."

I punched him in the belly before I had time to consider it.

Luckily, he laughed.

The other four Thornes were glaring at both of us when Gavin released me.

"Let us in on the joke," Jessie said tartly.

Gavin shrugged.

"He said I was like fine wine," I said tartly, shrugging his arm off and getting up abruptly. "I'll do clean up."

He swatted me on the ass as I went by him. I decided to ignore it.

Jessie sighed. "Well, I don't know about the rest of you, but that kind of pulled the rug out from under me."

Luke and Gavin grunted agreement.

"You should've known she'd be down here if you didn't go to her," Jared said irritably. "Now we're going to have to stay on our toes."

Chapter Eleven

I glanced up sharply when someone slipped an arm around my waist from behind. I was only partially relieved when I saw it was Jared. I reached to turn off the faucet as he leaned to nibble at my ear.

"Hey! You aren't buying into that horseshit, are you?"

I glanced at him uncomfortably. Ordinarily, I never gave my age a thought. It was hard not to when I knew damned well I was the 'senior' in the crowd.

He shook his head at me. "Hell! It isn't but a handful of years. What the fuck difference does that make?"

It was a lot closer to a decade than a 'handful', too close for my comfort.

To say nothing about the fact that I was 'getting on' in years to be producing a grandchild.

Not that that made a bit of difference, I reminded myself sternly. I wasn't 'dating' any of them. It was just that that had made me feel completely inappropriate as nothing else. All other considerations paled beside the one most important—these were young men and not one of them had had a child. I looked away from him. "I don't guess it does, really," I mumbled.

He caught my chin, forcing me to look at him. "Damned straight! You want me to go kick his ass?"

I couldn't help but smile at that chivalrous offer to defend my honor. "No, I don't." I didn't want them fighting at all and I especially didn't want anyone trying to kick Gavin's ass. Not that I was convinced Jared could do it, but then I didn't want any of them hurt. "It was stupid to get upset. I guess it just unsettled me finding myself in the middle of a family gathering."

"You mean the interrogation," he said dryly. "Baby, that unsettled the hell out of all of us. I thought I was going to have a heart attack. She's a scary broad. It's a damned good thing we'd moved our toys to the main bedroom. Aunt Clara finding them just doesn't bear thinking on."

"I heard that," Luke growled, entering the kitchen. "I *know* you didn't just refer to my mother as a broad."

"I noticed you didn't dispute the scary part," Jared retorted.

"Hell no! She scares the piss out of me. Why do you think I beat you out the back door?"

I covered my mouth, trying not to laugh. It was so absurd to think of a great, hulking brute like Luke trembling in front of his mother, though!

He dragged me away from Jared. Looping his arms around my waist, he tilted his head, studying me. "You think that's funny, lady?" he demanded, mock stern.

I shook my head.

"Good, because it was a damned unsettling experience. I need sympathy. I'm going to have nightmares."

I couldn't help but chuckle, but I could certainly see his point. I think I would've just died of mortification if she'd managed to find any of the sex toys and demanded an explanation. Horrible thought! "I'm glad it was your mother and not mine."

"You call that sympathy?"

I laughed. "I call that self-preservation."

Grinning, he released me and glanced at Jared. "I guess it'd be safe to move her things in now."

The reminder that Jared's SUV was full of my personal belongings sobered me instantly. I looked at the two of them worriedly. "You think it's a good idea to bring them in now? I mean … for me to stay here?"

Both of them sobered, as well, at my questions. "Don't worry about it," Luke said coolly. "Mom will just have to be unhappy about that if it bothers her. In any case, Gav will take the heat. He's the one that decided to tell them you were his girlfriend."

It was immediately clear that he wasn't irritated with me for suggesting he would allow his mother to run his life. That might have been some of it, but I realized it was primarily because Gavin had claimed me. I wasn't sure *why* that bothered him, but, given his earlier anger, it seemed clear that that was the main source of annoyance.

Puzzling over it, I returned my attention to cleaning up while he and Jared left the house to bring in the boxes and bags I'd packed. I didn't see why it would bother him. Gavin had been right in one sense—well a couple. *Someone* needed to claim me to keep their mother from asking awkward questions about one woman in the midst of the five of them and, as much as I hated to admit it, he'd been right about the other, too. Jared *was* younger than me and looked it, and it was just the sort of thing to set off alarms in any mother—the possibility that some older, manipulating woman had gotten their hooks in their 'baby'.

It wasn't a very pleasant thought, particularly when it resurrected the accusations Gavin and Jessie had lobbed at me before.

It was completely unfair when they were the ones who'd made the decision to hold me accountable in such a way, but I supposed it could be argued, however unreasonable I thought it was, that I'd seduced them into the idea.

My thoughts switched from discomfort over the age gap to discomfort over the economic gap when Jared and Luke began to troop through the back with my things. The assortment of mismatched hangers my clothes were hung on, old boxes and worn, faded stuffed pillow cases that I'd thrown my things in just seemed to make it more noticeable that everything I had was cheap and old. I suddenly regretted bringing anything at all, regardless of the inconvenience to me not to have my personal things when I had no idea how long I'd have to do without them. It didn't take a lot of effort to visualize how my things were going to look next to everything in this house.

Most of it was new—like the house—and none of it looked liked it had been purchased at the local budget department store, which mine had.

It depressed me. I wasn't exactly sure of why depression settled over me as I stood washing dishes, but I suspected it was because I'd been forced to face a few uncomfortable truths that I hadn't wanted to face.

Clean up didn't take long. Bret, Gavin, and Jessie cleaned off the table, raked the plates, and brought them to me, and the kitchen hadn't actually been used.

Gavin had 'the scepter' when I went back through the living area and was idly flipping through the channels. He glanced at me as I started through. "I don't suppose you have any movies? There aren't any games on."

A flicker of amusement went through me. No games, nothing to watch! One more thing we *didn't* have in common! I was probably as passionate about hating sports as they were about watching it.

"I brought some of my collection," I said a little doubtfully, "but I doubt there's anything you'd care to watch. I'll get the box."

He got up. "Sit down. I'll get it."

I didn't especially want him digging through my things, more because I didn't want him examining the 'quality', but I dismissed it and headed toward the couch. "It's the biggest box."

Jimmy and I didn't go out—ever, so I was a pretty avid movie collector since that was practically our only form of entertainment—well, besides books and video games. I was the reader. Jimmy was the game buff.

Just about the time I remembered that I'd packed a stack of the romance books I was addicted to that I'd bought at the local used bookstore and hadn't had the chance to read Gavin came back with the box of movies. Relieved, I settled back in my seat again.

Gavin emptied the box on the coffee table and the five men gathered around to look them over. They seemed surprised to discover I had a fairly wide range of tastes in entertainment. I supposed, with a mixture of amusement and irritation, they'd expected to discover I never watched anything but 'girly' movies. In point of fact, although I was addicted to romance novels, I didn't particularly like Hollywood's notion of romantic comedies and they apparently couldn't do a good historical if their life depended on it. They were inevitably slow and boring or completely inaccurate.

After some squabbling, they finally settled on a Sci-fi Horror trilogy I'd bought. It was one of my favorites, but I hadn't watched it in a while and I hadn't had the opportunity to watch it on a big screen since it had been at the theater. The prospect perked me up immediately.

"I don't suppose there's any popcorn?" I asked a little hopefully when Bret took the movie and loaded it into the DVD.

Gavin sent me an amused look.

"I've got some," Bret said. "I'll throw it in the microwave."

I got up. "Who wants a drink?"

Jared got to his feet. "I hid the rest of the beer in my SUV. I'll get it."

I couldn't help but grin. I had to suppose Aunt Clara disapproved of beer, too, or maybe it was only because it was Sunday? Some people had strange taboos. I didn't particularly approve of it on any occasion, not because of morals, but because it just wasn't a healthy way of relaxing.

"Beer with popcorn?" Luke asked with revulsion. "I think I'll just have a cola."

Jessie and Gavin agreed and I went to the kitchen to get four out of the fridge while Jared went to grab beer for Bret and himself and Bret popped a huge bowl of popcorn.

It seemed almost strange to settle in the living room with them and watch a movie—more like a group of friends than what we actually were—which was a little hard to define if it came to that. Strictly speaking, I suppose it was jailers and con, but they'd never actually acted that way. I caught the looks now and then that made it clear they still regarded me with a healthy dose of suspicion and distrust, but it didn't show in the way they treated me.

The couch, which as it turned out was the best seat in the house, was full when I got back. I passed out the bottles and looked around for a place to sit. Luke grabbed me and pulled me down on his lap. It wasn't particularly comfortable for me and I doubted it was for him, but I didn't protest.

Jared returned after a few moments and we settled to watch the movie, passing the popcorn bowl back and forth. "You don't want any popcorn?" I whispered to Luke when he didn't take any.

"I'll just eat what lands in your lap," he said in an amused voice.

I looked down automatically when he plucked a piece from lap. "You're so very funny," I said irritably.

"I've noticed only half of it actually makes it to your mouth."

"I have poor hand to mouth coordination."

He chuckled.

Jared glared at him. "Are you going to talk through the damned movie?"

"There's no dialogue," Luke retorted.

"Yeah, but you're ruining the damned mood."

Luke shot him a bird. Jared reciprocated and they both settled to watch the movie. As soon as the room got quiet, I sank completely into the movie. It was ten times more intense on their huge TV screen than on my little, tiny TV. As luck would have it, Gavin had just handed me the bowl of popcorn when the monster burst from the man's chest. I jumped, throwing what remained in the bowl up in the air. It rained down all over me and Luke.

Gavin, Luke, and Jessie all burst out laughing. Bret and Jared, who were seated in chairs they'd dragged to either side of the couch, hadn't actually witnessed the event but they turned and grinned when they saw the popcorn.

"It's a damned good thing you didn't have the cola in your hand. I'd have been pissed if you'd poured that all over me."

"Sorry," I said, embarrassed. Climbing off his lap, I quickly collected the popcorn. "I'll make more."

"I think we've had enough," Gavin said, eyeing me with amusement.

Shrugging, I finished clean up and set the bowl down on the coffee table.

Jessie grabbed me and pulled me on to his lap before I could sit down on Luke again. It was actually more comfortable since I was sitting across his lap and could prop my back against the high arm of the couch. It took me a few minutes to get back in to the movie, but it never failed to scare the piss out of me, mostly, I thought, because the aliens were very spider-like and spiders had always given me the creeps. Of course, there was the teeth, but I was pretty sure it was mostly because they reminded me of spiders.

I discovered the guys found my reaction to the movie almost as entertaining as the movie itself.

I suppose the parental visit really had put a damper on everybody's enthusiasm for romping with me. When the movie was over, they split up to use the showers and then headed for the bedrooms at the other end of the house, leaving me in sole possession of the master bedroom.

It figured. The one night when I would really have relished company in my bed and none of them were interested.

The house was empty when I woke. It unnerved me when I realized I'd overslept. I'd already jumped up and rushed to the bathroom before it dawned on me that I was to start working from the house. Since I was already up, however, I went ahead and performed my morning ritual except, instead of putting on dressier clothes for the bank, I put on a comfortable pair of jeans and a t-shirt. I decided to leave my hair down, too. It usually gave me a headache to wear it on top of my head anyway. Brushing it, I tied it back out of my way and headed to the kitchen to make my coffee.

Luke came in carrying computer parts while I was curled up in one corner of the couch with my cup. Setting it down, he went out again. When he'd assembled all the parts, he headed toward an armoire that stood in a corner of the living room and opened it, revealing a home office. It was empty, but he took care of that, quickly and efficiently connecting all the wires to the computer. When he'd strung a phone wire from it to a jack in the wall, he dragged one of the chairs from the table, sat down and booted the machine.

Quickly finishing my coffee, I took it to the kitchen to wash the cup and then returned to stand behind him. He was waiting for me when I came back. I saw the screen was displaying the bank's homepage. He told me the login and password. "All lower case."

"I should find something and write that down so I don't forget it," I said, looking around hopefully for a pen and piece of paper.

"No," he said implacably. "You *never* write down the login and password—ever."

I looked at him in dismay. "But ... nobody ever comes here."

"Ever."

I bit my lip. "Couldn't I just ...."

"No."

"I was just going to say write it several times until I'd memorized it and then destroy the paper."

"No. Repeat it in your head until you've memorized it."

Nice suggestion, I thought irritably, but that didn't work for me. I had to see it and write or type it to memorize it. Realizing there was no hope for it, I closed my eyes and obediently repeated it over and over.

I got it wrong two out of three times.

"I'll log you in in the morning before I leave," he said, disgust evident in his voice, "but that means you'll have to get up before I leave. We don't leave the system connected and unattended."

I wasn't very happy about that if it meant getting up really early and I had a feeling it did, but I merely nodded. He was already irritated with me. I didn't want to anger him any more.

He told me to drag up a chair. I did. I discovered Luke was brilliant when it came to computers—which meant he was a damned poor teacher and an impatient one. People who were really good at something simply couldn't grasp when someone else had a really hard time with it. I did my best to follow his instructions, but he explained everything too fast and he gave me too much at one time. I got more and more confused as time went on instead of more enlightened. By the time he'd finished 'taking me through' what I was supposed to do I had a headache and I felt like crying because I knew there was no way in hell I could do what he'd just shown me and I didn't want him to yell at me.

I also didn't want him to think I was stupid.

So ... I lied and told him I'd gotten it.

I didn't know if it was fortunate that he was in a hurry to get back to the bank or a bad thing. He didn't question me too closely, but then I didn't know what the hell to do.

Satisfied, he got up, paused long enough to kiss me stupid, and then patted my ass and left.

I stared at the screen glumly when he'd left. Finally, trying to dismiss the horrible feeling that I was going to fuck something up that was really important, I struggled to put my fear to the back of my mind and sat down, staring at my fingers on the keyboard and trying to remember where I was supposed to start. There was a file on the computer itself that contained the information I was supposed to be putting in to a working file in another program and then ftp over to the main computer at the bank.

I realized I'd forgotten the login and password for the ftp. A lump of misery rose in my throat, but then what did that matter when I couldn't remember the rest of it? I couldn't ftp when I hadn't done anything.

Deciding to dismiss that for the moment, I focused on trying to remember how to get to the first screen. It was a nightmare. I spent hours going from one screen to another and couldn't find the one I thought I was looking for.

After a while, deciding the headache was partly from emptiness, I logged off and got up to find food. There were leftovers in the fridge from at least two meals. The disorder prompted my OCD. I'd emptied the fridge and was sorting what should be thrown out from what should be kept when I heard the front door open and close—hard.

I jumped guiltily, glanced around at the mess I'd made of the kitchen in sudden horror.

Luke appeared at the door of the kitchen, his expression thunderous. It didn't improve when he'd surveyed the kitchen. "What the hell are you doing? I've been waiting for those files for hours."

I stared at him in dismay. "I was hungry," I said weakly.

"Jesus fucking Christ!" he muttered, staring around at the contents of the refrigerator as if he thought I'd meant to eat all of it.

It sent a spark of reviving anger through me which, unfortunately, didn't outlast the realization that I was actually supposed to be working at the computer.

"So you figured you might as well do some housekeeping while you were at it?"

"I didn't think you'd object," I said a little stiffly.

"Well, you should've, damn it! It isn't your place and you're supposed to be working anyway."

I knew it wasn't my place. They'd just moved me in to make Miss Puss more convenient for them, and it still hurt—however stupid it was to be hurt when forced to face the truth. He was right about the work, too. I was supposed to earn my paycheck.

I still felt my chin wobble uncontrollably, mostly because I didn't want to tell him I didn't have any idea how to do the work I'd been assigned.

He was probably equally ticked off about having to drive to town and back—twice—and the knowledge that he was going to have to make two more trips. No doubt burning up the road between the house and the bank wasn't his idea of a fun way to spend his day.

I managed to regain control of my emotions. "I'll just clean all this up and get to work."

I could see he was studying me keenly. "You're probably right. Half of this ought to be pitched out."

He helped me sort the food and put it back in the fridge. I wished he'd just go away. I didn't want him hanging around when I got back to the computer and settled to trying to figure it out again. To my dismay, he decided to stay and have lunch while he was there anyway. "It's going on two and I haven't eaten yet. What were you going to have?"

"I'd thought I'd fix a grilled chicken sandwich with the leftover chicken."

"I'll have one, too."

We ate in uncomfortable silence. I did anyway. Luke wolfed down two sandwiches and got up, thankfully, to leave. He paused by my chair. Dropping a hand to my shoulder, he squeezed it. "I'm sorry I jumped down your throat. I need those files, alright?"

I nodded miserably. I didn't look at him.

I hadn't managed to eat much and I thought I was going to throw up what I *had* swallowed. If I hadn't been such a coward I would've asked him to show me one more time before he left, but I *was* a coward. I was hopeful I could figure it out now that I'd had a little time away from the keyboard to calm down.

Hah!

I discovered when I went back to the computer that I couldn't even remember the damned login and password. I tried it over and over until I got kicked out.

When all else failed …. I covered my face with my hands and wept with a mixture of despair and frustration until the front door opened again. I jumped, scrubbing the tears from my face and wiping my nose hurriedly.

Vaguely relieved when I discovered it was Jared, I pushed my chair back and made a dash for the bathroom to hide. He intercepted me. Catching my chin, he forced my face up and examined it with a frown. "What the hell is going on?"

I stared at him, trying to regain my composure, and lost the battle. "I don't know how to do it!" I wailed. "I can't even get back in now!

Luke's going to be so angry with me!"

Thankfully, he let me go when I pulled away from him. Retreating to the bathroom, I slammed the door behind me, dropped the lid of the toilet and flopped down on it to weep. I'd used half the roll of toilet paper to mop my nose and wipe my eyes when I heard sounds of an arrival. Shortly behind that, I heard more angry voices than it seemed to me ought to be in the house.

The bathroom door opened a few minutes later. My heart jumped uncomfortably. A mixture of dismay that I'd forgotten to lock the door and uneasiness filled me when I saw Luke studying me. He approached me, crouching down in front of me. "Why didn't you just tell me you didn't understand?"

I stared at him miserably. I didn't want to tell him it was because I was worried that he'd think I was completely inept. Good thing I didn't tell him! Now he'd never know! "Don't be mad at me."

He released a sound of irritation. "I'm not angry."

I sniffed. "You aren't?" I asked a little doubtfully, because he'd sure seemed thoroughly pissed off and that was only after the first trip back to the house after the trip he'd made to bring the computer and set it up.

He straightened, pulling me to my feet. "Wash up. Jessie brought supper in a bag. They're heating it."

I would've liked more reassurance, but I could see I wasn't going to get it. Truthfully, I was so dismayed to discover I'd lost an entire workday that I was more concerned about that than anything else.

After supper, Luke sat down at the computer with me to give me another tutorial. Jared, much to his irritation, stood over us, pointing out the flaws in Luke's instructions—when he was going too fast, when he failed to explain something he assumed I already knew.

I'd never had to learn under duress before, but by the time we shut the computer down I thought I could muddle through the process without screwing anything up. Luke still wouldn't let me write down any of the logins or passwords, but he made me open and close and enter them over and over until I'd memorized them.

I was exhausted when we stopped for the night, mostly emotionally exhausted, but my head was whirling from trying to take in so much information so fast and I had an ungodly headache. Excusing myself, relieved when no one objected, I went to take a shower and pop some painkillers.

* * * *

Jared broke the tense silence that had gripped all of

time Stephanie retreated to the bedroom. "I knew she didn't have anything to do with the break in," he said to the room at large.

Gavin studied Jared a moment and glanced at Luke questioningly. Luke scrubbed a hand along the back his neck, massaging the tense muscles. "Assuming she really didn't understand what I showed her—and she either didn't or she's the best actress I've ever seen—I don't see how she could've."

"She doesn't know enough about using a computer to have helped," Jessie retorted irritably. "That doesn't mean she didn't have anything to do with. Her son knows. She could've hatched the idea and gotten him to do it. That's what she said."

Jared and Bret both glared at him. "You're just saying that because you'd rather believe she was guilty," Bret said coolly.

Jessie glared back at him but shifted uncomfortably. "So I don't want to believe it." He shrugged. "If we accept that possibility, then we also accept that what we're doing here is unconscionable if not downright illegal—which means it needs to stop."

"Nobody is stopping anything. She accepted responsibility—claimed it," Gavin pointed out coldly. "We're well within our rights, particularly since she signed the disclaimer relieving us of any and all responsibility."

"The question here," Luke said tightly, "is whether it's right or not."

Gavin stared at him for a long moment. "It feels damned right to me."

"I've got to agree with that, speaking of which we need to draw to see who gets what night," Jared said, getting up and heading to the cabinet where they kept the gaming supplies. He returned with a pack of cards, shuffling them.

"Just like that?" Luke asked. "It doesn't bother any of you? No pangs of conscience?"

"Nobody's hurt her, Luke," Gavin said irritably. "Nobody's going to. I can live with it—a hell of a lot better than the alternative. You think if we cut her loose now she'd let any of us within a hundred yards of her?"

"Maybe we should find out."

"You find out if you want to," Jared said irritably. "I'm not interested in breaking up the party yet. Gav's right. Don't get me wrong. I'm not saying I'm completely comfortable or that it doesn't bother me at all, but I can live with it. At least we're protecting her reputation by ~eping her here. You know how people are. If the five of us were creating a traffic jam at her front door there'd be no living with all the fucking talk—especially for her."

Jessie rolled his eyes. "You want to look at it like that?"

"Yeah, I do. Unless, of course, the rest of you are ready to back off and leave her to me. In which case, I'll be happy to take her home and move in with her."

"You think she'd let you?" Gavin asked tightly. "You're that sure of yourself?"

Jared narrowed his eyes at him. "Why the fuck wouldn't she? I guess you think she's too hot for you to consider any of the rest of us?"

"I think she's hot, period."

"What the fuck do you mean by that?" Luke growled, glaring at Jessie.

Jessie glared back at him. "Not what you obviously thought I meant," he snapped.

Luke studied him suspiciously for a moment and finally snatched a card from the deck Jared was holding out. Jared made the rounds and finally picked one for himself. "Ascending or descending order?"

"Ascending," Gavin replied promptly.

Jessie grinned. "My night," he said, tossing his card down.

"We didn't all agree on whether it was ascending or descending, damn it!" Jared growled.

"I don't feel like bickering over it all night," Gavin retorted, tossing his own card down.

"That's because you've got tomorrow night!" Jared responded in disgust when he'd looked at the card.

"But not tonight. I'm going to bed."

Luke, Jared, and Bret tossed their own cards onto the table and studied them. "I don't see that you've got much room to complain," Luke muttered, getting up to follow Gavin. "I'm low man."

* * * *

As tired as I was, I doubted very much that I was going to be left completely alone for two nights running. I'd put on one of my loose sleeping shirts for comfort, but hadn't bothered with panties since I doubted I'd be wearing them long.

I'd just begun to drowse when the bedroom opened. It was dark in the room, but I heard the rustle of clothes as he undressed. The light came on in the bathroom as he went in. When he came out a few minutes later, he left the light on and the door ajar. The bed dipped and he slid over next to me.

"What's this?" Jessie asked, plucking at my t-shirt.

"Removable," I said sleepily, my eyes closed against the light spilling from the bathroom.

Tossing the cover aside, he rolled me onto my back and pushed the t-shirt up, cupping my breasts. I'd lifted my hands above my head for him to remove it. When he didn't, I simply tucked my arms beneath the pillow, enjoying the feel of his hands on my breasts and the tingling that immediately began to flow through me like warm, sweet molasses.

He focused on teasing my nipples with his fingers and lips and mouth lazily, stroking his hand down my body from time to time. "You've got the most beautiful body of any woman I've ever seen," he murmured huskily.

The compliment startled me, but it sent a thrill of pleasure through me, too. "Thank you," I whispered a little uncomfortably after several moments passed while I tried to decide whether to break the spell or not.

He lifted his head to look at me and finally shifted to pull the t-shirt completely off, tossing it aside. When he had, he gathered me into his arms and rolled to his side. His engorged member settled heavily against my belly as he pulled me close, stroking his hands over my back and buttocks while he nuzzled my neck, sucking little bites of flesh here and there.

I found a place to rest my hands while he indulged his senses, but discovered I was equally curious of his body. The wild, often hurried, couplings I'd experienced with them hadn't given me a lot of opportunity to explore any of them.

I wasn't sure if I should. Would it feel too much like making love when it should feel like nothing but fucking?

Deciding finally that if he didn't like it he'd tell me, or I'd at least sense his withdrawal, I began to stroke his back in exploration as he caressed me. His skin was smooth and silky, delightful to touch, his back surprisingly muscular. No doubt he'd built a lot muscle in his youth working on the farm, but I thought he must work out fairly regularly to maintain such a beautiful physique.

He tensed slightly when I found my way to his ear and explored it with the tip of my tongue but even as I began to pull away, he speared his fingers through my hair, cupping the back of my head. He studied my face a moment and tilted his head, bringing my face to his and sucking at my lips. For a few moments, we teased one another, brushing lips, nipping, and then he settled his mouth over mine and thrust his tongue inside my mouth. I closed my mouth around his tongue, sucking.

He released a gusty breath, breaking contact for a moment. Covering my mouth again, he rolled, carrying me beneath him, kissing me with far more fervor than a moment before. When we'd dueled tongues until we were both breathless, he broke away to explore further a field, tracing a path down my throat to my breasts, where he lingered long enough tugging at the sensitive tips that I'd begun to feel feverish with need. Instead of shifting upward to mount me, however, he moved lower still, nipping at the extremely sensitive area of my lower belly and upper thighs until I was tugging at his hair.

Disentangling my fingers, lacing them through his own and manacling them to the bed on either side of my hips, he settled his mouth on my clit. I hadn't even realized that he'd managed to wedge himself between my thighs until I felt the felt heated drag of his tongue. I gasped, struggled to untangle my hands from his, but he tightened his grip, holding me down so that he could tease me until I was so drunk and feverish with need I couldn't catch my breath or lie still.

"I'm going to come," I gasped warningly.

Apparently, he wanted me to.

Either that or he didn't hear me.

He continued the wonderful assault until I went off like a rocket.

And kept caressing me until was screaming hoarsely and trying to escape.

Releasing me finally just before my heart exploded, he rolled off.

I lay as he'd left me, sprawled limply.

"Put this on me," he said, dropping a tube into my hand.

Closing my hand around it, I struggled up, studied the tube with drunken confusion for a moment and finally got the cap off. I'd squeezed a dollop into my palm and grasped the root of his cock before it dawned on me that turnabout was fair play.

Instead of smoothing the lubrication over his cock, I leaned down to cover the head with my mouth. I thought for a moment it was going to unhinge my jaws. Sucking at the tip for a moment, I lifted my head, worked my jaw trying to loosen up the joints and tackled the project again.

He settled a hand on the back of my head almost as if to push me away. Instead, as I sucked on the end of his cock and began stroking my hand up and down the length I couldn't possibly cover with my mouth, his fingers tightened in my hair. I wanted to bring him off with my mouth as he had me. Almost the moment it had occurred to me to try I'd begun to feel lightheaded with excitement.

Jessie had other ideas. He was nearing climax, which had me nearing the peak myself, when he abruptly broke contact, pulling away. Fairly mindless in my pursuit by that time, I tried to follow. He grabbed me beneath the arms, though, and hauled me atop of him. I sat up dizzily, when he pushed at my shoulder, watching hazily while he squeezed more lubrication out and coated himself with it.

My hands were sticky with the lube I'd gotten but never gotten around to spreading more than half the length of his cock. Reaching between my thighs, I stroked what I could on myself, using my fingers to spread my sex as wide as I could as I lowered myself on the waiting shaft.

It was lovely torture trying to engulf it within my body. My thighs were quivering with the effort of holding me at such an awkward position by the time I managed to slide all the way down and feel the lips of my sex kiss his belly. Jessie looked as if he was in agony. He dropped his hands to my thighs, kneading them, releasing small grunts of breath. I watched his face as I rose to allow his cock to glide from me and then slowly lowered myself again. His face twisted. Fascinated, feeling a thrill go through me merely watching the pleasure on his face, I began to move a little faster.

He arched his head back, lifting his hips to meet me when I lowered myself again. After a few moments, I became too caught up in my own pleasure, however, to be more than vaguely aware of his any longer. Finding the pace and angle that pleased me the most, I kept it until I began to come. The convulsions were so wonderful, I lost track of everything else then.

He grasped my hips, lifting and lowering me a couple of times and then holding me and driving up into me until he reached his own peak. He drove deeply then, curling his arms around me and holding me in a near crushing embrace until his cock ceased to jerk and buck inside of me. I dragged in a deep breath when his hold slackened, shuddering with the little quakes, drifting toward darkness with the languor from my release. Slowly my heart and respiration returned to normal. I roused drowsily a little later when it dawned on me that I was still draped limply over him. He tightened his arms around me, though, holding me as I was and I desisted, falling asleep still mounted on his cock.

I woke the same way.

Chapter Twelve

A sudden burst of light woke me. I squeezed my eyes more tightly shut, but finally opened them to see what was going on when it didn't magically disappear again. When I lifted my head sluggishly, I saw that Luke was just disappearing into the bathroom. He met my gaze for a moment before he shut the door.

I dropped my head to the hard pillow I'd been using all night.

Jessie rolled over, taking me with him. It should have been enough to disconnect us, but he'd gotten hard. Burrowing his face against my neck, he began to move very slowly in and out of me. Warmth stirred in my belly. It generated a scant amount of moisture to coat the walls of my sex, making his movements less uncomfortable. The moment he discovered he could move more easily, he pushed his hands beneath my hips and began to plow into me in deep, short, quick strokes.

I was just starting to get really warmed up when he came.

Mildly irritated about being left, I rolled over and presented him with my back when he moved off of me, burrowing my head under one of the pillows. I was just beginning to drift asleep again when someone smacked me on the ass hard enough I shot up off the bed like a scalded cat.

Amusement flickered in Luke's eyes. "Work now, sleep later."

Jessie had the bathroom, I discovered.

I fell back against the bed, closing my eyes.

Jessie flicked water on me when he came out of the shower. I opened my eyes wide enough to glare at him. He grinned at me and strolled out of the bedroom buck-naked. I lifted my head high enough off the pillow to enjoy the view.

"Nice ass!" I called after him.

He halted abruptly in his tracks and swiveled around to look at me.

I couldn't tell what was going through his mind, but I was shocked at my own audacity. Scrambling out of the bed, I galloped toward the bathroom and slammed the door behind me.

Thankfully, I was left to attend my morning needs without interruption. When I came out again, I was slightly more alert but still dead on my feet. Coffee! After searching around the bed for the t-shirt I'd put on the night before, I dragged it over my head and headed toward the kitchen.

Gavin, already drinking his coffee, watched me until I'd mixed mine and then slid his hand over my ass just about the time I got the cup to my lips. I dribbled it down my chin. He grinned unrepentantly at the glare I sent him as I swiped at my chin with the back of my hand.

"Here. Let me take care of that for you," he murmured, amusement gleaming in his eyes as he bent down until his face was level with mine. He sucked my chin before it even occurred to me what he intended and then settled his mouth over mine. By the time he'd thoroughly kissed me, I'd poured half my coffee out on the countertop.

He chuckled outright when he saw what I'd done. "Guess you'll have to start over."

Jared breezed in while I was mopping up the mess on the counter. Slipping up behind me, he slid a hand between my thighs, tickled my clit while he bumped my ass with his dick a couple of times, bent his head to bite my neck, and then breezed out again.

Uttering a sigh, I drank what little was left of my coffee and set the cup down to start over. Bret and Jessie paused behind me to fondle me and then left.

Luke came to the door of the kitchen just about the time I finally managed to get my coffee mixed again. "I logged in for you."

"Ok," I said, carefully balancing my coffee cup as I headed for the living room.

"You going to start work like that?" Luke asked, his voice carefully neutral.

I looked down at myself. I'd only meant to make my coffee and then return to the room to dress while I sipped it. "I should get dressed."

He followed me to the room. Moving up behind me as I reached the dresser where I'd put my clothes, he took my coffee from my hand and carefully set it aside and then slid his hands under the t-shirt, cupping both breasts. His cock rose between us while he was nibbling my ear. My nipples rose in his palms.

He plucked at them, reminding me that Jessie had left me hanging.

Luke left me hanging, too, damn his hide! He got me all stirred up, then checked his watch and decided he didn't have time.

Uttering an irritated huff when he left, I got dressed, took my coffee to warm it in the microwave and finally settled in front of the computer. Trying not to panic, I stared at the screen and struggled to bring up the instructions from the night before. Thankfully, it came back to me. I managed to open the screen I needed and set to work.

I was so pleased with myself when I managed to ftp the completed file over to the bank I was beside myself. Getting up, I went to the kitchen to celebrate with lunch. The computer made a chiming noise when I'd fixed my sandwich and headed back.

I saw there was an email message. Clicking on it, I opened it and read it.

Good job, Luke had written. *I got it. Hold on to that 'thought for the day' I left you with this morning. I'm going to collect on it later.*

I wasn't sure which pleased me more, the praise or the promise. I was oh so tempted to write something really naughty back, but I was afraid someone else might read it. *I will as soon as I remember it*, I wrote back. *I wasn't really awake when you left. Can you give me a hint of what it was about?*

I'll give you a stiff cock. Maybe that'll jog your memory.

Ah! Jogging! Now I remember.

I thought you might.

I was a little disappointed when he didn't write back again, but opened a new file and set to work. The mail chimed again.

Feeling a little thrill run through me I opened it. *Luke isn't going to be jogging you tonight. It's my night. Both of you behave and get to work—Gavin*

A shiver went through me that was equal parts excitement and fright. I hadn't realized anybody else might access the mail. I'd thought more in terms of someone looking over Luke's shoulder. I saw the email had been carbon copied to both Luke and me. A moment later, the mail chimed again. When I opened it, I saw it cc'd to me and Gavin. *Bite me!*

I'll do it! I volunteered.

Behave! Both of you!

It was easier to fall into the new routine than I'd expected—once I got the hang of working online. In some ways, I also liked the 'other' arrangements, too. Sunday through Thursday, they rotated. Friday and Saturday they tried to fuck me to death. To keep their parents off their backs—and away from the playhouse—Gavin and Luke went to their parents' house every other week and their cousins the alternate week.

I'd thought when the gang moved to the sex toys that they were already getting bored with me.   Apparently, they just liked to experiment.

It was exhausting trying to keep with up with them, but after about a month, I'd hit my stride and reached the point where I wasn't quite as exhausted as I had been at first. Regardless, they kept me so busy that I completely lost track of time.

I'd been living with them a month when I decided I just couldn't take grilled food or take-out any more. The entire group was clearly deeply suspicious the first time I cooked. They thoroughly appreciated it, but I could see what was going through their minds.

I was getting too domestic and that meant trouble.

I could see they didn't believe me when I informed them that I liked to have something home cooked at least once in a while, but they didn't pursue it or argue with me. I started out by cooking once a week. By the time another month had passed, I was cooking five days a week and I wasn't totally happy about that, either.

On the other hand, the full extent of their cooking skills was throwing meat on the grill.

At least they took care of clean up. I decided I could handle the cooking if they did the cleaning or least most of it.

I didn't go out much, needless to say, but then I hadn't before so I didn't particularly miss it. I'd taken on the additional job of buying the groceries because the men never came home with the right stuff no matter how carefully I made out the list.

Apparently, despite the efforts of the guys to keep their parents in the dark, Clara Thorne wasn't easily fooled. She showed up one day in the middle of the day, catching me completely off guard.

As panicked as I was when I peered out the window and saw whose car was parked out front, I at least had the presence of mind to race across the living room on tiptoes and lock the bedroom door. Coward that I was, I huddled in one corner in quivering silence while Clara walked around the house, peering in windows and checking all the doors.

I'd just breathed a sigh of relieve when I heard a key in the lock of the front door. Wide eyed, I watched as it opened and Clara poked her head in.

She jumped when she met my horrified gaze. "Oh! I didn't think anyone was here!"

Obviously! I was holding a hand to my heart because it felt like it would beat it's way out. "I thought I heard somebody at the door!" I lied. "I was in the bathroom."

She looked me over and stepped inside. "Is Gavin here?"

"He's not home yet."

She nodded, but I could the wheels turning—me at the house and Gavin at the bank—to say nothing of the fact that I'd said 'home'. Oh god! I could've bitten my tongue off. "I guess I'll be going then. Tell him I said I expect him to bring you over for dinner this weekend."

Oh god! Gavin was going to be fit to be tied!

He wasn't the only one.

He nearly slammed face first into the bedroom door when he headed in and discovered the door was still locked. "What the hell's the door locked for?" he demanded irritably.

"I couldn't unlock it."

"Why did you lock it to start with?"

I shrugged. "Your mother came by."

"Oh hell!"

I grimaced. "I'm sorry! I hid! She had her own key."

Gavin studied me for a long moment. "What did you two talk about?"

"I didn't talk. She didn't actually stay long. I think she was surprised when she found out I was here."

"I'll just bet she was," Gavin said grimly. "What did she want?"

I reddened. "She said to tell you to bring me when you came to dinner Sunday."

"Well fuck!"

"You don't have to take me. You can just tell her I didn't mention it," I said quickly.

He shook his head at me. "There's no avoiding it. Once Mom gets something in her head …."

He made the announcement to the others as we sat down to eat. "Well fuck!" Luke snapped. "We can't take Steph!"

"We can. We have to," Gavin said grimly.

I'd tried really hard not to let it bother me that they didn't want me around their family, but I knew deep down that they didn't like the idea of taking a woman like me around their mother.

Jared, who sitting next to me, tapped my chin. "She can handle Aunt Clara," he said, winking at me when I looked at him.

"*Nobody* can handle Mom," Gavin retorted dryly. "We'll just have to time it out so that we arrive in time to sit down and think of a damned good reason to leave as soon as we're done eating."

"She'll go all out since she's expecting Steph," Luke said warningly. "Steph'll be miserable."

Feeling a good bit better that it seemed they were more concerned that I'd be overwhelmed than ashamed to take me, I told them I'd be careful not to say anything I shouldn't. The doubtful look I encountered from all the Thornes didn't make me feel a lot better.

"We should all go," Jessie said decisively. "That way we can run interference."

Gavin thought it over. "Not a bad plan. You'll need to give her a call and tell her you're coming. You know she'll be put out if you show up unannounced."

It made me feel better that they were so supportive, even though they clearly thought I was going to blow it, but I wasn't thrilled about going to Sunday dinner with the family. I *was* thrilled with the dress Gavin brought home for me to wear for the occasion, though.

Alright, a little embarrassed that there wasn't anything 'appropriate' in my wardrobe until I saw what he considered appropriate, but it was the most beautiful, elegant thing I'd ever seen. He turned red when I squealed with pleasure and flung myself at him—a good indication that I shouldn't have given in to the impulse. I was too happy, though, to crumble when I saw I'd made him uncomfortable. "Sorry. I got carried away."

"You can get carried away with what I brought you if you want to," Luke said, smiling faintly when he held out the packages he'd brought in.

It felt like Christmas—except better than any Christmas I'd ever had. I took the packages and tore into them with excitement—heels to match the dress, hose, a garter belt and matching panties and bra. Laughing, I threw myself at him as I had Gavin, but I also kissed him all over the face. "Thank you! Thank you! They're beautiful."

He tightened his arms around me for a moment before he released me. Reaching into his coat pocket, he pulled out a small box. I almost had heart failure. I knew it was a jewelry box. My hands were shaking so badly I had a hard time even opening it. I caught my breath when I had. The necklace was absolutely beautiful.

"It's just a little trinket, but I noticed you'd didn't have any jewelry," Luke said a little uncomfortably when I didn't say anything.

I couldn't. I swallowed a couple of times against the lump in my throat.

"If you don't like it …."

I blinked, trying to flush the tears from my eyes, but I could barely bring him into focus when I looked up at him. "I do. I really do."

He grinned at me a little lopsidedly. "Well, don't cry about it. It confuses the hell out of me. You're sure you like it?"

I uttered a watery chuckle. "I'm sure. It's beautiful. It'll be perfect with the dress." I sniffed. "I'll feel like Cinderella."

"Well, get dressed, Cinderella," Gavin said huskily. "We're going to be unfashionably late and Mom will be fit to be tied if her dinner isn't perfect."

Grabbing up the things they'd brought, I dashed into the room to change. I desperately wanted to simply stand in front of the mirror and stare at the way I looked in the dress, but he'd warned me his mother wouldn't be happy. I draped a towel over the dress to protect it when I got into the bathroom. I'd been so anxious before, and so excited after

I'd gotten the outfit, I'd forgotten to put on any makeup. I couldn't wear anything like this without doing my face, too. I used the makeup sparingly, focusing mostly on my eyes. I was so flushed with excitement I didn't think I really needed blush, but I added a light swish of color to my cheeks.

I studied myself when I finished and decided it was the best I could do.

My hair was another matter.

I didn't think I should wear it loose, even though the guys liked it that way. The bun on the top of the head certainly wasn't going to set off the dress, though. After a little thought, I combed it, braided it and then formed it into a crown around my head and pinned it in place.

It looked elegant and stylish to me.

I wasn't so sure his mother would agree, but I didn't know anything else to try.

I hadn't put the necklace on. The chain was so delicate I was almost afraid to try, and my hands were too shaky to fasten it.

Sighing in defeat, I held it carefully in my hand and went out to ask Luke to put it on for me.

All five of the Thorne men were standing in a nervous cluster near the door, glancing at their watches. All five of them looked up when I came out and all five of them looked like they'd just been brained. I stopped abruptly. "Something's wrong?"

The question seemed to bring them out of trance.

Jared plowed through the group, grabbed me around the waist and waltzed me in a tight circle. "You look like …. You're beautiful."

Maybe it was a little exaggerated as compliments went, but he looked sincere enough to make me feel dizzy with delight. "Thank you."

"You decided not to wear the necklace?"

I looked at Luke when he spoke, holding it out to him. "I'm so shaky I couldn't fasten it. I was afraid I'd break the chain."

He took it from me and I turned so he could put it on me. It took him so long, I'd begun to wonder if he could fasten the tiny catch. After all, his hands were a good bit bigger than mine. Finally, he managed it, though.

I turned to display it. "How does it look?"

He scanned my face. "Beautiful."

It was a good thing they bolstered my ego. The dinner was every bit as much of a trial as Gavin had suggested it would be. I'd never *been* to a formal dinner, but I realized as soon as we'd been ushered into the living room that I wasn't overdressed at all, although that fear had certainly assailed me when we'd pulled up at the house and gotten out.

I'd ridden over with Luke and Gavin and they walked me to the door together.

A maid let us in and told us Mr. and Mrs. Thorne were in the small salon.

My god!

It was good thing Gavin and Luke had a firm grip on me. I think I would've retreated right then.

Since he hadn't wanted it to be too obvious that him and his brothers were trailing us, Jessie had given us a five-minute head start. His timing was perfect. Jessie, Jared, and Bret arrived just about the time Clara asked me if Gavin and I were serious and before I had time to ask, about what?

Gavin grinned at the look on my face. Seeing that Jessie and the others had claimed his mother's attention, he leaned down. "She wants to know if we're thinking about marriage," he whispered.

I felt my face turn beet red.

Clara missed nothing. "Behave yourself, Gavin! You're embarrassing the girl."

He grinned at his mother unrepentantly. "You don't know what I said."

She gave him a reproving look. "I don't want to either, thank you! I'm sure it isn't fit for polite company."

Gavin glanced at me and chuckled outright at that.

I was totally entranced. This was a side of Gavin I'd never seen—completely relaxed without a sign of the stony suit of armor he usually wore.

Evidently, Gavin knew his mother's habits to a T. We'd barely gathered when we were informed that dinner was served and moved from the living room—small salon—to the formal dining room. It looked a banquet room. It was so huge our footsteps actually echoed as we walked across the marble tile floor.

The table was long enough it was still half-empty when we'd all settled at our seats at one end. A tall arrangement of flowers decorated the center of the table. Above it was a huge chandelier.

I knew it was gauche to gawk and I didn't—not really. I just took a few casual glances around when someone spoke and I had the opportunity to look toward them and gawk at another part of the room. The table was unnervingly formal. There were two plates stacked in front of me and more silverware surrounding it than I owned all together.

Luke leaned close and spoke quietly near my ear. "It isn't as complicated as it looks. Just watch me."

Relieved, I sent him a look of gratitude as he straightened.

The first question out of Clara's mouth when we sat shattered my composure completely. "Where did you go to school?"

I blinked at her. I didn't make the mistake of thinking she was talking about school. She meant college. I hadn't even graduated from high school. I'd taken a GED and then managed to get through a couple of years of junior college—and it certainly wasn't ivy league. I felt pale. I'm sure I looked pale. Gavin found my hand under the table and squeezed it.

"She went to a small college near her home," Gavin said smoothly. "You won't have heard of it."

"Nothing wrong with that," Robert Thorne said before his wife could ask for more particulars. "How are things going at the bank?"

The men managed to dominate the conversation with a discussion of banking matters while the maid moved around the table removing the top plate and replacing it with a salad plate. When she'd made the rounds, she returned with a vinaigrette.

Luke picked up his salad fork and stabbed a piece of greenery. Taking my cue from him, I found the correct fork and took a bite of my own salad.

The dressing was tart. I hadn't expected it and I couldn't prevent myself from screwing up my face or shuddering.

Robert Thorne choked on his water. He cleared his throat. "Tart my dear?"

I smiled at him a little weakly. "Just a little."

"It tastes fine to me," Clara said coolly.

"It's very good ... just ... tart."

I noticed Gavin's eyes were gleaming with amusement when I glanced at him. I decided to avoid the vinaigrette.

The maid circled the table with rolls, which she very carefully removed from the basket with tongs and placed on the small plates just above the dinner plates. I wasn't sure whether I was supposed to pick it up or not.

When she'd made the rounds, the maid returned with a plate that had small pats of butter that had been shaped into some sort of design.

We hadn't even gotten through the salads, I thought unhappily. At this rate we were going to be here until doomsday. I could see Clara was just waiting for another opening to ask me something else.

It wasn't that I didn't completely understand. I knew if my son was dating anyone and I'd thought he might be serious about the relationship, I'd want to know about her and her family.

I just hadn't expected it because I knew it wasn't a relationship at all.

No wonder the guys had been so dismayed about the 'order' to bring me. They knew my background wasn't something the Thorne family would approve of.

Actually, in all honesty, I doubted very many families *would* approve of me.

I wasn't ignorant or stupid. I hadn't managed to make it through school because I'd gotten pregnant, but I was interested in the world around me. I *sought* knowledge. I'd learned a lot through books even if I'd never been tested or graded on it.

Of course the lack of formal education was only the icing, really. My getting pregnant as a teenager was enough by itself to make me the last woman in the world any mother would want her son involved with.

Clara Thorne would probably drop dead of heart failure—and have her house fumigated—if she knew what sort of woman was sitting across from her.

I wished I hadn't thought of any of that. It made it harder to hold my head up and try to carry off the dinner with the Thornes. I had my pride, though, whether anyone thought I was entitled to feel any or not. So what if I was a mutt and white trash as far as people like the Thornes, people in general, were concerned? I had worth. I was a good citizen. I worked, paid my bills, supported myself and my son, didn't run afoul of the law, and I didn't do drugs.

I was honest.

Of course, my son was a bank robber.

The food was delicious, but it might as well have been sawdust. My stomach was tied in so many knots I had a hard time appreciating any of it.

"So …," Clara asked the first time she had a chance. "What do you do, Miss Bridges?"

Fuck your sons until they pass out. I smiled at her with an effort. "I'm a clerk at the bank," I responded, ignoring the warning glance Gavin sent me.

Clara's brows rose almost to her hairline. "Really?"

"We promoted her to another department. She's doing data entry at the moment."

Clara smiled at him thinly. "She works from home?"

Gavin squirmed a little uncomfortably. "At the moment, yes."

"Your home."

Gavin's lips tightened. "As a matter of fact, yes. She does."

Clara sent her husband a look.

"Amazing thing the internet," he said jovially. "I imagine we're going to be seeing the world change even more in the next few years."

She kicked him under the table. I was sitting across from them and I saw it.

He sent her a look, but he ignored her prompt to 'say something'. I knew that was what it was. I also realized no one had fooled her for a minute. She'd known, or at least suspected, the first time she set eyes on me that I was Gavin's fuck buddy. That was why she'd come to the house—to look for evidence.

If she only knew the scope of it!

Jessie brought the conversation back to banking. They managed to keep the discussion going until the desert arrived. Gavin waved it off. "None for me. We really need to be going. I have a long day tomorrow."

Relieved when Gavin got up and pulled out my chair, I thanked Mr. and Mrs. Thorne for inviting me and told them how much I'd enjoyed the visit and the delicious food—which was sitting in the bottom of my stomach like a rock.

Jessie, Bret, and Jared excused themselves hurriedly and nearly raced us out of the dining room.

Their desperation to depart before their aunt could corral them and pump them for information might have been funny if I'd been in any mood to laugh.

Luke settled his arm around my shoulders and pulled me close once we'd gotten in the car, brushing a kiss along my temple. "You did good."

"Don't do that!" Gavin said testily. "You know that damned maid of hers will have her nose to the window and report right back to Mom. She's supposed to me my girlfriend."

"Well, she isn't and I don't give a fuck," Luke said coolly, releasing me in a leisurely manner and straightening in his seat.

"Well, you should."

"Except I don't."

"She can make life hell if she's a mind to."

"Maybe, but I won't give her the chance. If she starts anything, I can leave."

"You would do that, you asshole," Gavin said irritably. "Then she'll cry all over me."

Luke snorted. It wasn't a laugh, although there was some humor in it. "So leave with me."

Gavin glanced at me. "How're you holding up, baby? Did the mean old woman scare you?"

As depressed as I was, I couldn't help but smile. "You two talk about her as if she's a terror. She doesn't look like she'd weigh a hundred pounds soaking wet."

"Yes, but she's our mother. There's no escaping that," Gavin retorted, grinning wryly. "Don't tell me you wouldn't be worried about it if it was your mother."

I thought that over. "If it was my mother, I wouldn't have gone at all. I would've been headed in the other direction."

"I rest my case."

He had a point.

* * * *

I came to a decision that was just shy of insane after the dinner with Mr. and Mrs. Thorne.

Actually, it wasn't shy of insane. It *was* insane.

The dinner was only part of it, though. Jimmy's call sealed the deal. I answered the phone.

"Mom?" Jimmy said blankly. "Did I dial the wrong number?"

I gulped. "Uh ... you weren't calling me?" I asked shakily.

"I was trying to call Mr. Thorne."

"Oh? What were calling Mr. Thorne about?"

He was silent for several moments. "Actually, I guess I should've called you first anyway. I just figured there wasn't any point until I'd talked to him. Who's that talking in the background?"

"It's the TV," I lied, turning a frantic look toward the Thornes, who immediately went dead silent.

"The thing is, I hate to transfer in the middle of the school year. I've only got two months to go on this boot camp thing, and I thought I'd just stay here and finish out this school year."

I felt a wave of dismay settle heavily over me. I couldn't think of anything to say for several moments. Only two months? Had it been that long?

"Oh?" I managed finally. "You're sure that's what you want to do?"

"I think it would be for the best. I'm sure. I'm just not sure Mr. Thorne will go for it."

"I guess you should ask him then and ... uh ... I'll call you back in about fifteen minutes or so and find out what's happening, ok?"

"I should probably call you. I might not get him."

"No! No, I'll call you. I was ... uh ... just fixing to take a shower."

"Ok."

My hand was shaking when I hung up.

"Who was it?" Gavin called from the living room.

"Jimmy."

"Jimmy who?"

"My son Jimmy."

"Oh shit!"

That brought him into the kitchen where I was standing. "What did you tell him?"

"He thought he'd called me by mistake," I said shakily, feeling awful that I'd lied to him, although I didn't think he'd have taken it well if he'd found out I was at Gavin's home at ten o'clock at night. He would know immediately what was going on—at least part of it. "I let him think he had. He's going to call you—uh—back, and then I told him I'd call him."

Gavin frowned. "What did he want to talk to me about?"

Before I could explain, the phone rang. Gavin picked it up that time. I studied his face for a moment and finally left. Without glancing at the men in the living room, I headed into the master bedroom and shut myself in the bathroom.

Chapter Thirteen

I wasn't happy about Jimmy's decision not to come home right away, but I could see that his reasoning was sound. He was nearing graduation. I hadn't liked the idea of sending him off to start with. He had plans for college and I wanted him to have what I hadn't had the chance of—a full education and the kind of job that went with it.

I'd missed him. I'd been looking forward to him graduating from boot camp so that I could see him.

It was the realization that I was nearing the term of my own service that had totally wrecked my composure, though. I felt like I couldn't breathe for several moments as I finally let that fully sink in. Two months. It didn't seem possible that I'd been with them four months, that I was looking at an end to life as I'd known it for months.

What was I going to do with myself? How was I going to go back to just being a clerk at the bank, seeing Gavin and Luke day in and day out and being nothing at all to them except another employee?

I couldn't live and bear it I realized abruptly. They were my friends and lovers.

I loved them, I realized. In spite of all the pep talks I'd given myself to beware of falling for them, I had.

God! And it had been so easy!

I couldn't begin to imagine life without them in it.

I wouldn't even have Jimmy, I thought with sudden fear—me—when I'd always been so independent, perfectly content with my own company when Jimmy was off with friends.

Before this, I hadn't even been particularly worried about the time when Jimmy would go off to college. I'd been excited for him. I'd known I'd miss him, but I hadn't been afraid of being alone. I hadn't thought about it with this horrible sense of dread.

I was too hurt even to cry. My chest ached. I could hardly breathe, but I didn't think I could cry if I'd wanted to.

I knew I could afford to. I had to call Jimmy. I couldn't be weeping when I did that.

I couldn't break down in front the guys. They'd want to know why and I couldn't tell them.

I splashed cool water on my face, composed myself the best I could, and returned to the living room. I knew I was pale. My face had looked colorless in the bathroom mirror. I had to suppose that was why the guys were looking at me strangely.

I leaned weakly against the couch when I reached them. "What did you decide?"

Gavin studied me for a long moment. "I told him he'd have to clear it with you but I was alright with it."

I nodded a little jerkily. "I guess I'll call him back."

Had it been fifteen minutes, I wondered? Five? I didn't have any idea. I decided to call him anyway.

He was enthusiastic. I realized after he'd talked for a few minutes that there was a girl at the heart of his decision.

Wasn't there always at his age?

I told him I'd try get down to see him when he graduated from boot camp, but I couldn't promise. The car wasn't really in any shape for such a long trip. He knew that. He suggested I take the bus. "I'll see. I love you."

"Love you, too, Mama."

Behaving normally after that was impossible. I tried, really hard, but I knew from the looks I encountered that I wasn't doing a very good job of it. I was really glad when it was time for bed.

It was Gavin's night to share the bed with me. I didn't know how they decided it, but, for once, I was sorry it was Gavin. I supposed it would've been as hard on me with any of them, but somehow it seemed harder that it was Gavin.

Did I love him the most? When I thought about it, I realized I couldn't say that. Despite the strong family resemblance between them all, they were all completely unique individuals and I'd found so many things about each one of them to love that I couldn't honestly say I loved any one of them more than any of the others.

Maybe it was because it felt like he was making love to me?

And maybe it only felt that way because, for the first time, I was fully aware that I was making love to him.

I think I always had been. I'd just tried to convince myself it was just healthy animal lust for an achingly handsome, virile male.

And when we'd finished, I waited until he'd fallen asleep and then slipped quietly out of the bed, locked myself in the bathroom and climbed in the shower so he couldn't hear my heart breaking.

That was when I made the insane decision.

I stopped taking my birth control pills. I had two months left. If I was really lucky for the first time in my life, I was going to be pregnant when I left. I knew it was an irresponsible thing to do. I was old enough pregnancy was risky even if it wasn't impossible, but I just didn't think I could live and stand it if I didn't have something to take with me, some part of them—at least one of them. I didn't care which. He, or she, would be a Thorne, my Thorne. He or she would be a little bit of all of them. And nobody could take that away from me.

They were going to be furious if they ever found out, but I didn't see why I couldn't keep it from them. I didn't *have* to keep working for them after the term of service. No doubt they'd be relieved to see me go. It couldn't be comfortable for them to have me underfoot when they were finished with me.

I could move down to live near my brother and Jimmy. Maybe they'd let him finish up his last year of high school down there?

If they didn't, I'd think of something.

I wasn't going to let anything—reason—interfere once I'd decided.

It unnerved me, a little, at first, but I overcame it. Actually, I discovered the thrill of possibility enhanced my enjoyment. Every time I had sex with any of them I'd wonder if it had taken, if I'd conceived and a baby was growing inside me. I was a nervous wreck, though, when it came time for Jimmy's graduation. I thought I might be pregnant, but I wasn't certain and it scared me that my time was up and I didn't know if I'd been successful or not.

Gavin had gotten me a cell phone after the night Jimmy had called so that there wouldn't be another chance for Jimmy to call the 'wrong' number and get me. When he'd called me to ask if I was going to be able to come down and visit, Jared had volunteered to drive me down.

It had nearly caused an argument. Gavin had informed him it would be better if he took me and Jared had taken exception. "Now you think her *son* is going to object to her dating a younger man? He's a kid! Everybody that's grown looks old to a teenager! And I doubt it would bother him even if he did notice. At least I don't look like a Thorne!"

"I'll take her," Gavin said implacably. "I imagine he'll think I've come down to check up on him and he won't be happy about it, but I doubt he'll think I'm a boyfriend and that'll make it easier on Steph."

Luke pointed out that the same could be said for him and he could take off the time more easily.

"If that's an issue, I'm just branch manager," Bret said pointedly. "I could take the time off easier."

"I'll just take the bus … if you're ok with me going?"

They all turned to look at me. "We'll draw for it," Gavin said in disgust.

Luke took me. I'd forgotten how much his driving terrorized me. To do him justice, he tried to keep to the speed limit, but impatience got the better of him and his foot got heavier the longer we drove.

He got a speeding ticket.

He was thoroughly pissed off about it, but he watched the speedometer more closely the remainder of the trip.

Gavin had been right. Jimmy took one look at Luke and bowed up like a cur dog. He behaved so badly I was almost sorry I'd made the trip and very sorry that Luke had won the draw. I was pretty sure it couldn't possibly have gone more badly if I'd showed up with Jared or Bret in tow and Jimmy had thought they were my boyfriend.

Not that I could agree that they didn't look like Thornes. Except for the blond hair, they looked as much like the others as peas from the same pod, but the hair color might have thrown Jimmy. After all, he hadn't really had the chance to get to know them all that well.

It didn't seem to bother Luke, but I thought that might be because he was still smoldering over the speeding ticket and too preoccupied to really notice how snotty Jimmy behaved.

It certainly answered one question in my mind, though.

Jimmy wouldn't take it well if he discovered my attachment to the Thornes.

And, of course, that was the first time my feet actually touched Earth and it occurred to me that Jimmy and I were in for a very rocky time if it transpired that I was successful.

Well, I decided, he'd just have to get over it. I had a right to a life of my own. I'd devoted myself to him. He was practically grown and he wouldn't look back once he was ready to cut the strings and run free.

Not that he should, but it meant that I was entitled to have a life, too, whether he agreed with it or not. I wasn't *just* Jimmy's mother. I was Stephanie, a person.

I'd never felt worse in my life by the time we got home—back.

It wasn't *my* home, wouldn't be for much longer, and that was the biggest part of why I felt so bad. Top that off with a drive that had been long and tiring, and the fact that I hadn't seen my son in months only to find myself at odds with him, and I was as miserable as I'd ever been in my life.

We had a quiet dinner—too quiet.

The boot I'd been expecting the following morning never came. Confused but feeling a slight budding of relief, I made it through the day without moping too much. It boosted my spirits a good bit when I my home pregnancy test came up positive.

By the time the guys got home from work, I'd decided I was just going to enjoy what time was left and stop dwelling on the negative.

Not one of them said a single word about my trip or the fact that it was the end of the six months they'd told me in the beginning that I could look forward to.

I wasn't about to bring it up myself.

I managed to get through several more weeks of total happiness before it dawned on me that I'd hanged myself. I was pregnant. I'd known when I decided to take a chance on it that they'd be furious if they found out.

They certainly weren't going to be thrilled.

I was at least a couple of months along, I knew, possibly as much as three, though I doubted that. They were a virile bunch, but I was no spring chicken. I didn't know how fertile my ground was.

True, I'd gotten pregnant with Jimmy without even trying, but I'd just been a kid then.

None of that really mattered. What mattered was that I *was* pregnant and I wasn't about to abort it. I could take my chances and hang around until there was no longer any doubt in their minds that I was pregnant, risk their wrath, risk having them demand I abort it, or I could go.

I didn't *want* to go. If I'd realized that they wouldn't boot me out as soon as the time was up I wouldn't have risked doing anything that would make them want to toss me out.

When another month passed and I could see that I was already showing, I realized I'd run out of time. I didn't have a choice anymore. They didn't seem to have noticed, but it wasn't going to be long at all before they did.

I decided I just couldn't *face* all of them. I didn't want to face even one of them, but I didn't have a choice about that. The next time Gavin spent the night with me I waited until we'd finished making love and told him I missed Jimmy.

He stoked my arm. "I know, baby. I'll take you down to see him in a few weeks."

I felt like I had a lump in my throat the size of a golf ball. I hadn't expected him to be so understanding. "It's been eight months, Gavin," I said tentatively. "You said ...."

He pushed himself up on the bed and studied me for so long I regretted bringing it up at all. Finally, he lay back down, staring at the ceiling. "You want to go," he said finally.

"Well, I know Jimmy's supposed to work in the bank once he graduates, but I thought I'd move down and stay with him and my brother. He really ought not change schools again. He'll be graduating next year."

He let out a long, slow breath. "When are you leaving?"

I don't ever want to leave, I thought, struggling to keep from squalling like a baby. "I don't know. I have to do something about the house."

I heard him swallow. "I'll tell Jared to take you home tomorrow."

I hadn't expected it to be so easy. I think, in the back of my mind, I'd hoped he'd tell me I couldn't go.

I know in the back of my mind I'd hoped he'd tell me he cared about me, that he wanted me to stay.

I suppose that wasn't fair. Even if he felt that way, he wouldn't want to say so when I'd just told him I wanted to go. "I'd rather you didn't," I said as evenly as I could. "I'll make my own arrangements."

He didn't say anything else. After a while, he turned onto his belly and went to sleep. I couldn't sleep. I lay fighting the urge to cry most of the night. It was already getting light outside before I finally fell asleep.

The house was empty when I got up.

I was glad. As hard as it had been to tell Gavin I wanted to leave, I didn't think I could've gotten through any kind of confrontation with the others without breaking down.

Of course, if I hadn't been such a coward I could've just said I was pregnant and waited for the fireworks. I hadn't wanted it to end that way, though. In all the time I'd been with them there hadn't been a single argument—not between me and any of them—very few even between them and those hadn't been serious disagreements that had caused hard feelings.

I called around until I found a car rental company that would bring the vehicle to me and made arrangements and then packed up my belongings and settled to wait. I'd debated over whether or not to pack the elegant outfit Gavin and Luke had bought me, but what possible use would I have for it? I wouldn't be going anywhere where I might wear it.

I still hated leaving it. I hated leaving the necklace Luke had bought me even more. I really, really wanted to keep it, but I could tell it was expensive. Maybe I hadn't been brought up like they had, but I knew a decent woman didn't take things like that from men they weren't related to. If nothing else, at least maybe they'd have a little higher opinion of me.

I doubted it, but I honestly thought it would hurt more to take something like that with me.

When the man brought my car, he was kind enough to help me load my things in it. I drove back to the agency with him and, after a little thought, decided to pay one way to my destination. I needed to go. The longer I stayed nearby, the more tempted I was going to be to run back to them and beg them to let me stay.

The house was a rental. I'd covered my lease.

The car—well, it wasn't much of a car. I emptied it and called a towing place that bought broken down cars and sold it for what I could get. It took me most of the day to pack up everything I wanted to keep, and I left the rest for the for the trash men. I didn't care, for once, if I did lose my deposit. It wasn't as if it didn't always turn in to a fight trying to get the deposit back and renters usually lost anyway.

I called my brother when I got to the edge of town and told him I was coming.

He wasn't really thrilled.

Big surprise!

He was still pissed off at me for getting pregnant. I had to suppose it was something he was never going to get over.

Boy was he going to be thrilled when he discovered I'd done it again!

Misery sat in the pit of stomach like a rock through most of the trip, but began to get a little lighter the more distance I put between me and the guys. I began to think I might just manage to get through it without falling apart. It was nearly one in the morning by the time I got to my brother's house. I had to beat on the door to get him to let me in, but the good part was that he was half-asleep and I managed to avoid an interrogation.

Jimmy was surprised but pleased when he discovered I'd moved down.

I had the feeling he was a lot more thrilled that I'd brought his things, but at least he included me amongst the things he was glad to see.

I left my brother's house as soon as I got up and went into town to grab a paper. I needed some kind of transportation that was fairly reliable, a place to stay, and a job. Thankfully, I didn't need the job with absolute desperation. I'd put just about everything I'd earned in the bank since I'd gone to live with the Thornes. It was a comfortable little nest egg. I could pay first and last month rent and utility deposits and I'd still have a nice little egg, but I had a growing egg in my belly and that wasn't going to be cheap—even if I could get help from welfare—which I really hated to do.

Beggars couldn't be choosers, though.

I decided I could put that off for a little while and focus on the job and the apartment once I'd tracked down a fairly decent ride. My brother looked it over and told me it was a junk heap, but he agreed he could probably help me keep it running for a while. Luckily for me, he was a fine mechanic and no matter how much he disapproved of me he considered that family should always stick together.

I discovered it was blessing that survival took so much effort. I managed to stay so busy at first that I hardly thought about the Thornes more than a hundred times a day. After a couple of weeks, I was so tired and disheartened from job hunting that I'd carved that down to not much more than fifty.

I had to settle for a cashier position at a 'shooting gallery'—which was how my brother described working at a convenience store due to the fact that they were so infamous about being robbed. At least it had bullet proof-glass that separated the cashier from the robbers.

Of course that didn't mean it was safe going to and from the 'cage', but I decided it would have to do until I could find something else. I couldn't afford to just live off the money I'd saved. I might need it for an emergency.

Jimmy surprised and pleased me by taking on a part time job without me even having to prod him into it. Of course, he spent most of his money on himself and the girl he was in hot pursuit of, but at least he was covering most of his own expenses.

I managed to make it all the way to my fifth month before either Jimmy or my brother said anything about the growing mound. I didn't know if they just hadn't noticed, though, or they'd decided I was getting fat and hadn't wanted to point it out.

Jimmy and I had a fight about it.

Then me and my brother had a fight about it.

Actually, it probably couldn't be described as 'a' fight. We went round and round about it regularly. Both Buddy and my son demanded to know who'd gotten me knocked up so that they could find them and beat the crap out of them for knocking me up and then dumping me.

They didn't believe I wasn't the dumpee.

I didn't suppose I could actually claim that I'd dumped the father—especially when I didn't know which one of them *was* the father—but I thought that was just a technicality. I'd chosen to leave. That made me the dumper. Of course, if I'd hung around I would probably have been the dumpee, but I hadn't given them the chance.

I was so sorry I hadn't. With the best will in the world, I couldn't put them out of my mind. I missed them so much it was a constant pain, no matter how much I worked at trying convince myself it wasn't.

And on top of everything else, I was so horny I could hardly stand it.

I hadn't expected that to be a problem. It never had been before.

I was sitting on my stool at work, pondering it, wondering if it was hormonal or just the sudden lack after having all I could possibly want for so long, when a car pulled up in front of the store.

Sighing, I got off my stool. I hadn't had a customer in hours and I'd actually hoped I wouldn't see another one before the other cashier arrived to take over.

The car hadn't even pulled to the curb when three more pulled in.

"Wouldn't you know it?" I muttered. "They must have discovered they were out of beer and it was close to midnight."

I plopped back down on my stool when I saw the man that got out of the first car, pressing a hand to my heart because it felt like it was going to beat right out of my chest.

Gavin looked the store over and then his gaze zeroed in on me.

My mind went chaotic with the thoughts tumbling through it.

What were the odds, I wondered, that he'd show up at *this* convenience store?

He scanned the store as he came in and then strode directly to the counter. The doorbell tinkled again—and then again. I stared back at Gavin for a moment and then flicked a glance toward the door as the other customers came in.

I went catatonic when I saw that it was Luke—and Jessie, Jared, and Bret.

I decided I'd completely lost my mind.

I couldn't think of anything to say.

"Gavin! What are y'all doing here?"

Alright, that was lame, but I was lucky even to manage that much.

Gavin scanned the bulletproof glass separating us. "What the hell are you doing here?" he demanded.

I gaped at him. "I work here."

His lips tightened.

"Is that why you left?" Luke asked.

I saw when I glanced at him that he was looking at my stomach. I covered it self-consciously. I realized when I glanced down at my belly, though, that by now there was no pretending it was anything except what it was and I glanced around at them uneasily.

"You thought we'd be pissed off that you accidentally got pregnant?" Jared growled angrily.

I felt my face redden, but that was a good thing. All of the blood had rushed from my head and I needed it before I fainted. "It wasn't an accident."

Their reaction wasn't what I'd expected. Some of the tension seemed to go out of them. "It wasn't?" Luke asked. "You're saying you meant to get pregnant?"

I shook my head. "It's alright. I signed the agreement, remember?"

"No," Gavin said implacably. "It isn't alright. You weren't going to tell us a damned thing about it, were you?"

I swallowed with an effort. My heart was beating so hard it felt like it was lodged in my throat. "I didn't think you'd want to know."

"That's cold," Bret muttered.

"And just plain wrong, damn it!" Jessie growled. "It's a Thorne."

I stared at him uneasily. "It's a Bridges."

"But it *belongs* to one of us!" Gavin growled.

"It belongs to me!" I said shakily.

"Shut up, Gav! Don't you see you've scared her?" Luke snapped. "That wasn't what he meant, baby. Honest to god!" He put his hands on the glass. "Come out of there and talk to us."

Actually, I was a lot more comfortable with the glass between us. I smiled at him a little weakly. "Not if you're going to be mad at me."

"I'm going to be seriously pissed off if you don't come out of there!" Gavin growled.

"That'll convince her to come out!" Jared said dryly.

"Nobody's angry with you, baby," Luke said coaxingly. "Just come out."

They looked pretty pissed off to me.

"We just want you to come home," Jessie said.

I shot a startled glance at him. I couldn't catch my breath for several moments. "You do? You mean it? You're not just saying that so I'll come out?" I added suspiciously.

"He isn't," Gavin said implacably. He met my gaze for a long moment when I looked at him. "We miss you. *I* miss you like hell!"

"I missed you." I glanced at the others. "I missed all of you so much."

"Why did you leave then?"

"I thought you'd be angry about the baby."

"You might at least have given us the benefit of doubt, Steph," Jared said angrily.

I shook my head at him. "If you'd said you didn't want it … if you'd demanded that I abort it …. I couldn't take a chance." I glanced at them all. "I wanted *your* baby, not just 'a' baby. I didn't want to know if you didn't want me to have it."

"Well, I hope you know this is going to be damned awkward!" Jessie said shortly. "We don't know who's going to be uncle and who's going to be daddy."

"Don't be a fucking jackass!" Jared growled. "Like it's *her* fault we don't know! Anyway, we can get a paternity test. Then whoever the father is can marry her."

"Like hell!" Gavin growled. "As if we don't know the minute you got the ring on her finger it would be 'my' wife and you'd cut the rest of us out!"

"And I suppose you wouldn't?"

"Well, there's not going to be a damned wedding till we get this straightened out," Luke said tightly. "We'll need a pre-nup or something."

Gavin stared at him. "Good god, Luke! They don't make pre-nups like that! I can just imagine the look on the lawyer's face!"

I could, too. I listened to them argue about it very happily until my relief came in the door. He stared at the men in front of the 'cage' for several moments and finally edged around them. I met him at the door and let him in.

Gavin wedged his foot in the door before I could close it again, shoved the door wider and snatched me out. "Better," he said complacently, hauling me up against him for a deeply satisfying kiss.

"You done here?" Luke asked when Gavin finally released me.

I nodded a little dizzily.

"She quits," he told the cashier.

"Luke!"

He gave me a look. I sighed. "I quit. I'm going home."

Luke pulled me into his arms, hugging me tightly for several moments before he drew away to kiss me. The minute he loosened his grip on me, Jessie reeled me in for a third. Jared shoved Bret out of the way and grabbed me up for a kiss.

"The clerk's going to think we're all crazy," I murmured when Bret had kissed me and we'd all left the store.

"We are … crazy about you," Gavin agreed. "Now all we have to do is hold Jimmy and your brother off while we collect your things and we can head for home."

"Oh hell!" I muttered. "This is going to be interesting."

"You think? Wait until Mom finds out you're pregnant and we don't if it's mine, Gavin's, or one of theirs," Luke said dryly, nodding toward his cousins.

I smiled at him. "It's ours," I said complacently.

* * * *

I've never been able to figure out why, in a supposedly 'free' country, people always watched other people resentfully whenever they chose a lifestyle *they* didn't approve of. The entire concept of freedom was that each person was free, not just the ones with the fucking opinions!

Needless to say, nobody approved. I wasn't even completely sure my guys would've approved if the circumstances had been different. We'd gone in to it together, though. We'd spent months growing together, growing comfortable, falling into a routine that worked, and pleased all of us most of the time.

If it hadn't begun like that—as a game nobody expected to last—I don't think it would've worked out.

Luckily, it did. The two months I'd been in hell sparked a solid month of getting reacquainted that was fun for all!

The rest of the world excluded, of course.

Marriage was a hot topic for a while, but eventually died off when nobody could agree on it. I was fine with it. I felt like I had all the commitment I needed, a total devotion to me that seemed likely to last as long as any marriage I was familiar with. I didn't feel a need to have a ring on my finger and besides that I realized the guys were right. Marriage always seemed to change things and not always for the better. As long as there was some doubt, as long as we all knew we had to work on our relationship, there was magic.

In due time, I produced a daughter—Jared's. He was like a rooster, crowing about it at every opportunity, which nearly got his ass beat by the others. They didn't complain, per se, but I could see they felt a little left out.

I gave myself a brief respite to recover and managed to produce a son for Gavin. I had my doubts for a while, but I finally succeeded in making each a father and they seemed happy enough with one—three girls and two boys.

Good thing, too, because that was five for me, six including Jimmy, who by that time was married and expecting my first grandchild, and I wasn't old fashioned enough to want a baseball team.

I don't guess anybody would consider me old fashioned, though, not with five men. I was hated all over half the state for being greedy and grabbing up all the Thornes, but my guys loved me, my babies loved me. I didn't suffer over the resentment of the single women.

Submission—who would ever have thought it was the most powerful weapon in a woman's arsenal?

The End.

Read an excerpt from Kimberly Zant's SURRENDER.

Surrender
By
Kimberly Zant

Chapter One

I suppose I should have found the wording of the contract reassuring, because it certainly indicated that everything was completely above board and the dark fears circling the back of my mind like a flock of black crows were groundless. Instead, a sense of unreality swept through me as I read back over the long list of terms I was agreeing to, tying my nervous stomach into a harder knot.

Desperation, I thought, looking up at the man seated across from me, was a hard task master—and destitution the equivalent of hell on earth because the fear of it was enough to make an ordinarily rational person, like myself, consider making a deal with the devil.

He didn't look like the devil. He looked like a completely ordinary mortal.

"Is there a problem?"

I cleared my throat, which felt as if it had closed together. "It says if I fail to … uh … fail to perform according to expectations, I can be terminated immediately without compensation."

He gave me an impatient look. "I explained that to you when you applied for the position. Would you like to go over everything again?"

He had. I'd just been too addled to really take it in, because from the moment I'd realized exactly what I was being hired to do my mind had gone perfectly blank.

I felt my face redden. "It's just … does that mean if he isn't satisfied with my performance? Or, by fail, does it mean if I refused to do anything I'd agreed to do? I did mention that I hadn't actually done much of this before? A lot of these things, I mean. The things on the list aren't … aren't really familiar to me, experience wise, so I couldn't really claim to be good at this."

He looked a little uncomfortable. "That clause goes to willingness to perform the various … acts that have been described. A refusal to do so upon demand would be a breach of contract, which would make all terms null and void. The client is aware of your relative inexperience."

I nodded at the clarification, though I didn't feel terribly reassured. I felt like kicking myself. The money being offered was staggering considering it was only for a six-week stint. I wasn't stupid. I had known going in to the first interview that it had to be something really radical for them to be offering so much. Lying to myself wasn't going to change a thing. I'd suspected, just from the wording of the ad, in spite of how carefully it had been composed, that this was, in effect, sex for hire. As shocked and horrified as I'd been once everything had been baldly laid out for me, though, I hadn't gotten up and walked out. I'd stayed and listened to the entire spiel, and I'd allowed them to interview me. The list of 'requirements' was part of the initial interview.

They'd been very cool and professionally impersonal about it, but I'd cringed inside and stumbled over every answer.

I suppose I'd never really believed that they would actually offer the position to me. I was hardly sex goddess material, and I was certain my prudishness must be glaringly obvious, which would also make it evident that my knowledge and experience of the subject under discussion was practically nil.

I'd known before I'd even arrived for the interview, though, that I couldn't afford to turn it down, whatever it entailed—short of murder. I needed the money way too badly to worry about silly old things like pride or morals or even doing things I might not especially like. People who weren't facing disaster and starvation could afford to have principles. I couldn't.

'Whatever sexual acts requested' though—why, I wondered, would they have any interest in me? I'd seen the competition. Most of the other women had been younger than me—college age young, pretty, well built. A lot of them had had that 'road weary' look that proclaimed a vast deal of sexual experience and I'd been sure one of them would be chosen. Why would they choose a 'ripe' tomato like me, who was not the least bit girlish in any way? I'd had two children and I had the 'womanly' body to prove it. Sure I'd tried really hard to battle nature, because my husband–ex husband–had brow beat me about 'letting myself go' until I was terrified gaining five pounds would earn me the boot, but no amount of dieting or exercise could undo what carrying a baby for nine months could do to a body, let alone going through it twice.

Maybe it was the 'submissive' thing?

I was certainly *used* to being submissive and I supposed that showed. I hadn't been terribly assertive before my marriage and having been a total idiot and bound myself to a tyrant with serious control issues the little assertiveness I'd had before had been crushed under his heavy hand.

Regardless, I still wasn't certain I could carry this off.

My ex was going to get my children, though, if I didn't come up with a *lot* of money fast, I reminded myself.

For *them*, I could be a tigress. I *would* be—a submissive one, granted, but the *will* to take this on, that was mine.

Smiling weakly, I took up the pen.

"If you decide to terminate the agreement at any time, you have that option, but the full payment will not be due to you. It will be prorated according to time put in."

I looked at him blankly.

"For instance, half if you only stay three weeks instead of the full six."

I nodded, dragging in a shaky breath. I could do this. I needed *all* the money.

When I'd signed it, he notarized the contract and got up to run off a copy for me. He handed me a card with an address on it after he'd handed me a copy. "You're to report to this address tomorrow morning."

I stared at the card, feeling faint that everything seemed to be moving so fast. "He didn't want to meet me first?"

"*They*," he corrected. "It was a group that selected this fantasy holiday. They were present at the interview, observing from the room adjoining, and selected you from among the other applicants."

"Group?" I asked weakly, feeling more faint. I wasn't certain what startled me more, the discovery that they'd been watching me while I was interviewed or the 'group' part. Actually, I was certain. It hadn't occurred to me, at all, that it would be a group. And that unnerved me a lot more than the fact that I'd been watched without my knowledge.

He gave me an irritated look. "Is that a problem?"

I swallowed with an effort. Safety was assured. I'd had a thorough health exam before I was even allowed to interview and the same was required of 'guests'. No one, least of all the company, wanted to have to face the unpleasant repercussions of a lawsuit. Moreover, I would be allowed to call it off at any point and a company representative would be checking in every other day to make certain none of the rules had been violated. It *had* to be voluntary. That was part of his—their—fantasy. "No," I said weakly, realizing that it had probably taken a group to fork out the money the company was asking for this arrangement plus the money I was getting.

"The money has already been deposited in a holding account. You'll be given the access number once you've completed the job. And, of course, if you decide to terminate early, the amount unearned will be removed from the account before you're given the number."

Dismissed, I had nothing to do but leave, but it took a supreme effort to push myself up from the chair. Wobbly kneed, completely addled by the thoughts rattling my brain, I stuffed the card and my copy of the contract into my purse and let myself out.

I sat staring into space for a while once I'd gotten into my car.

I'd just signed away six weeks of my life to play submissive sex toy to a 'group' of men I'd never even set eyes on.

Think positive, I told myself. Six weeks wasn't a lot when it meant at the end of it my troubles with my ex would be over.

I can do this, I told myself.

My mother was never going to know. All she knew at this point was that she was babysitting for six weeks so I could take a job that would guarantee I had the money to win my case and get custody of my children.

If I didn't freak and do anything stupid, *nobody* was ever going to know.

* * * *

I ran out of steam before I got to the door of the mansion. Breathless with fear and weak all over, it took all I could do to manage the last few steps and ring the doorbell … and to fight the urge to whirl around and flee, though, in all honesty, I wasn't sure I had the strength to flee.

Partly, it was the mansion itself that intimidated me. I was certain, at first, that I must have the address wrong, but after studying the card and the house number for ten minutes, I decided I wasn't hallucinating. The mansion, I decided, must belong to the company, the 'game group' that arranged these entertaining little fantasies for the truly wealthy and jaded, or in my case, the well-to-do and jaded and/or kinky. I wasn't certain where that put my little group, but I had already decided that it was a group because they couldn't afford an individual 'game', which still put them in a staggering income bracket if they could afford to pay me thousands *and* take off for a six week 'vacation'.

Facing the unknown was rather akin to facing a firing squad, though, and that was the biggest part of my anxiety. True, I had a dim idea of what I was facing, but it was just enough to scare me shitless.

The man that answered the doorbell didn't look like a butler, despite my expectations to the contrary. In point of fact, and despite my anxieties, the moment we made eye contact a stunning force of attraction rolled over me that demolished the last of my wits.

He was tall and dark—thirtyish I thought, maybe late twenties. His face was unquestionably attractive in a very manly-male way, though not precisely handsome, his build, at least from what I could tell considering the expensive suit he was wearing, was just as appealing as the face.

He looked me up and down with a slow thoroughness that made me feel naked which should have insulted me, or intimidated me even more, but instead had the effect of making my heart rev and warmth flutter in my belly. "Anna," he said finally. "Prompt. I like that."

He didn't sound like a butler either. His voice was deep and fired synapses in my brain as if he'd reached out and run a caressing hand over my breasts.

He didn't look at me like a servant … or at least the way I thought a servant would look at a guest.

"Come in," he said after a moment. "I'll show you to your room and then we can get down to business."

I blinked, undecided now whether he *was* in fact the butler, or one of the 'group' I was to meet. Nodding jerkily, I followed him across the expansive marble tiled foyer and up a wide, winding stairway to the second floor. Carpet, so thick I felt as if I was wading through water, covered the upper hallway. He led me down it to a bedroom on the back side of the house and opened the door, indicating that I was to go in.

My heart was in my throat as I preceded him and set my small bag on the floor by the huge four poster bed that held center stage in the room. I got a fleeting impression of opulence everywhere, in the massive, ornately carved furniture, the heavy drapes, thick carpet and expensive knickknacks here and there, but I was too nervous to gawk. As soon as I'd set my battered little suitcase down, I turned to face him uneasily.

He closed the door. Folding his arms, he leaned back against the panel, studying me. It made me uneasy that I couldn't tell anything about his expression.

"You were acquainted with the rules and the list of what we expect of you?"

The question was unexpected. I blinked at him and finally nodded speechlessly, unable even to find my voice for a polite 'yes'.

His dark brows inched up his forehead. "Just the same, I think I'll go over them," he said. Pushing away from the door, he approached me and I realized abruptly that he was a good bit taller and broader than I'd first thought.

"You are a submissive and as such will be expected to obey without question anything I, or the others, ask of you. We are familiar with the list. We compiled it and nothing will be asked of you that you have not willingly agreed to, in writing. Therefore no, is no longer a part of your vocabulary. You have been given a safety word, but I will not expect to hear it unless you are ready to throw in the towel."

My mouth felt like the Mohave desert. I swallowed with an effort and managed to nod again that I understood.

"Take off your clothes and let me have a look at you."

I felt my eyes widen, but as his dark brows descended, I looked down and began to fumble nervously with the buttons of my blouse. He watched me keenly while I stripped, unnerving me more. By the time I'd stripped down to my bra and panties my face was flashing like a neon sign and the red went all the way down to my breasts. I looked up at him a little hopefully when I'd gotten to that point—hopeful that was as far as I would be expected to go.

No such luck.

"The rest," he said implacably.

Dragging in a shuddering breath, I complied, resisting the urge to try to cover myself with my hands and completely unable to figure out what to do with them when it dawned on me that I shouldn't try to cover myself. I flinched in spite of all I could do when he reached for my breasts, but gritted my teeth and held perfectly still while he examined them, letting out a shaky breath when he released them after a moment and walked around me, looking me over with a slow attention to detail that I felt sure missed no flaw.

His eyes were dark and smoldering with heat when he faced me again. Reaching down, he dragged his fingers through the curls at the apex of my thighs, making me jump. "Au natural," he said speculatively. "Appealing, and yet I like to be able to see my pretty thing."

I felt my face heat again as he withdrew lifted his gaze from my mound and met mine. As if that settled something in his mind, he moved away, striding toward a door I hadn't noticed before. Opening it, he turned to look at me expectantly. "Come along, Anna. First a bath and then I'll trim that."

Trim that? My hair *there*?

Submissive! I reminded myself and moved toward him jerkily, standing dumbstruck while he adjusted the water in the huge tub that looked as if it could easily accommodate a half a dozen people at one time—three or four anyway.

Indicating with a nod that I was to get in, I did so, settling almost with a sense of relief because me legs had felt as if they would give way and dump me in the floor at any moment.

Taking up a position near the door, he watched me bathe. I wasn't sure if that was because he wanted to make certain I was thorough, or if he merely wanted to watch, but I reminded myself, again, that I had, to all intents and purposes, contracted to be his sex slave for the duration and that meant he did whatever he pleased and I submitted to whatever he pleased—as long as it didn't violate the rules I'd agreed to.

And it occurred to me rather forcefully as I mentally reviewed those rules that I'd agreed to pretty much anything so long as it didn't entail injury to me.

Either the hot water or just plain old weariness began to dissipate the tension as I bathed, slowly, not because I was trying to give him a show, but because I felt awkward at being watched. I wasn't even *almost* relaxed, but the edge wore off.

It felt strange to be watched, made me conscious of every moment of my hands in a way I never had been before. On the other hand, despite my nervousness, there was no doubt in my mind that his gaze was appreciative and it warmed me in a purely sensual way.

I would've been willing to sit in the tub until my skin pruned since being watched wasn't nearly as unnerving as some of the thoughts rambling through my chaotic brain, but he moved away from the door after a few minutes and picked up a thick towel. Instead of handing it to me, he settled it on the top step of the two that led up to the tub and indicated that I was to get out of the tub and sit on it. My belly instantly knotted up, but I complied, sitting on the towel uneasily and placing my feet on the step below me.

Crouching in front of me, he grasped first one ankle and then the other, moving them wide apart, and then pushing my thighs wide when I kept my knees together. The instinct to snap them back together the moment he let go was strong, but one look at his face was enough to convince me not to try.

He combed his fingers through the hair on my mound and then placed his thumbs on my nether lips, pushing them apart and studying me. My color fluctuated two or three times during the process. My belly clenched and unclenched frantically, but warmth flooded my sex in spite of that and I wondered uncomfortably if he would be able to see he made me wet just looking at me.

After studying my pussy for a handful of seconds, he grasped my hips and slid me forward until my buttocks were resting on the edge of the step and I had to put my arms behind me to keep my balance. I watched him as he got up and collected a razor and shaving cream. When he returned, kneeling between my thighs, he grasped my knees and spread my legs as wide as they would go.

The shaving cream was cold, but it was the stroke of his fingers as he applied it that made me jump, that sent shockwaves of anticipation through me and stole my breath. He flicked a glance at me as he smoothed the shaving cream between my thighs, all the way back to my rectum.

I hadn't even realized I had any hair back there. It embarrassed me to learn that I did. I tried to focus my gaze elsewhere as he began to shave me, but I couldn't help it. My gaze kept wandering back to his face.

His expression was one of concentration. It accentuated the almost harsh plains and angles of his face. His hair, somewhat longer than was currently fashionable, was very dark but not ethnic black. Rather, it was a deep, almost black, brown with just a hint of russet highlights. His brows were thick and virtually straight. His eyes would've made any woman envious. His lashes were thick, black, long, and curling, shielding eyes that were somewhere between gray and green, a pale combination of the two colors.

His nose was exceptional, too, a hawkish sort of blade but far more appealing for the sharp definition of bridge and nostrils than a fleshy blob, even though the cut of his nostrils was perilously close to a perpetual sneer. I thought it made him look extraordinarily aristocratic.

Next to eyes, his mouth was his best feature. Wide, but not overly so, his lips were as well defined as his nose, neither too thin nor too full, and looked firm and hard like the rest of him. My belly fluttered as I stared at that mouth and images flooded my mind of what it would feel like.

He was clean shaven, but dark hair shadowed his lean cheeks, strong jaw, and forceful chin. High testosterone, I mused, realizing that was probably a good part of my nervousness. I'd read somewhere that it actually oozed from their pores and women, even though they weren't aware they could smell it, in fact could, and it effected their libido.

As he shaved me, his brows slowly inched together in a frown of concentration and a thick lock of hair fell across his brow. He used the fingers of his free hand to stretch the fleshy outer lips of my sex taut while he shaved. It seemed impersonal and yet I noticed after a few moments that his hand wasn't quite as steady as it had been when he'd begun.

When he flicked a glance at my face again, the green irises had virtually disappeared for the darkness of his dilated pupils.

Rising, he rinsed the razor and returned, stroking his fingers along the area he'd shaved to test his thoroughness. Apparently satisfied, he studied the wedge of hair on my belly above my cleft and trimmed it down to a small wedge that made me wonder why he'd left anything at all. I'd been denuded of hair from the beginning of my cleft all the way back and the hair on my mound trimmed until it hid nothing at all.

Leaning back slightly, he studied the effect and finally nodded. "Rinse and dry off."

He left the room while I was drying.

Wondering if we were done for now, or if he was waiting in the bedroom for my first sexual performance, I followed him uneasily after several moments and discovered that he was selecting—*something* from the armoire. My suitcase had disappeared. I felt my stomach take a freefall as I studied the garments I was, apparently, expected to wear.

Dropping them onto the bed, he summoned me to stand before a full length mirror. "This is the way I expect you to groom yourself for the duration," he said in a deep voice that sounded more than a little husky as he stood behind me and stroked a hand over my denuded pussy.

A jolt went through me at his first touch for I discovered the skin that had been covered with my pubic hair was far more sensitive than I'd ever noticed before—as if it wasn't shocking enough to *see* so clearly what had been veiled by hair before!

As I'd suspected, the little 'moustache' he left didn't cover anything. It was almost more like an exclamation point to draw attention to my pussy than anything else. The outer lips that hid my sex looked plumper than I'd thought they were and actually pretty obscene to me, but I was still relieved because my nether lips felt swollen and pouty from his focus on them and I was glad that *that* part wasn't visible.

"The correct response is 'yes, sir'."

I struggled to find my voice and dutifully repeated the words.

"Wait here."

I watched his reflection in the mirror as he moved briskly toward the garments he'd selected. He picked up a bustier and returned. When he'd fitted the black leather piece around my waist and told me to hold it while he fastened the back, I saw that the piece only covered me from just beneath the breasts to a little more than mid-way down my hips, stopping just above my new exclamation point patch of hair. When he'd fastened it, he moved around in front of me and adjusted my breasts which were half in and half out of the thing. Scooping them from the restricting garment, he almost seemed to be 'fluffing' them. After staring at them a moment, he caught a nipple between the thumb and forefinger of each hand and plucked at them until my nipples were standing at attention and the rest of me was quivering weakly.

I saw when he moved away at last that the top of the bustier formed more of a shelf for a display than a cup, lifting my breasts as if in offering but covering nothing.

He stood behind me for several moments, studying my reflection and finally summoned me to follow him back to the bed.

He caught my chin in one hand when we stopped there, tipping my face up so that I had to meet him eye to eye. "Have you ever engaged in anal sex?"

My eyes widened. I'd been asked that as part of the interview, but I'd, conveniently, closed my mind to that. I shook my head.

He studied my face for several moments, as if he could read my mind, and finally nodded as if it was the answer he'd expected. "Turn around and lean over the bed."

I gulped, my stomach clenching harder, but oddly enough I discovered my sex was damper than before, when, by rights, the comment and all it entailed should have been enough to dry up all my juices with anxiety. Dragging in a shaky breath, I turned and did as I was told, spreading my legs wide for him and turning my head to watch as he moved to the small cabinet beside the bed, taking something from a drawer.

I'd never seen anything like the thing he pulled out. It looked strikingly similar to a dildo except that it was tapered to a narrow tip at one end and it looked as if it was made of a far softer material than dildos generally were. He squeezed lubricant out of a tube and spread it over the thing thickly. I caught my breath as he moved behind me again and pushed the cheeks of my ass wide with the fingers of one hand.

"Relax. As I insert this, you need to bear down with your stomach muscles to open the rectum."

My heart was in my throat, but as I felt him begin to push, I did as I'd been told, panting as I felt the thing penetrating me. Discomfort went through me as it penetrated, a sense of fullness followed as he pushed it slowly inside until it could go no further, but, thankfully, it wasn't nearly as uncomfortable as I'd expected.

"Now clench and hold for me and stand upright."

Disconcerted that he obviously meant to leave it, more embarrassed than uncomfortable, I pushed myself up from the bed as he returned to the nightstand. The sense of fullness increased as I straightened. It wasn't comfortable by any stretch of the imagination, but I was relieved that it wasn't painful.

I was still focused on that strange sensation of having something up my ass when he moved up behind me again. I felt a tug along the back edge of the bustier, as if he was attaching something. Catching my shoulders, he turned me to face him and knelt down. I merely stared at him when he pushed one hand between my legs. He looked up at me, his dark brows rising and nudged at my legs with his hand until I shifted them apart. Reaching between my thighs, he caught hold of whatever it was he'd attached to the back of the bustier and pulled it between my legs—into the cleft of my ass. I frowned, thinking it was just something that would be adjusted. I discovered otherwise.

It tightened as he pulled on it, pressing against my rectum and pushing the thing he'd inserted deeper. Trying not to wiggle, I stared down at the top of his dark head and his hands, unable to see what he was doing. I felt the thing cinched upward, though, felt it compress one side of the outer lips of my sex. He drew it up and fastened it to the front of the bustier, cinching it uncomfortably tight. I reached down instinctively to adjust myself, but he slapped my hand—not hard, but in rebuke.

I snatched my hand back, feeling mildly embarrassed and rather like a child that had been chastised. He delved between my legs again and pulled up another strap catching the other lip my sex as he had the first and making it obvious that it had been no accident. As he fastened the strap to the other edge of the front, cinching it as he had the first, I felt his hot breath waft over the very delicate and sensitive inner lips of my sex. My clit swelled instantly to a hard, throbbing knot and felt about twice its normal size.

He flicked a glance up at my face when he'd finished fastening the 'binding' then returned his attention to his handiwork, making minor adjustments with his fingers that made my knees feel like jelly.

"You will keep the plug in at all times unless it is necessary to remove it for your needs, then you will replace it and reattach the restraints between your legs just as I've adjusted them. In a few days, once you've grown accustomed to this one, we'll move up to a slightly larger size plug."

I stared down at his dark head, abruptly feeling mulish. I didn't want anything bigger in my ass! I already felt uncomfortable and it boggled my mind to think I was supposed to walk around, sit, stand, whatever—trying to carry on as if I *didn't* have something shoved up my ass that was impossible to ignore or get used to.

Although the first moments of sheer terror had long since worn off, though, it had left me vulnerable to my desperate needs, allowed me the calm to realize that however reluctant I might feel, I had better keep it to myself. I hadn't expected this, but I realized I probably should have—would have if I'd had any clue about this business.

It didn't hurt. I couldn't complain to the referee, not honestly, that it did and I knew my acceptance, and my money, depended on complete submission, which meant compliance to anything they wanted of me.

No, as he'd said, was no longer a part of my vocabulary. If I uttered my safety word, we were done and I went home as bad off as before.

He told me to sit down on the bed. When I did so, he lifted one of my legs and slipped a sheer hose over it, adjusting the elasticized upper edge on my thigh. Bending that knee, he settled my foot on the bed and lifted the other leg, repeating the process.

He sent me to stand before the mirror and study what he'd done so that I'd know how I was expected to dress hereafter.

Despite my suspicions about his adjustments, I was horrified to discover that the 'restraints' which I'd thought were primarily there to make sure the plug stayed put, pulled the outer lips of my sex back so that the darker pink inner petals were fully, obscenely exposed. It had felt 'airish'. I'd felt the brush of my thighs against sensitive flesh with every step I took, but I'd still thought I couldn't possibly *be* as exposed as I'd felt like I was.

He came to stand behind me again, this time slipping my arms into a filmy robe that was the next thing to completely transparent. He tapped my chin to make me look up at him as he tied the thin ribbon at the neck of the thing. "One final thing—You aren't allowed to cum unless you're given permission. At any time that you feel that you are about to cum, you must announce it and request permission. If, and only if, it is granted, you may cum. Otherwise, you'll be punished for disobedience. And if you make a habit of disobeying, you've failed to live up to your part of the agreement, which means it will be terminated at my discretion."

My heart tried to beat its way out of my chest at that. I stared at him owl eyed, wondering what sort of punishment they had in mind.

Nothing to do with pain or that could cause injury! That was absolutely forbidden.

I hoped he realized that.

Not that I thought I had anything to worry about. According to my ex, I was frigid. I didn't agree with him, but I'd certainly never been oversexed and I couldn't imagine having a problem containing myself.

It wasn't until a good bit later that I realized that there were ways to be punished that didn't fall under either category that were nevertheless excruciating. And not being allowed to cum, no matter what they did, was the worst of all—until I discovered the other!

Chapter Two

A pair of heels finished the ensemble. He knelt before me to slip them onto my feet. When he'd adjusted both shoes, he simply stayed where he was, looking up at me for several moments … or rather the exposed pink lips of my sex. After a brief hesitation, he caught my legs, urging me to part them.

I stared down at his dark head as I did so, wondering what he meant to do.

A shock wave rolled over me when he opened his mouth over my clit. My knees instantly turned to water as he tugged at it with his mouth, sucked it, and then tugged again. Heat rolled through my mind, making me feel weak all over and making it almost impossible to maintain my balance. Mindlessly, I dug my fingers into his hair as he continued licking and sucking until I was shaking all over and thought I'd wilt to the floor.

He disentangled my fingers, caught my wrists and held them at my sides.

A soft moan escaped me in spite of all I could do to contain it. Almost as if he'd been waiting for that reaction, he stopped. Rising to his feet he studied my face for several moments and finally told me to follow him.

I stared after him blankly for several moments and finally, as he reached the door, managed to command my feet to move. I was in a daze, however, as I followed him down the stairs and it took every ounce of concentration to keep my wobbly legs from buckling.

I was so dazed still as I followed him down the lower hallway and into a room that it was several moments before I realized there were men in the room awaiting us.

"There," the man leading me said, pointing to a spot on the floor.

I stopped, wondering if I was supposed to sit down or just stand.

The other men rose and approached me.

There were four—five if I counted the first.

Surprise was my first impression, because I was still too rattled by what he'd done and my racing pulse to feel much of anything else. Not one of them looked to be more than their late twenties and the plainest of the group was what I would've considered 'nice' looking any day of the week.

I'd been trying very hard since I discovered the day before that I was to entertain a group *not* to consider what sort of men would pay so much for a submissive, but it had nagged at the back of my mind that they would *not* be the sort of men who could get a woman without paying for her.

These men were as far from hideous, wrinkled old men as they could possibly get. I was fairly certain that not one was even as old as I was. They were clean cut, well dressed—expensively dressed, handsome, well built.

Why in the world, I wondered, would they even consider hiring a woman, much less me?

But then maybe the buzz from that tongue lashing I'd gotten on my clit had really scrambled my brains?

I studied them uneasily as they studied me, flinching in spite of all I could do as first one and then another lifted a hand and caressed a breast, an arm, a thigh, my buttocks. One of the men bore a striking resemblance to the man who'd been grooming me and I knew he had to be related. He was a little taller, I thought, and had a slighter build, though he was a long way from skinny. Two of them were blonds, although one of the two had more of a strawberry blond hair color and the other an ash blond. The fifth had blue black hair and was swarthy enough I thought he might have had a drop or two of some ethnic mix—but it eluded me what that might have been. Of them all, he was the most exotically, classically handsome, borderline 'pretty boy' but just a hair too manly looking with his square jaw and five o'clock shadow to earn that sobriquet.

Their personalities, I fancied, were reflected on their faces as they looked me over. The one with ash blond hair was either shy or just reserved. His expression was guarded. He didn't touch, but he looked me over thoroughly. I saw a deep hunger in his gaze as he lifted his head to study my face that made everything inside of me grow hot and jittery.

'Pretty boy' had the look of a player. He was struggling to maintain an air of bored interest, but I could see that his eyes were stormy and his hand shook faintly as he stroked it over my breast and watched my nipple pucker and stand erect. I sensed a good deal of tension in him, as if he was controlling himself with an effort, but that made it all the more obvious that what he really wanted to do that very moment was to throw me down on the couch or floor and fuck me senseless.

The man with the strawberry blond hair was open faced and, I thought, probably impetuous. He looked more like a randy teenager who could hardly contain his glee than a man approaching thirty.

The one I'd decided must be related to my groomer also had the 'air' of a player.

My groomer, who'd taken up a position by the fireplace while the others looked me over, seemed by far the most dark and dangerous of the bunch and the hardest to read. I had the impression that he was eldest, certainly the ringmaster, but it was more a matter of his aplomb than that he actually appeared older.

They moved away after a few moments, settling in their seats again.

I was told to sit by the man who'd prepared me. Moving to the couch he'd indicated, I sat—very carefully. Sitting, I discovered, nearly coming up off the couch again the second my ass hit it, pressed the plug I'd almost been able to dismiss from my mind more deeply inside of me and the restraints pulled uncomfortably at the lips of my sex. He shook his head. "Not like that. We like being able to see you."

He moved toward me. Directing me to put my arms behind me to brace myself and lean back, he grasped my knees and parted my thighs and then stepped back to study the effect. "When you're allowed to sit in our presence, you will sit like that to display our pretty pussy for us."

I felt my face reddening as he moved away again and I saw that the others were studying me. A warm wetness filled my channel, however, as I felt their gazes on me—or rather their 'pretty pussy'. It was more than a little unnerving to draw that many avid gazes, because none of them made any great attempt at that point even to pretend they weren't interested in what I was displaying for them. I saw Adam's apples bobbing. It made my own mouth go dry and the fear assailed me that, displayed as I was, they were going to see the effect their interest had on me.

I'd gone beyond damp. I felt downright wet, and I feared they already could see the effect and that was one of the reasons I could see a definite response against their breeches.

"Yes. I like that," said one of the men, clearing his throat before he spoke, the strawberry blond who looked to be around twenty five but might have been older.

"Anna, this is Chance," my groomer said, indicating the man that had spoken. "I'm Kaelen. The tall guy with the black hair is Dev, the blond, Cameron, and the skinny one there is my brother, Gareth. You may refer to us as by our given name, or sir."

I was actually surprised he hadn't ordered me to refer to them as lord, or master. I blinked a few times as I assimilated that and finally merely nodded, wondering if I would remember a single name if it actually became necessary to use it.

Submissive, I reminded myself—whatever he'd said, they were all my lords and masters for the duration and whatever doubts I'd had before that they would take full advantage and enjoy it thoroughly vanished. There was no reluctance and no conflict on any other their faces. Rather, they seemed to be struggling to hold back the urge to instantly sample their submissive.

I could do this, I thought, fighting a battle of my own.

The plug was an uncomfortable reminder that they were going to expect things of me that I wasn't used to doing, had never done, but they weren't at all hard on the eyes. That, I felt sure, would make it easier.

I hoped.

To my surprise, once he'd made the introductions, the other men got to their feet and left. Kaelen settled in a chair across from me, studying me through slumberous eyes for several moments before he lifted a hand and crooked a finger at me. I got up with an effort and crossed to him. "Down on your knees."

My sex clenched spasmodically and so did my rectum around the plug, or maybe it was the second that caused the first? I got down on my knees waiting for further instruction, watching with a mixture of uneasiness and, surprisingly, to me at least, almost a sense of breathless anticipation as he unfastened his belt and then pulled his zipper down. "Pleasure me."

My mouth went dry, but not from reluctance. After staring at him for several moments, waiting for him to produce the cock I'd been told to suck, I realized he was waiting for me to get it out myself. My hands shook as I delved the folds of his trousers and found the opening in his shorts. His cock was already hard and throbbing when I pulled it free of his clothing.

It was huge, to my eyes at least, but then again I wasn't used to looking at one quite this closely in broad daylight. It was long and thick, though. I discovered as I curled my hand around the hard shaft that my hand didn't span the circumference. His skin was smooth and surprisingly silky to the touch. The veins that ran the length were prominent. The rounded head was glossy. A tiny drop of moisture beaded the slit in the end.

I stared at that drop of moisture feeling my belly go weightless. My salivary glands went into over time, burning as they spasmed.

I flicked a glance at his face and finally shifted closer, opening my mouth and engulfing the glossy head. Surprise and pleasure flooded me as the taste and texture of his cock filled my mouth. Without conscious intent, I licked the slit at the tip, collecting the drop of moisture that had mesmerized me. A dizzying wave of heat rushed over me and I sucked the head with far more enthusiasm, using my tongue to explore the shape of it and trace the ridge just beneath his cock head.

He shifted a little restlessly. I wasn't certain if it was because he was impatient for me to take the whole thing into my mouth or because he liked what I was doing, but I opened my mouth wider and allowed his cock to slide as deeply into my mouth as I could, sucking on it as I lifted my head again. I released it, looking up at him. "Like that?"

I knew the mechanics of giving head, of course, but I'd never gotten the impression that I was particularly good at it.

His voice was harsh when he spoke and gravelly, as if with disuse. "Just like that. I want to cum in your mouth. I want you to suck me dry. You'd like that, wouldn't you, Anna?"

His voice, his words were strangely seductive, evoking a response inside of me I hardly recognized at first. My gaze flickered over his lean, handsome face, lingered for a long moment on his mouth and finally settled on his eyes. "Yes," I answered finally, realizing that I did, recognizing finally that the unidentifiable sensation I'd felt was a hunger that demanded appeasement.

"Yes, what?" he demanded, his voice a little hoarser than before.

"Yes ... Kaelen," I responded, my own voice husky with arousal.

Something flickered in his eyes. I had a sense that it was part surprise and, strangely enough, that my response had worked on him much the same as his had worked on me, aroused him even more. He settled his hand over mine where I gripped his cock. His hand dwarfed mine, covered it completely. Slowly, he guided my hand over his cock, teaching me the way he wanted to be pleasured.

"My dick is sensitive all over, root to tip, and all the way around," he murmured huskily as he guided my hand in a massage that brought pressure to bear all the way around and from root to tip. My balls, too." His eyes slid almost shut as he guided my hand to his testicles and I massaged them carefully, a little unnerved because I knew how easily a man could be hurt there.

The weight of his hand on mine stirred currents inside of me as surely as the feel of his cock beneath my hand did. I was almost disappointed when he lifted his hand at last.

Dragging in a shaky breath, I continued to massage him as he'd shown me, pausing now and then to suck the head of his cock and tease it with my tongue, sometimes taking as much of his cock into my mouth as I could and sucking his flesh. He remained perfectly still at first, but then, almost as if he could no longer bear to remain still, he began to move with me, thrusting upward as I stroked downward on his cock, surging into my mouth when I closed my mouth around him. My excitement seemed to grow apace with his and I began to stroke him faster as he moved more and more restlessly, his breath hitching in his chest and then sawing outward in harsh bursts of breath that grew more and more ragged. The hunger in me grew until I was suckling his flesh greedily, more focused on that than massaging him with my hand.

Uttering a sound that was part growl, part groan, he speared his fingers through my hair, clenching them tightly against my skull as his cock bucked in my mouth. My heart clenched. Drawing him deeply inside my mouth, I sucked harder. The hot, salty taste of his semen filled my mouth. I groaned, swallowing and lapping at him hungrily, sucking on his cock as if I could suck his seed from him. A shudder went through him as his body convulsed in orgasm. His harsh breaths became almost pained grunts as I milked him until he had no more to yield and continued to suck at him hungrily until he finally pushed me away.

He was gasping for breath when I lifted my head, his head tipped back against the chair. As if he felt my gaze, he lifted his head after a moment. His eyes were blazing as he stared down at me. His hands tightened around my skull, tugging me upward as he leaned forward, his gaze fastened with intent upon my mouth.

For several painful heartbeats I was certain he meant to kiss me. He hesitated within inches of my lips, though, his gaze flicking to mine. Something flickered in his eyes, caution, doubt, a sudden realization. I had no clear idea if I was right on any point. Slowly, he released his grip on my head and leaned back. I saw his throat move as he swallowed.

"Good girl," he said finally, his voice still hoarse.

It took me several moments to realize that it was a dismissal.

Disappointment flooded me as he looked away from me, focusing his attention on adjusting himself, and then zipped his pants. Anger flickered to life behind the disappointment, because my body was screaming for release—as certain as I'd been before that that was not going to be an issue for me. He'd made a point of telling me, in point of fact, that I wasn't allowed to cum without permission.

With an effort I tamped it as it dawned on me that I'd been hired— hired to submit to them, not to receive pleasure. I was a toy, not a person, and my feelings were of no consequence—in fact shouldn't even be an issue, I realized.

He wasn't my lover. He was my employer.

I felt like kicking myself, then.

He wasn't in the wrong. I was. I'd let myself get carried away and 'forgotten' that this wasn't something I was doing because I wanted to. It was a job I'd taken because I desperately needed money.

Uncertain of what I was supposed to do now, I returned to my seat on the sofa. He glanced at me frowningly as he got to his feet. It took me a second to realize what that frown was for.

Leaning back, I spread my legs, trying to ignore the fact that my clit was swollen with my own needs now and throbbing hard enough to make me miserable.

His brow cleared. He moved toward me, stood over me for several moments and finally leaned down. Currents of heat went through me and directly to my core as he sucked one of my nipples into his mouth, bit down on it just hard enough to make me suck in my breath and then lathed it with his tongue.

And then abandoned me.

Despite the pep talk I'd just had with myself, I sat fuming when he'd gone. Contrary to all that was logical, having my nether lips exposed to the cool air did *not* cool me down. As time passed, I began to realize that it was the very fact that I was so exposed that my engines refused to cool.

Left alone, I began to wonder if the rule of 'sitting' still applied when no one was around. Before I'd entirely decided whether I could get comfortable or not, the door opened.

Much to my disappointment, I saw it wasn't Kaelen.

Gareth looked like a leaner, slightly scaled down version of his brother, at least physically, though I thought he might be a fraction taller. His hair, although still closer to black than brown, was a lighter shade than Kaelen's, his face slightly less angular. Studied objectively, I supposed his features were actually closer to handsome than his brother's, too, and yet, to me, Kaelen seemed to exude a more powerful magnetism.

He took the seat Kaelen had sat in earlier, crooking a finger in me in a gesture strikingly familiar. I got up and crossed to stand in front of him.

"On your knees, here," he said, indicating that I was to get into the chair with him.

Hope and doubt instantly warred within me. I was still buzzing from my last encounter and I couldn't help but hope he meant to satisfy my discomfort. On the other hand, I'd started with Kaelen. I really, really wanted Kaelen to pleasure me as I'd pleasured him. More distressing than that thought, though, was the fear that he was only going to tease me more and I might 'slip'.

Swallowing against the reluctance in my throat I placed a knee on either side of his hips and settled on his lap.

"That's not what I said, is it?"

I stared at him blankly, searching my mind, and finally remembered he'd said on my knees. I pushed upward. Reaching for the tie at my throat, he pulled on it, releasing the bow and then shoved the sleeves of the sheer robe down my arms. He lifted his hands, cupping a breast in each and plucking at my nipples until they stood erect. He settled his hands on my waist then, pulling me forward until my breasts were inches from his face. I caught my breath as he opened his mouth. It wasn't his mouth that closed on the tip, though, but his teeth. He bore down slowly on the distended tip and then stripped it with his teeth. My nipple exploded with sensation closer to pain than pleasure. I gasped, began to shake as he raked it over and over with the edge of his teeth carefully applying just enough pressure to keep me teetering between pleasure and pain.

I was already feeling weak and faint before he turned his attention to my other nipple. Again, using only the edge of his teeth, he plucked at that nipple, pinching it and raking it just hard enough that it seemed to get more sensitive and more swollen each time. The restriction of the bustier on my ribs didn't help my desperate attempts to drag in a decent breath of air.

I moaned when he turned his attentions to tormenting the first nipple again, this time sucking it so hard I felt my belly quiver and hot moisture flood my sex. My legs began to quiver with the strain of holding myself up. I felt faint with the heat swirling through me, faint with breathlessness.

I'd begun to make little whimpering sounds I was hardly aware of by the time he stopped and I didn't know if I was glad he'd stopped, or very, very sorry. Every nerve ending in my body felt as if it was on fire.

He stroked his hands downward along the curve of my hips and then around me to cup the cheeks of my ass, digging his fingers into the cleft. Slipping down in the seat, he lifted me, thrusting my hips forward. An electrifying jolt went through me as he caught my clit between his lips, tugging at the painfully swollen nub in a way sent shockwaves of lava pouring through my veins and seemed to suck all of the air out the room. Clutching desperately at the back of the chair, I struggled to suck in a breath as he closed his mouth over it at last and began to suck it with a feverish zealous that made my eyeballs roll back in my head, left me gasping hoarsely in an effort to breathe.

I thought I would faint with the pleasure of it, die. My body, already teased and allowed to cool twice, skyrocketed toward completion. I groaned, struggling against it, fighting to reach it. I was nearly there when it abruptly flickered through my frying brain that I wasn't allowed. I had to announce it and beg permission.

I didn't want to. I had a bad feeling permission would be withheld.

I struggled with the consequences for several moments more and finally gasped out the words I didn't want to say in the worst way. "I'm ... I'm ... coming!"

He lifted his head abruptly. "Did you cum?"

I groaned, shuddering at the painful throbbing of my clit as it screamed at being abandoned so abruptly. "No," I gasped shakily, shivering now as the heat wafted off my burning body.

"You are not permitted to cum."

I swallowed with an effort, but the tension had already begun to ease. I dragged in another shaky breath just as he closed his mouth over my clit again. My belly clenched painfully at the fresh assault. Fire coursed through me. I realized I'd only thought my nerve endings were frying before. Now, as he suckled the nearly painfully sensitive bud, I began to feel as if fire ants were stinging me all over. I groaned, squeezed my eyes tightly, trying to focus my mind on something else.

I couldn't. I could feel my body gathering to take the leap despite my struggle to hold it at bay. "May I?" I gasped out desperately.

He stopped again, allowing me a moment's respite. "No."

I groaned as he plucked at the painfully swollen nub again, sucked it.

"That's enough, Gareth!"

A jolt went through both of us at the sound of that implacable voice.

I hadn't heard Kaelen enter the room, but that was hardly surprising considering my heart felt as if it was going to explode and had been pounding against my eardrums deafeningly.

Gareth lifted his head to stare at his brother. I was only peripherally aware of it, however. It was all I could do to hold myself up any longer.

After a moment, Gareth shifted upward in the seat again. As he did, he shifted me downward until my legs slipped from the seat of the chair. I was too wobbly to actually catch myself, but he didn't release me until I'd settled on my knees. I watched him dully as he unzipped his pants and pulled his cock out, but I didn't need to be told what to do. I'm not sure I would've listened if he'd informed me I wasn't to have it.

My brain was still frying. My body was on fire. I had a mindless need to have a cock in me and I wasn't particular, at the moment, where. I opened my mouth as he speared his fingers through my hair and guided me to him.

He was definitely Kaelen's brother, I thought dizzily as his flesh filled my mouth!

"Suck me," he ground out.

Ecstasy flooded me as I took him into my mouth and began to suckle him as greedily as he had me. I was burning up, fevered. I needed release. I pulled and sucked on him with all that need boiling inside of me until he was shaking all over, groaning as incessantly as I had been. His hands tightened abruptly against my skull, holding me still for a split second and then he uttered a choked groan as his seed began to spill into my mouth. I almost came with the powerful surge of pleasure that flooded me. I sucked at him hungrily until I'd drained him and his cock went flaccid in my mouth. I would have continued to suck in desperation if he hadn't finally pulled away from me.

I sat back on my heels, gasping for breath, still aching all over with the need thrumming through my veins.

"You have permission to go up to your room and rest for now. You'll be serving us luncheon in the dining room," Kaelen said, his voice even but threaded with anger. "Don't change."

He looked away when I finally lifted my head to look up at him. Turning, he strode to the door and went out. I stared at the door blankly after he'd left. My jaws were aching from sucking the two brothers off, but my whole body was on fire, throbbing painfully with disappointment. After a moment, realizing I'd been given an order, I got up, and headed upstairs, leaving my robe on the floor at Gareth's feet.

Dev was leaning against the banister as I made my way down the hall on wobbly legs. He watched me through narrowed eyes as I drew nearer. Catching me around the waist as I passed him and mounted the first stair, he halted me, pulled me to him and sucked one of my throbbing nipples into his mouth. An almost painful shaft of pleasure shot through me at the tug of his mouth on my swollen nipple. My knees threatened to give out. When he'd sucked on it till I lost my breath, he released the first and caught the second. That time there was more pain that pleasure, but my sex still went wet at the heat that scoured my insides. He slipped his hands down from my waist and over my buttocks as he suckled the tip and finally released it. Watching my face, he slipped one hand down my belly and flicked at my swollen, exposed clit, sending another jolt through me.

He hesitated then, and I could see he was debating countermanding the order for me to go upstairs, but finally he dropped his hands and stepped away.

Thoroughly shaken, so weak I wasn't even certain I could make it up the stairs, I climbed them with a great effort and made my way down the hall to my room. Once I'd closed the door, I collapsed on the bed. Every nerve ending in my body was still smoldering, sizzling as if I could still feel the touch of their mouths and hands on me. I ached with the need for fulfillment in a way I'd not only never experienced, but never considered possible. I'd almost felt like scoffing when Kaelen had said I was not allowed to cum without permission because I'd been certain then that it wouldn't be a problem for me.

I could see right now that it was going to be a *serious* problem.

They were all attractive men, and I was still confused as to why I was so hot I felt as if I was on fire. My breasts had always been sensitive but not so sensitive that teasing them could arouse me almost to the point of orgasm. I was lucky if I warmed up enough to have a possibility of climaxing after penetration. Giving head had certainly never been a turn on for me and if my ex had cum in my mouth I wouldn't have given him any head again.

I found it hard to accept that it had been so hot and exciting just because I'd been ordered to do it. There was no denying I had found both Kaelen and Gareth very attractive even before they'd driven me half out of my skull with their teasing, and certainly Gareth's determined assault on my clit had been enough to make me cum, but I'd been the next thing to frantic before he'd gotten that far. I'd been so ready, I'd almost cum the moment he'd started.

I didn't even think it was the fact that I'd been made to wear this 'fuck me' outfit that left my most sensitive areas exposed.

It was undoubtedly all of it together, though, and the fact that I wasn't allowed to cum only made me want to that much more.

If this wasn't their idea of punishment, I was pretty sure I didn't want to know what the 'punishment' for not obeying was going to be like because this was already hellish and I knew damned well the other three were going to expect much the same. I rolled onto my back after a while, staring up at the drapery canopy above the bed and trying to will my body to cool down. It wasn't easy when every current of air that wafted over me brushed my nipples and my sensitive nether lips like a caress.

The straps were digging into my outer lips, too, restricting blood flow and making everything else ache that much more. I shifted, trying to get comfortable, but no position seemed to ease the ache, either there or in my rectum … which I couldn't get my mind off of because of the plug.

The plug Kaelen was going to replace with a larger plug.

My belly clenched.

I hadn't even been here half a day and I was already miserable.

Closing my eyes, I sought calm. My body ceased to throb quite as uncomfortably as it had at first, but it didn't return to 'rest'.

Finally, I got up, kicked the heels off my feet and explored the room.

There were scarves tied around each of the four posts of the bed, I discovered, and I knew the moment I looked at them that they weren't there merely to hold the drapes. Feeling my belly shimmer, I turned away from the bed and moved to the armoire. The wardrobe inside was in a variety of colors, but I could see at a glance that each and every garment was pretty much like the thing I was already wearing, designed to offer me for their pleasure rather than to cover me.

Closing the doors again, I glanced at the bedside cabinet that Kaelen had pulled the plug from and finally yielded to curiosity. There were three more plugs I saw in dismay, each about twice the size of the one before. The largest was the size of Kaelen's cock.

Shivering, feeling oddly more turned on by that discovery than repulsed, as I was sure I should be, I closed the drawer again and looked around, wondering if I actually wanted to know what else the room contained.

I did, and I didn't.

It seemed inescapable that whatever I found was meant to be used on me, and I was still torn. I didn't actually want any surprises, but I wound never have known what the plug was for before Kaelen had shown me. The chances were I wasn't going to be able to figure out any other toys either, and it might just shake my nerves worse than they were already.

I looked anyway.

And mostly I was mystified, as I'd expected I would be, but along with the pangs of fear of that discovery sent through me were currents that were definitely erotic.

I was so busy checking everything out that I was nearly late for luncheon. Galvanized when I saw the clock hands nearing noon, I slipped the heels on again and headed downstairs, wondering where the kitchen was, and the dining room. No one had enlightened me. I'd just been told to appear and serve.

I found the dining room easily enough. The men had gathered there and I could hear them talking. Resisting the temptation to move close enough to tell what they were talking about, I moved further down the hall, knowing the kitchen would almost certainly adjoin the dining room and wondering abruptly if I was just to serve, or to prepare.

And if I wasn't supposed to prepare, who was going to be doing that?

And was the cook going to pass out when he or she got a good look at my outfit?